The Casterglass Heir

The Casterglass Heir

A Keeping Up with the Penryns Romance

KATE HEWITT

TULE
PUBLISHING

Chapter One

"UH, SAM?"

Sam Penryn looked up from the paperwork he'd been staring at with what he hoped passed for intense focus but was really just a blank, buzzing brain. How long had he been looking at this brochure, needing to sign off on it, without taking in a thing? He blinked the world back into focus and saw his sister Althea was standing in the doorway of the spare larder he'd converted into a small office, the look on her face a weird mix of apprehension and intense curiosity.

"Yes?" He spoke moderately enough but he heard the impatience in his voice, felt it in himself. He'd been back at Casterglass for just over two months and the surging restlessness hadn't yet gone away. Neither had the memories.

"There's someone here to see you."

There was no disguising the avid gleam in his older sister's eyes. Sam had a feeling it couldn't just be a deliveryman who wanted to see him, but then who? He'd made sure to avoid anyone from the village since he'd been back, and he didn't have any friends here. He never had.

"Who is it?" he asked, and Althea bit her lip.

"It's a woman. She said you won't be expecting her... Her name is Rose."

Rose? Sam felt a jolt go through him and then he went completely still, as if he'd been electrocuted and was now absorbing the shock. And it *was* a shock, because Rose, his Rose—except of course she hadn't been his at all—she was in New Zealand. And the last time he'd seen her, before he'd flown home to help turn their family home into a tourist attraction, he'd never expected to again. Rose had made that abundantly clear. *It was fun, but...*

Yeah, yeah, he'd said so quickly he stumbled over his words. *Yeah, exactly.* As if he'd felt the same.

"Rose...Lacey?" he asked, hearing how befuddled he sounded, like his brain was misfiring, but he simply could not compute that Rose would come all the way to Casterglass. He hadn't even told her where he'd lived, not really, although he'd probably mentioned Casterglass once or twice. They hadn't talked very much about personal stuff, which at the time had suited him fine. When they'd said goodbye, she'd been talking airily of heading to Jamaica next.

"She didn't give her last name," Althea told him, "but she's quite petite with lots of strawberry-blonde hair?" She raised her eyebrows, while Sam nodded dumbly. That definitely was Rose. "And...she's pregnant."

What? Another jolt went through him, this one worse

than before, causing his whole body to tingle. He could only stare at his sister as her words reverberated through him. Pregnant…impossible.

Not really.

"She's in the morning parlour," Althea finished helpfully, and then, although she looked as if she wanted to ask a million questions and demand their answers, she slipped away, back to the kitchen.

Sam sat there for a moment, staring into space, his body still tingling. He was remembering when he'd first met Rose just over five months ago, at a bar by the beach in Tairua, a surfing town on the Coromandel Peninsula in New Zealand. She'd been mixing cocktails with an assured gracefulness, her slender arms moving so quickly as she'd poured and shook the drink that he'd been transfixed. He wasn't normally the kind of guy who chatted up a woman at a bar, especially not one serving behind the counter, but he'd been drawn to Rose like metal to a magnet.

He'd slid onto a stool and watched her for twenty minutes without speaking, as she whirled from customer to cocktail and back again with lightning speed, pouring drinks, trading witty remarks and barbs with the other bartender as well as some regulars who were clearly as besotted as Sam was, although perhaps they hid it a little better. They were able to joke with her, at least, while Sam had simply stared gormlessly.

Her red-gold hair had been piled messily on top of her

head, and her body, in a midriff-skimming T-shirt and gauzy sarong over bikini bottoms, had been slender and lithe. There had been a whimsical energy to her, along with a steely focus, and Sam had been entranced by both.

The other bartender had taken his drink order, and he'd been halfway through his beer, having still said not a word the entire time, when she'd turned to him, hands planted on her hips, one eyebrow cocked in mocking challenge. "Well?" she'd demanded. "Are you going to ask me out or what?"

He'd spluttered his drink, nearly choking, wiped his mouth, and then said, sounding surprised, "Why, yes. I think I am."

Sam started from his reverie, blinking the tiny office back into focus. He'd been back two months, but it still felt like a surprise, to be here at all. To choose it…although he wasn't sure he really had. When your whole family decided to pitch in and help out, it felt mean and small not to come along for the ride.

Except he hated being here. Hated being home.

Outside rain clouds were homing in on what had been a beautiful, blue-sky morning. Typical Cumbria. It was the middle of July, but the thermometer hadn't pushed much past fourteen degrees, hardly the balmy weather they wanted for tomorrow's big opening of Casterglass Castle, *your ultimate Lake District tourist destination!* Poppy had designed the banner now strung between the gateposts, proudly proclaiming they were 'Fully Open!' Sam had six bookings for the glamping yurts for the weekend, and it was meant to be pouring with rain.

And Rose was here.

Slowly, as if walking through a dream, Sam rose from his seat and then headed down the narrow, stone-flagged corridor that had once been the domain of servants, past the kitchen, where he saw his sisters Althea and Olivia hunched over the table, whispering madly. As he walked past the open doorway, they both threw him not-so-covert, deeply speculative looks before they turned away quickly, and went back to their gossiping.

Pregnant.

She couldn't be. He'd left her only two months ago. She hadn't been pregnant then. Had she just found out? Then how on earth would Althea have known? Sam didn't know all that much about bumps and babies, but he could count at least, and a woman who was two months pregnant wasn't showing. Was she? Besides, they'd used protection all during their brief, intense yet casual affair. He'd made sure of it.

He stood in front of the doorway to the morning parlour, a small, cosy sitting room on the side of the Georgian addition to the thirteenth-century castle, where they had always received visitors, since the drawing room was too grand, and often too cold. He rested his hand on the doorknob, his heart starting to thud.

Rose. Pregnant. Here.

It was way too much to take in.

Realising he'd left her waiting for long enough, he opened the door and stepped into the room.

Rose had been standing with her back to him as she looked out the window at the side lawn, a verdant swathe of green, thanks to the rain, with a cluster of huge rhododendrons hiding the sea from view. Olivia and Will, who were responsible for the garden, had trimmed the enormous bushes substantially but they were still gigantic, now in full flower, their bright fuchsia blossoms looking like something you'd see in the Amazon, not the chilly, wet Lake District.

As Sam opened the door, Rose whirled around, her long, tumbled hair flying out, her golden-green cat's eyes widening. Sam remembered those eyes. He remembered how they were flecked with gold, with luxuriant lashes, and how they crinkled at the corners when she was smiling at him. She wasn't smiling now.

He couldn't tell if she was apprehensive or angry or something in between, but she didn't look happy. She was wearing a long, loose patchwork dress, and there was definitely a bump underneath it. Smallish but very much there. How far along could she be? Slowly, still feeling as if he were in a dream, he closed the door behind him.

They stared at each other.

A million memories tumbled through Sam's mind—their first date, where they'd walked along the beach at Tairua as the sun set and the stars came out, one by one, filling the sky with flickering glimmers of light. He'd never seen stars like he had in New Zealand, and he'd been to a lot of places in this world. The night sky had been like a living, pulsing map scrolled across the heavens, twinkling with promises. They had kissed on the damp sand as the sky had lit up with the Southern Lights, a riot of pink and orange, green and gold, better than fireworks, more beautiful than anything he'd ever seen.

He remembered too how she'd danced away from him as they'd walked along, doing a cartwheel across the sand, tanned legs flying out, seeming so free, so wonderfully reckless, completely unburdened by responsibility, by family, by life…unlike him.

She'd been travelling the world for five years, never staying anywhere for long, all her worldly possessions kept in a single rucksack, which was exactly how she liked it. She'd been impossible to pin down, like a rare and beautiful butterfly, and he'd loved that about her, but he'd also fought the urge to do exactly what he knew she didn't want, and trap her in his hands, let her wings beat between his palms.

Of course she'd never let him, and in truth he'd never really tried, not properly. He didn't want to be pinned down either, even if he was fascinated by her. He travelled almost as much as she did, signing up for one charitable venture after another—climbing Kilimanjaro, scaling the Eiger, crossing the Kalahari—in between freelance work in data analysis. He convinced themselves they were both free spirits, even though he'd never felt particularly free.

They'd lasted for nearly three months, off and on, before he'd reluctantly decided to return to Casterglass, to take up the glamping and outdoor adventure course at his family's home, a wreck of a castle that was slowly, so slowly, being renovated.

And now Rose was here. Her lips were pursed, her eyebrows raised, as some emotion flashed in her eyes in a shower of golden sparks.

"Well?" she asked, a bit tartly.

Sam's mind spun. He still couldn't actually process that she was here, that she was pregnant. And so he found himself asking, stupidly, the one question that was blazing through his brain, because how could it not be, considering the casual nature of their relationship? The dates?

"Is it mine?"

WOW, OKAY. GREAT start. Rose stayed still, trying to keep her expression neutral. Sam was looking poleaxed, which she supposed was to be expected, but *was it his?* Why on earth would she be here otherwise?

"Is that seriously the first thing you're going to say to me?" she asked when she trusted her voice to be level. The truth was since she'd arrived at Casterglass this morning she'd felt as if she were jumping out of her skin. She had not expected a castle, and when she'd found out about *that*, she had not been expecting Sam to be the owner's son, the son of a baron, as a matter of fact. He'd never mentioned anything about either. All he'd said was he was from a little village in the Lake District called Casterglass. *You can't say it's in the middle of nowhere because it's by the sea. It isn't in the middle of anything.*

"Sorry," Sam said. He rubbed a hand over his face. "I'm just...surprised. I didn't expect..." He shook his head slowly, as if to clear it. "Do you want to sit down?"

She didn't really, because she felt too nervous to keep still, but she was also feeling faint, and the only thing she'd eaten today was a plastic-wrapped croissant bought at the train station in Lancaster that had managed to be both tasteless and disgusting. Her stomach was roiling now, even though it was empty. Wordlessly she nodded, and sank a bit unsteadily into a small, elegant chair with wood-carved arms and velvet upholstery. Sam was still staring at her as if she wasn't real.

Okay, she'd known this was going to be a surprise, a big one. She'd made it very clear when they'd said goodbye that their fling was over, that she was off to Jamaica. Then she'd started having second thoughts...about a lot of things. But even though she'd had plenty of time to think on the twenty-four-hour flight to London, not to mention the six-hour train journey to this far-flung place, she still had no idea what to say, or even what she wanted. So she simply looked at him, waiting for him to speak.

Slowly Sam lowered himself into a chair opposite her,

resting his hands on his thighs, like he was bracing himself. Somehow she'd managed to forget how crazily good-looking he was, which was a bit annoying. It made her feel off-kilter, because she just wanted to stare at him. His hair was a little darker and a lot shorter than it had been in New Zealand when it had a messy mop of sun-bleached curls. His eyes were the same deep, piercing blue, the colour so intense that Rose had teased that he wore coloured contact lenses. She remembered how he'd sputtered in outrage when she'd said it, which was one of the things she'd loved about him. How could someone who was so outrageously handsome be so shy and unsure of his own overwhelming appeal? And yet Sam was.

She hadn't *loved* it about him, Rose automatically corrected herself. She'd liked it. They'd had a case of deep like—that was all. A fling, like she'd said, but now there was a baby.

"So it is mine?" Sam asked, and Rose let out a huff of breath.

"You're kind of fixated on that," she remarked, and he shrugged, spreading his hands.

"It's just…I'm gobsmacked, I guess. Considering…I mean…" He shook his head as if to clear it. "How far along are you?"

"Seventeen weeks." She patted her bump. "I'm showing quite a lot, I know, but when you're short, apparently that's what happens." She looked like a toothpick with a bowling ball sticking out of its middle. Not exactly the best look.

"Seventeen weeks…"

He was clearly doing the math in his head. Rose couldn't keep from rolling her eyes. "It probably happened the first time. You remember?"

He blushed. He actually blushed. Yes, he remembered, and so did she. She didn't have flings, even though she acted as if she did, all part of the persona she'd taken on at eighteen and was now so much a part of her it had to be real, at least a little bit. She usually kept herself to herself, but something about Sam had slid right under her skin. They'd slept together right there on the sand, on their second date. She *never* did stuff like that. Never, and neither, it seemed, had Sam, because afterwards he'd looked as shellshocked as she felt.

"Wow," he'd said, shaking his head slowly, and she'd burst out laughing, even though part of her had felt like crying, and she didn't even know why. She'd felt exposed and vulnerable and outrageously happy all at once. Way too many emotions.

"But we used protection?" he asked, and Rose shrugged.

"Protections fails, I suppose. Ninety-eight per cent rate and all that."

He nodded, accepting but clearly still reeling. When were they going to get past the shock? Although what came next Rose still had no idea. She wasn't even sure what she wanted to happen next.

She really had not thought this through. Now, she realised, would be a very good time to have a plan, but the reality was she was reeling as much as Sam was. Yes, she'd had time to get used to the idea that she was having a baby, *sort of*, but she still had no idea what the future might look like. Coming here had been her end point rather than her beginning.

"Okay," Sam said, apropos of precisely nothing, and they both stared some more. All right, she needed to get to grips with this conversation.

Rose drew herself up, ignoring the dancing of spots before her eyes, the wave of dizziness and nausea that crashed over like the white-capped surf at Tairua. The taste of that croissant was in her mouth, along with something nastier. She swallowed it all down.

"I came here because I thought you should know," she stated as matter-of-factly as she could. "I'm not expecting anything from you, and you don't need to panic that I want a wedding ring or something ridiculous like that." Sam blinked, said nothing. After a second's pause Rose continued, her voice growing steadier even as her conviction that she was doing the right thing started to drain away. "You don't need to be involved at all. I won't ask for money or anything. I just think a man ought to know if he's got a child in the world, that's all."

Sam was silent for a few seconds. "You couldn't have sent an email?" he finally said, and Rose made a choked sound that she bit back as soon as she could.

Seriously? "I didn't have your email address."

"Text, then."

She felt tears crowding behind her lids and she blinked them back fiercely. The dizziness came back, along with the nausea. She realised, with a distant sort of surprise, that she might actually vomit. *Breathe. Blink. Swallow.* Sam was staring at her, his expression so nonplussed Rose had no idea what he was feeling. Not much, it seemed, at any rate. He looked annoyed, if he looked anything. *Sorry for this minor inconvenience of bearing your child.*

Well, what she expected, really? The truth was she hadn't let herself expect anything, because she knew how people let you down, even, *especially* the people closest to you. And yet his cool indifference hurt more than a little. A fricking *text?*

"Sorry to have bothered you then," she managed, the words coming out thickly because she suddenly realised that she actually was going to vomit, and the carpet looked very old and expensive, if rather threadbare. She lurched out of her seat, way too fast, because in addition to trying to swallow down the need to retch, she also felt like she was going to pass out.

The room swam and Sam's face loomed up in front of her, looking weirdly pale.

"Rose—"

He sounded panicked, which she supposed was better than annoyed. The room was lurching about like they were on a ship, and her stomach was too. She *really* wished she hadn't eaten that stupid croissant. Or come here, actually.

Sam grabbed her arm. "Rose—"

"Sorry," she mumbled, and then she felt herself crumple.

Chapter Two

"**R**OSE!"

Sam watched as Rose sank to the floor, her head lolling back, and he just managed to catch her in his arms before she hit the deck. Her face looked too pale, a scattering of freckles across her nose like gold dust. He remembered once trying to kiss every single one while Rose had laughed and squirmed away. And now she was slumped against him, pliant and boneless and very much unconscious.

"Rose," he said again, desperately, and she didn't so much as stir, sagging in his arms like she was a bowlful of jelly.

He scooped her up—even pregnant she was tiny—and carefully laid her on the divan. Now what? He was usually pretty good in a crisis; when they'd run into a thunderstorm on top of Kilimanjaro, he hadn't panicked at all. Why was he freaking out over a single woman who had fainted?

Because she's pregnant with your baby and you basically acted like an arse.

In retrospect, he could see that the questions he'd asked

about the baby being his and why she hadn't texted instead might have been *slightly* insensitive, but he'd been shocked by the news and stung by her insistence that she wasn't asking him for anything. *You don't need to be involved.*

It had brought him right back to their goodbye in Tairua, when he'd fumbled through saying he still cared and he wanted to keep in touch, and she'd looked as if he'd just spat on her.

It's been fun, but...

Right. Not only had she not wanted to keep in touch, she also didn't want him involved in their child's life. It was hard not to let that hurt, at least a little bit.

Had Rose known she was pregnant when they'd said goodbye? That had been only eight weeks ago. She was seventeen weeks now. He could do the math, but did women who were nine weeks along know it? He would have to ask Althea, except...he did not want to ask his bossy, interfering older sister anything, although he had a feeling she would be asking him a lot.

He had a lot of questions for Rose, though, if she'd just wake up.

"Rose." Gently he touched her cheek; it was soft and cool. "Rose, can you hear me?"

Her eyelids fluttered once, showing a flash of green and gold, and then closed again. She breathed in deeply, as if she were asleep. Did people stay unconscious for this long? It had to have been a couple of minutes, at least. What if she'd hurt her head? Except she hadn't even hit her head; he'd caught her before then. What if she'd had a *stroke* or something awful like that?

"Rose…"

Nothing. Sam glanced at her lying on the divan, slim tanned ankles peeking out from beneath the frayed patchwork of her dress. Her hair was in a golden nimbus about her heart-shaped face, like a tangled halo. He'd forgotten how beautiful she was, as well as how feisty. The strength of Maleficent in the body of Tinker Bell. And, like some sort of Snow White, she wasn't waking up.

"Rose," he said, "if you can hear me, I'm just going to get you a glass of water, okay? I'll be back in a couple of ticks." He hesitated, resting the back of his hand against her forehead, which felt cool and clammy. What if she was seriously ill? Or what if something was wrong with the baby?

The baby… Good Lord. He really could not process that reality yet. Right now, he needed to focus on the current crisis, which was Rose being unconscious.

Taking a deep breath, Sam rose from where he'd been crouching by the sofa and headed for the kitchen. Olivia and Althea were still gossiping like a pair of fishwives, heads together and elbows planted on the table, but they both sprang to attention as he came into the room.

"Well?" Althea demanded, her voice full of both curiosity and disbelief. They'd clearly put two and two together and come up with about forty-six, which was about right. A *baby*.

Good heavens.

"I need a glass of water." He went to the tap, waiting the requisite three seconds for the rusty-brown water to flush out before he filled a glass. Ah, the joys of ancient plumbing. They'd done a lot of work to this place, it was true, but it was still more or less falling down. It always had been.

"Sam." Now his older sister was sounding huffy. "Are you going to tell us what's going on?"

"Rose fainted."

"What!" Althea looked alarmed while Olivia's expression had softened into sympathy.

"Oh, poor thing—"

"You just *left* her?"

"To get a glass of water!" What should he have done? "I'm going back now. Obviously."

"Is she all right?" Althea demanded, sounding outraged on Rose's behalf, as if her fainting was somehow Sam's fault, which, on second thought, maybe it was. He hadn't said any of the right things, but then neither had she. Not a good start, he realised. Not a good start at all.

"Does she need a doctor?" Olivia asked. "I could ring the GP in Brough—"

"I don't know. I don't think so." Although he really *didn't* know. There might be something seriously wrong with her. Maybe she'd come to Casterglass to tell him that, in addition to being pregnant, she had a life-threatening illness, as unlikely as that seemed. Still, they'd barely spoken before she'd fainted—a couple of sentences, him asking her why she hadn't sent a text. *Why* had he said that? Because he hadn't been thinking, clearly. He'd just been hurt.

"Why don't we check on her," Althea said in a teacher-ish, no-nonsense sort of voice, like he was a little boy who had forgotten how to do his sums. Sam gritted his teeth on any possible reply and, knowing there was no point in arguing, he let both Althea and Olivia follow him back to the morning parlour, where Rose was still lying on the sofa, looking like Sleeping Beauty in need of a kiss. That was definitely not how he intended to wake her up.

"Rose?" he asked hesitantly. Her eyes stayed closed. "Rose, I've brought you some water."

"How long has she been unconscious?" Olivia asked in a whisper.

"Umm…a few minutes." That really was a long time, wasn't it? Didn't most people come to right away?

"Hmm," Althea said, folding her arms. She sounded sceptical.

Sam crouched by the divan, near Rose's head. He wanted to stroke a tendril of red-gold hair that had fallen across her cheek, but he didn't feel he had the right. *She's having your baby.* He was really struggling to process that fact. The word kept echoing emptily through his brain, like some kind of endless echo. *Baby…baby…baby…BABY.*

"Rose?" he asked again. She didn't stir.

"Rose," Althea said, and now she really sounded like a

teacher, calling on a pupil who had been daydreaming.

"*Althea,*" Olivia whispered. "Really, I don't think—"

Althea ignored her. "Rose," she stated firmly, "wake up."

ROSE CRACKED OPEN an eye to see three people staring down at her. Sam looked abject, one woman looked concerned, and the woman who had answered the door earlier looked both stern and unconvinced. Rose quickly closed her eyes again.

She'd come to almost as soon as Sam had laid her down on the sofa, but it had been so nice to hear the concern in his voice—to feel like the whole world had disappeared for a few moments—that she'd kept her eyes closed. All right, so it wasn't the most mature thing to do, pretending to be unconscious, but she'd been in desperate need of a break. She still was, but she had a feeling the stern-looking woman didn't miss a trick, and already knew she was faking. Darn.

"Rose, can you hear me?" Sam asked, and he sounded so troubled that Rose felt she had no choice but to face the music—and the three people gazing down at her in various states of emotion.

"Sorry…" she said, and her voice came out all wavery. The older woman looked as if she might either glower or burst out laughing or both, and Rose squashed a flicker of guilt, along with one of annoyance. She hadn't faked *that*, but clearly the woman thought she was an actress missing out on her Academy Award.

"Here, have some water." Sam pressed a glass into her hands while he helped her up to a seated position. Rose lowered her gaze as she sipped from the glass, conscious of the two women's curious stares. This had all gone so very wrong, and she knew she had no one to blame but herself. She should have had more of a plan before she'd come all the way to Casterglass, which really was as remote as Sam had said. She should have, but she hadn't, besides: *Tell Sam and then…*

Not much of a plan at all.

"Are you feeling better?" the older woman asked rather pointedly. Rose was starting not to like her.

"Yes, much, thank you," she murmured, her gaze still lowered. "I'm sorry, I just came over dizzy for a few moments. I haven't eaten much today…" She let her voice trail off as she realised how stupid she sounded, like some damsel in distress, and worse, one who was *faking* being said damsel. No wonder the woman looked so unimpressed. She was unimpressed with herself. "If you could just give me a few minutes, I'm sure I'll be fine and then I'll be out of your way."

"You're not *going*," Sam stated, one part disbelief to three parts outrage, or maybe it was the other way round.

Rose took a sip of water, not knowing how to reply, especially with these two women as an audience to this torrid little drama. *You asked me why I didn't text you the news,* she thought, but didn't say, because she didn't want to admit it in front of these strangers. There was only so much humiliation a girl could take.

"If you haven't eaten, why don't I make you something?" the other woman, the friendlier one, asked. Her long, blonde hair was piled up in a messy bun and she had eyes the colour of violets. She was very pretty, in a fragile sort of way. "What would you like?" she asked. "I could run you up an omelette or a cheese toastie…"

Both sounded delicious, and the truth was Rose was absolutely starving. "Oh, I couldn't—" she began only for the other woman, the one with ash-blonde hair and a rather hard expression, to interject in a no-nonsense voice.

"Why don't you make her an omelette?"

Whoa, bossy much? What if she didn't like omelettes? Or was allergic to eggs? "Thank you," Rose said, sincerely, but she could tell the other woman didn't believe her. She'd marked her down as a chancer and Rose supposed she wasn't far wrong, all told. But she'd come here to let Sam know he was going to be a father, not to ask for anything.

Hadn't she?

She didn't even understand her own motives anymore.

"I'll just be a few minutes," the woman murmured, and hurried out of the room. The other woman was still watching Rose with narrowed eyes.

"Althea," Sam said, "can you give us a minute?"

For a second Rose thought she was going to refuse.

Then, with a single terse nod, she left the room. Rose breathed a sigh of relief.

"Are you feeling better?" Sam asked.

"Yes, a bit. I'm sorry I collapsed." At least she hadn't vomited. She'd had that much self-control, at least. She could just imagine Althea's horrified expression at seeing a puddle of coughed-up croissant on the Turkish rug. *You know that was a precious family heirloom?*

"You don't need to be sorry, Rose." Sam was silent for a moment. Rose had finished the water, so she simply stared into the glass, not sure she wanted to see the expression on his face. "I think I'm the one who should be sorry," he continued, seeming to need to feel his way through the words. "I shouldn't have said that thing about texting—I didn't mean I wished you'd texted, or hadn't come, or something. I was trying to say, if that's all you wanted from me, why did you come so far?"

Which was, Rose supposed, a reasonable question. "I don't know," she admitted, and it was the most honest thing she'd said so far. *I really don't know anything at all.*

Sam eased into a chair opposite her. Rose kept her eyes on the empty glass. "When did you fly in?" he asked, and she breathed a tiny sigh of relief. So they were going to do chitchat? Good.

"This morning."

"So in addition to being hungry, you're completely jet-lagged."

"Pretty much." She hadn't slept much on the plane, and she'd been travelling for thirty-six hours, all told. No wonder she had fainted.

"What happened to Jamaica?" Sam asked, and Rose finally looked up from her glass.

"This baby happened."

"I know, I know. I mean…" He ran a hand through his hair, ruffling it up. "You just seemed so determined to go somewhere new. To…not stay in touch."

She heard the slight note of accusation in his voice, as if not staying in touch had been entirely her idea, when he'd been the one to say, so half-heartedly, they should keep in contact, without offering her so much as his phone number. She knew a cheap sentiment when she heard one. She'd heard plenty.

"Well, obviously things changed," she said stiffly.

"Right. Right." He shook his head with a sheepish smile. "Sorry…I'm just trying to get my head around it all."

"I know." She also knew she needed to cut him some serious slack. She'd known she was pregnant for months, but this was a very recent bombshell for him, and a big one at that. But not *that* big, because… "I meant what I said, though," she told him. "You don't have to be involved at all. That's not what this is about."

He gazed at her, his eyes narrowing. "What is it about then, Rose?"

"I told you. I just thought you should know." She

sounded defensive. She *felt* defensive. She'd meant to reassure him, but he sounded annoyed.

"Yes, but why is it so important for me to know, if I'm not meant to be involved?" His voice had gone sharp. "What's the point of that?"

Rose stared at him, trying to figure out what he was attempting to say. What he really wanted. "It just seemed important," she said at last, with a little shrug. What else was she supposed to say? She had no idea how he felt about any of this. Maybe he didn't either, not yet anyway, but what did he want from her? Maybe he didn't know that, either. What a pair they were, except of course they weren't a pair at all.

"Okay." Sam raked his hand through his hair again, before dropping it to his side. He was staring at the floor beneath his feet, his forearms braced on his thighs. "Okay," he said again, almost to himself.

"Omelette's ready," a voice called from the hallway.

Sam looked up. "You should eat."

"All right."

He stood up and then he reached out a hand to help her up from where she was still half-sprawled on the sofa. She hesitated for a fraction of a second, which she saw he noticed, and then she took his hand.

The slide of the warm, work-roughened skin of his palm across hers had sudden sparks shooting off in her belly as she remembered, all too well, how good they'd been together. Surprisingly good, because she had never been one for relationships and she didn't think he was, either.

But *that* way…they'd been very good, indeed. Or so it had seemed to her, at least.

As soon as she was on her feet, she slipped her hand from his. Sam's mouth twisted again and then he walked out of the room, leaving her to follow.

He led her to the back of the house, past about half a dozen doorways, into a kitchen the size of a tennis court, or very nearly. A huge Aga took up one wall, several Welsh dressers full of dusty willowware another, and a large, squashy sofa was at the other end. The room managed to be cosy even though it was huge, and it was also a mess. The kindly looking woman—Rose still didn't know her name— was flipping a fluffy omelette onto a plate while Althea stared at her rather beadily.

"So, Rose," she said. "Where are you from?"

"Althea…" Sam began, a bit half-heartedly. "She's only just got here."

"And I'm just making conversation." Althea raised her eyebrows, gave a little shrug as if to ask *what's the big deal?*

And really, what *was* the big deal? Except Althea was looking so sceptical and there was no easy answer to that question.

"I'm not really from anywhere," Rose said as the other woman placed the omelette in front of her. She smiled up at her. "Thank you, that's so kind of you. I'm sorry—I don't know your name."

"I'm Olivia, and this is Althea." Althea, Rose saw, had the grace to look slightly abashed by the lack of introductions. "We're Sam's sisters. Two of them, anyway."

"Right. Well, I'm Rose."

"What do you mean, you're not from anywhere?" Althea asked, after an only-just-suitable pause.

This was starting to feel a bit like an inquisition. A friendly one, sort of. "I moved around a lot growing up," Rose answered as she cut a piece of the omelette. It looked perfect, golden and fluffy and hot. "But I was born in Reading."

"Ah." Althea nodded, folding her arms, as Rose popped a bite of omelette in her mouth and closed her eyes briefly in bliss. It had been days since she'd eaten properly, thanks to travel and the usual lack of money. Something she did not want to think too closely about right now, with three people staring her down, wondering why she was here, and perhaps when she was going to go.

"I didn't know you were born in Reading," Sam said, and Althea and Olivia both swivelled to look at him.

"I don't know why you would," Rose replied, before she realised how that sounded. Like they didn't know each other at all, but she was carrying his baby. Which was more or less the truth. Olivia was looking sympathetic, and Althea was trying to school her face into some sort of semi-friendly expression. Oh dear.

A sudden wave of exhaustion crashed over her, as overwhelming as the ones of dizziness and nausea before. She hadn't slept in forever, and she hadn't showered in the same amount of time. She felt grubby and worn down and so very tired. She ate another bite of the omelette, and then another, and then put her fork down because she feared she was going to fall asleep right there. Keel over, yet again, because really, this was just all too much.

"You poor thing," Olivia murmured. "You look absolutely knackered." Rose opened her mouth to deny it, and then found she couldn't. "You need a good, long sleep," Olivia said firmly. "Why don't I show you to a guest room?"

"I couldn't—" Rose began. She could hardly bear to look at Sam, who was probably appalled by the thought of her staying under his roof, especially after she'd promised him she wouldn't stay long.

"You certainly can," Olivia replied. "Can't she, Althea?" This with a quelling look for her sister.

"It seems she can," Althea replied neutrally, and before she could protest, Rose found herself bundled along by Olivia as if she were an unruly child, out of the kitchen, down the hallway, and upstairs.

Chapter Three

THE SILENCE IN the kitchen was absolute. Sam stared at the doorway Olivia had just steered Rose through, and Althea stared at him. The clock above the Aga ticked the seconds by with loud deliberation.

"Well?" Althea said finally, when at least sixty of those seconds had passed painfully by.

Sam jammed his hands into the pockets of his jeans. "Well, what?"

"What do you mean, well what, Sam Penryn? That—that *girl* is carrying your baby!"

"She's twenty-four."

"She looks about seventeen."

"Althea."

"I'm sorry, but what? You left a girl pregnant in New Zealand?" She sounded so aggrieved, it almost made Sam laugh. And he'd been wondering if his sister was suspicious of Rose...but, no. She was suspicious of *him*. Of course she was.

"I didn't know she was pregnant when I left, Althea. Obviously."

"I thought maybe it was why you were so reluctant to come home."

"It wasn't." No, he'd been reluctant because he'd *liked* Rose, and also because he didn't like being back at Casterglass. Hated it, in fact. Strange how the hard memories were so much more powerful than the good ones, because he knew, in his head anyway, that there were plenty of both. But it was the bad ones that stayed with him. That kept him lying in bed, trying not to remember and failing. Always failing.

"How well do you know her, Sam?" Althea asked quietly. "I mean, really? Was this a one-night stand? A fling?"

Sam hesitated. He didn't particularly want to talk about his sex life, such as it was, with his sister. And yet Althea was looking at him expectantly, and Rose was *upstairs*, and heaven knew what on earth he was going to do about any of this.

"I don't know what it was," he admitted quietly.

"Hmm." Althea shook her head slowly. "So how well do you know her?"

How well? Not at all, and yet completely. She'd lain in his arms while the sun had risen and he'd felt happy and whole, and yet he hadn't known that she'd been born in Reading, or what her favourite colour was, or what she was afraid of. He didn't actually know her at all, because they'd kept it light. That was how she'd wanted it, and maybe that was how he'd wanted it, too.

"I don't know," he said.

"You don't know much, do you?" Althea remarked tartly.

Sam gave her the ghost of a smile. "Nope." He suddenly felt very tired, felled by a bone-deep exhaustion born both from working flat out and not being able to sleep. With this new emotional tsunami of realising he was going to be *a father*…well, it was enough to make him want to sleep for a year.

He ran a hand through his hair. "I can't think about all this now. I've got the opening tomorrow—"

"We've all got the opening tomorrow," Althea reminded him. "But you can't put this off, Sam. What are you going to tell Dad? And Mum? And what are you going to do about Rose?"

He blanched, although he tried not to show just how terrifying and dispiriting the prospect of telling his parents was. He could already picture his father's droopy, disappointed expression. Except of course he wouldn't *say* he was disappointed. He would just look it, which was worse.

"I don't know, Althea—" He started to turn away, only to still completely when she spoke again, her voice quiet and serious.

"Sam, look, I don't mean to be, well, rude, but…are you sure the baby's yours?"

He stiffened. "Why wouldn't I be?"

"Well, because you don't know her." Althea hesitated. "I know it sounds cynical, but if she knew you were the son of a baron and the heir to—"

"What? This mouldering pile?" He let out a huff of humourless laughter. "She'd probably run a mile."

"She wouldn't know about any of that," Althea persisted. "All I'm saying is, it looks good on paper. Title, castle, et cetera. How far along did she say she was?"

"Seventeen weeks."

Althea frowned. "So over four months? And when did you meet her?"

"I can do maths, Althea." Sam tried not to sound annoyed, but she was treating him like a child. "I met her just under five months ago."

"So you would have…"

"Yes." He willed himself not to blush. "For heaven's sake, enough."

His sister pursed her lips. "To be honest, she looked more than seventeen weeks to me. First time, with a bump that size? Doesn't seem likely."

"I'm sure every woman is different." Now he really was out of his depth. But what was his sister saying? That Rose was pregnant with another man's child and trying to fob it off as his because one day he was going to be a baron? It sounded a little archaic and far-fetched to him.

"It's just, she seemed a bit…desperate."

"Desperate!" Sam exclaimed. "Desperate to leave here,

maybe. She made sure to tell me repeatedly that I didn't need to be involved."

Althea shrugged, unmoved. "That could be a ploy to make sure you were."

"Wow, cynical much?" Sam shook his head. He couldn't believe his sister was suggesting such thing, and yet already the seeds of doubt had been sown. He really didn't know Rose at all. And he still didn't understand why she'd come all this way, just to tell him she didn't want anything from him. What *did* she want, then? It had to be something.

"I am cynical," Althea agreed, "because I've learned to be. Jasper—"

"Rose is not Jasper." His sister's ex-husband had been a schmuck of the first order, cheating on Althea practically since their honeymoon. She'd put up with it for twenty years, so she was understandably a little scarred.

"No," Althea agreed, "but she might be like Jasper. You said yourself you don't know her all that well—"

"I know her better than that."

"How did you meet her?"

Sam hesitated, then accepted the inevitable. His sister wanted an inquisition, and so she'd have one. "At a bar in Tairua, a surf town on the Coromandel."

"A bar," she repeated, clearly struggling to keep her expression neutral.

"Loads of people meet in bars, Althea. You don't need to sound so scandalised." He tried to inject a note of humour in his voice, but he feared he just sounded truculent.

"I know that, Sam, it's just…did you spend much time with her?"

"A fair amount." He found he couldn't bear any more of this grilling. "Look, it's my life, Althea, all right? And Rose's. And—and the baby's. We'll figure it out." If Rose would even let them have a discussion about it.

"At the very least, please ask for a paternity test. Then you can discuss options—once you know for sure."

And *that* would go over well. Not. "I'll talk to her tomorrow," he promised. "Let her rest and recover first." And let him figure out what his plan was, because he really didn't have one. He'd have to tell his parents—ugh. He couldn't stomach the thought. Everyone in Casterglass would be buzzing with the news, something he told himself he didn't care about but knew he did.

"I need to check the yurts," he said, although what he really needed to do was just be alone. His head felt as if it was going to explode, and his heart was aching. "If Rose wakes up…"

Althea raised her eyebrows. Again. "Yes?"

"Be nice," Sam told her, and then he headed outside.

The air was fresh and damp, the sky the colour of slate as the promised thunderstorm started to roll in. Not great weather for the weekend of their big opening, but this was Cumbria, after all. In any case, the darkening skies suited his mood. His thoughts were all tangled up, his stomach in similar knots. He was going to be a *father*.

Sam struck out from the castle, past the walled garden that was his sister Olivia and her boyfriend Will's pride and joy, with the path leading out the other side towards the river and the wood. The glamping yurts were in a meadow on the other side of the wood, up a steep hill and far away enough for privacy but still within reasonable distance of the castle's amenities.

He'd actually enjoyed setting up the campsite, somewhat to his surprise. If it had been anywhere other than Casterglass, he would definitely have relished the challenge, but this place simply had too many memories. So while he'd enjoyed being outdoors and active, he'd been fighting his memory every step of the way. Still was.

Sam hiked through the wood, up the hill to the wooden gate that led to Casterglass Camping Site. Seph had carved a little wooden sign, complete with a toadstool and a frog, to mark its boundary. The six yurts were pitched for maximum privacy, but with a communal firepit and a set of deluxe Portaloos everyone could use. With the fells to one side and the sea on the other, the views were unparalleled. Standing there looking out at all that beauty, Sam felt as if he could finally breathe.

The trouble was, he still had no idea what he was going to *do*.

ROSE WOKE UP groggily, sunlight filtering through the floral curtains of the quaint if rather dated bedroom Olivia had led her up to yesterday afternoon. She'd been so kind, and Rose had been so exhausted, that she'd barely processed what Olivia had said about where the bathroom was, and something about the water pressure being a bit low. When Olivia had left her with a smile and several fresh towels, Rose had been about to fling herself into bed, only to catch raised voices from the kitchen downstairs.

Knowing she shouldn't and suspecting it would only hurt her, she'd tiptoed down the stairs to listen to Althea tell Sam he should ask for a paternity test. And Sam hadn't said no. Then she'd gone on about how Rose might be more pregnant than she was, lying to get hands on Sam's money and title. Like this was some Austen novel or something! Rose had crept back upstairs, peeled back the covers and then huddled in bed, feeling utterly alone and completely miserable, grateful when exhaustion gate-crashed her consciousness, and pulled her irresistibly into sleep.

Now, an astonishing fifteen hours later, she was staring up at the brown rabbit-shaped water stain on the ceiling and wondering what on earth she should do. Leave, probably. Her preference would be to slip out without telling or seeing anyone, but that hardly seemed gracious, considering how hospitable at least Olivia had been.

No, she'd say her thank yous and goodbyes, and then she'd scarper, because clearly that was what everyone wanted.

They'd labelled her a scheming gold digger, and she'd prove them wrong by leaving.

Unfortunately, she had nowhere to go, but that was hardly Sam's problem.

Was that why you came here? Because secretly you wanted to be asked to stay?

Rose shifted uneasily in bed, the thought like a tickle at the back of her throat, making her want to cough and her eyes water. Had she tricked herself into thinking she was oh so independent, when actually she wasn't? Did she want to be taken care of, just as Althea suspected?

No. She'd been taking care of herself for a long time, and she'd keep doing it. Her and the baby. She rested one hand on her bump, small but definitely there. She hadn't felt any kicks yet but the midwife back in New Zealand had said she should soon. She couldn't wait for that connection.

Resolutely Rose swung her legs over the side of the bed, blinked back the wave of dizziness she invariably felt, and then pulled some fresh clothes out of her rucksack. Would it be rude to ask if she could do some laundry before she went? No, she'd find a laundromat. She wouldn't ask these people for anything more. They could take their doubts and suspicions, their texts and paternity tests and shove—

No. She was going to be gracious. And then she was going to go.

Downstairs the kitchen was empty save for Olivia, who was tackling a huge pile of dirty dishes by the sink. Rose lingered in the doorway, unsure how to handle this moment, wondering where everyone was. Or even who everyone was, besides Sam and Althea. Judging by the number of dishes, about a dozen people had eaten breakfast.

"Hello," she finally ventured, her voice sounding uncharacteristically shy. Her feisty persona seemed to have abandoned her since she'd come to Casterglass. She needed to find it again, fast.

Olivia turned around, a ready smile lighting her fine-boned features. "Oh, hello! I hope you had a good sleep."

"Yes, and a very long one. I had no idea I'd sleep for so long."

"I'm glad you did," Olivia replied warmly. "Come, sit down. I've saved you some breakfast."

"Oh, that's so kind of you."

"No trouble," Olivia assured her, and as Rose took a place at the table, she placed various dishes and delicacies in front of her—a rack of toast, a pot of jam, a pat of butter, several rashers of bacon and a bowl of yoghurt.

"Coffee?" Olivia asked. "Or tea?"

"Neither, I'm afraid. I've gone off both since…" She touched her bump self-consciously. "But thank you."

Rose braced herself for some questions as she filled her plate, but Olivia had gone back to her washing, and so she was able to sit there in a surprisingly contented silence, eating a massive breakfast and watching the sun disappear behind some clouds the colour of a bruise. "Where is everyone?" she asked eventually. "Although I suppose the question really is, who is everyone? It looks like you were feeding an army."

"It feels that way sometimes." Olivia turned around again, leaning against the sink as she brushed a tendril of hair away from her face. "Let's see, there are my parents, Walter and Violet, and my older sister, Althea, who you've met." She gave a slight, apologetic grimace while Rose merely smiled. "And Althea's children—Ben, who is usually at uni, Poppy, and Toby. Then there's my younger sister Seph, she's about your age, and Will, my...my boyfriend." She ducked her head, almost embarrassed. A new relationship? Rose wondered. "And his two children, Lally and Jake. Oh, and Althea's fiancé John, and his daughter Alice. They don't all live here, but today's the grand opening of Casterglass Castle as 'the Lake District's premium tourist destination' so it's all hands on deck."

"Not a great time for me to drop in, then," Rose remarked.

"Well, you can't time these things, can you?" Olivia replied cheerfully. "Anyway, we're glad to have you."

Are you? Rose thought, but didn't say. There was no need to be snarky. She'd be leaving soon anyway. "Thank you for your hospitality," she told Olivia. "I'm really very grateful."

"Of course—"

"I'll finish up here and then I'll be out of your hair, I promise," she added, while Olivia looked at her in confusion.

"Out of…?"

"I'm going," Rose explained, and thankfully her voice came out firm. She was getting herself back together, at last.

"Going?" Olivia looked shocked. "But…but you can't yet, surely? You and Sam haven't talked properly."

Rose felt her smile turn brittle at the edges, like a leaf in autumn. "I think we've said enough."

"Oh, Rose, no." Now Olivia looked alarmed. "Sam has barely been able to process it yet. It came as quite a shock to him, as I'm sure you realise. Give him a chance, though. I know he'd want to be involved in his child's life."

"Well, I won't stop him," Rose replied dubiously, "but he hasn't said anything like that to me. And in the meantime, I don't want to be an inconvenience."

"You're not," Olivia assured her. "In fact, we could use another pair of hands around today. As you might have realised, things are a bit chaotic here. We open at ten and I'm supposed to be out in the garden, helping visitors with our treasure hunt, but…" She gestured to the dishes.

"Let me do the dishes," Rose offered. She would be glad of a way to pay back Olivia's kindness and generosity, and a few moments alone would give her time to formulate a plan that was not just walking out into the world with less than a tenner in her pocket. "And you can do whatever you need to do."

"Oh, you don't have to—"

"I want to. Please."

Olivia hesitated, and then said, "Okay. But...please. Promise you'll talk to Sam before you go."

Now it was Rose who was hesitating before she reluctantly nodded. Sam deserved a goodbye, at least. And she ought to give him her number, since he didn't have it. He'd never asked for it before. "Okay."

Olivia reached over to squeeze her hand. "I'm glad you're here," she said, and as Rose smiled back, she didn't miss the *I* rather than the *we*. Well, it was a start.

After Olivia had pulled on a pair of mud-splattered wellies and a mac and then left, Rose sat alone at the kitchen table, her chin in her hands, as she let the silence soak into her. Her gaze moved slowly around the room in all of its cluttered loveliness—the photo collage on the wall that looked at least twenty years old, the Penryn children a bunch of blond, gap-toothed kids; the mismatched teacups and saucers filling an entire Welsh dresser; the stack of newspaper supplements on the end of the sofa that looked like a collection of culture sections from about a year's worth of papers. It all spoke of a lovably aggravating mess, and it made her wonder about all the people Olivia had mentioned. Walter and Violet. Althea and John. Olivia and Will. Sam and Seph, and the kids whose names Rose couldn't remember. So much family, and she'd had basically none—just one dad who had disappeared from her life at the worst possible moment, and a mother who had never wanted to be involved.

She couldn't imagine living in a place like this. Growing up in a place like this. Something twisted inside her, a pang of longing, a frisson of fear. She knew she couldn't give her baby this kind of upbringing, and it looked like Sam didn't want to, so, well, neither would she.

Chapter Four

I T TOOK ROSE an hour to wash up; she actually enjoyed it, humming as she moved around the kitchen, figuring out where to put things away. She did her best to tidy up the mess without being invasive—straightening the pile of newspapers, lining up boots by the door—and then she found herself rearranging the spice rack by alphabetical order, because she couldn't resist and why *wouldn't* you do that? Strange, how she was compelled to neatness when her own life was so messy.

She'd just put the tarragon next to the thyme when a woman wafted into the room—at least that's what it looked like, almost as if she were floating. She was wearing some sort of mud-coloured kaftan and a lot of dangly necklaces of glass beads, and her faded blonde hair was piled up on top of her head with no less than three pencils stuck into it at various angles. Her pale blue eyes widened as she caught sight of Rose.

"Oh, how interesting," she remarked. "Someone I don't know cleaning my kitchen! What a *lovely* surprise." Rose swallowed a surprised laugh as the woman continued with her own gurgling giggle, "Do you make coffee, too?"

"I can," she said, and the woman gave her a beatific smile. "I'm Rose," she offered, as she set the kettle to boil.

"Violet." Violet sank elegantly onto the sofa, regarding Rose with unabashed interest. "Who are you related to? I simply cannot keep everyone straight anymore. I don't think we've had so many people here since Walter's sixtieth birthday. Or maybe it was his fiftieth. In any case, a long time ago."

"I'm not related to anyone," Rose said, "but I suppose I'm here because of Sam." Too late she realised how sticky this could get. Violet was Sam's *mother*. When she'd first come into the room, Rose had assumed she was a dotty aunt or something. Had Violet noticed her bump? Would she start asking awkward questions?

"Sam…" she mused, almost as if trying to place him.

The kettle started to hum, and Rose set about making coffee. "Just a quick visit," she told Violet. "I'll be off again."

"Oh, but you must stay at least through the weekend," Violet replied instantly. "We're having a house party—I do love house parties! We used to have the most amazing ones when the children were younger. I remember a cricket match that lasted nearly a week…and Walter's cousin stayed right through till September, which was a bit much, but there *is* room, isn't there?" She beamed at Rose. "Do say you'll stay. We're having a ceilidh tomorrow night, in the old barn. I do love to kick up my heels on occasion. And a pig roast, on the beach, as well."

"Oh, uh…" Rose's mind was racing. It did sound kind of fun, as well as incredibly awkward. *Why don't I just insinuate myself into your family, Sam?*

He would *love* that.

"So you'll stay?"

"I'm not sure," she hedged. "I have, um, a friend I need to visit…"

"They can come, too," Violet proclaimed grandly. "The more the merrier!"

Rose smiled weakly. "Here's your coffee," she said.

AN HOUR LATER, having put on a spare pair of wellies found in the appropriately named boot room, along with a waxed jacket that looked like it had last been worn for a pheasant shoot circa 1920, Rose headed outside.

The air was fresh and damp, and the rain had held off, save for a few sudden splatters, like the sky was spitting. Blue sky peeked from behind dark, rain-swollen clouds, so the heavens could open at any moment, but Rose didn't mind. She was used to rain, and she liked walking. She was looking forward to clearing her head, which was a complete jumble after talking to Violet for nearly an hour. She couldn't tell if the woman was off her rocker or just very, very shrewd. She'd managed to wrangle an agreement to stay for the weekend out of Rose, and she still wasn't sure how she'd done it. She dreaded to think how Sam would react, or Althea for that matter. Her suspicions, whatever they were, would seem likely to be proved. *Yes, I'm a gold digger,* Rose thought wryly, *looking for a square meal.*

She skirted through the walled garden, which looked lovely, with lots of hidden corners and secret paths amid a colourful tangle of blossoms, but was also full of children and their parents, and she didn't feel like seeing anyone. On the other side there was a set of stone barns built around a courtyard, which seemed to be another hive of activity— there was a little café, a gift shop, and what looked like several workshops for various kinds of craftsmanship. It all looked rather fascinating, but Rose was keen to avoid company and so she headed for the woods.

Damp mulch squelched under her feet as she headed up-hill, wet branches catching her coat and spraying her with drops. The noise from the garden and the courtyard fell away as the deep stillness of the forest fell on her like a blanket. Rose let out a gusty breath. *What was she doing here?*

She still had no idea.

She tried to think back to when she'd left New Zealand, just over forty-eight hours ago. Not that long, but it already felt like a lifetime. She'd decided to move on from Tairua, just as she'd told Sam, and she'd had a friend of a friend of a friend who ran a bar in Kingston, so she'd thought she might try Jamaica for a while. That had been the plan, but the reality of her pregnancy—something she hadn't let herself think about too much, because it had felt so overwhelming—had made her pause. And then, when she'd been walking along the beach, wondering how she'd managed to make a life for herself that felt so empty, she saw a father hoist his little girl onto his shoulders. She heard the girl's squeal of delighted laughter, and her heart had clenched hard.

She'd had that, as a child. She still missed it, so much, even if in the end it had turned out to have been not all that real. But she knew in that moment that she wanted more for this baby than what she could provide. A father. A family. A home.

All here in this place; yet the very last thing Rose knew she would ever do was beg for someone to love her. To take care of her.

Never again. Never, ever again.

Even for the sake of your baby?

That little voice in her head was really annoying, telling her truths she did not want to hear. For the sake of her baby, she should be willing to do anything, even beg, even though she'd insisted to Sam that she didn't want anything. She wouldn't ask.

Her hands instinctively clenched into fists and her body tensed, as if readying for a fight. She'd long ago developed a policy of doing the rejecting first, along with a persona of devil-may-care recklessness, because if you acted like you didn't care, then nobody would ever know when you were hurt. If you were lucky, you wouldn't even know yourself.

But a baby made doing both of those hard, even as they were more tempting. *Reject me, but don't reject my baby.* She had a duty as well as a deep-seated desire to protect this little life from being hurt the way she had been. Because one thing Rose knew was she would never let this child of hers down. Not the way her own parents had.

She stopped at the top of the hill, her breath coming out in great big huffs, because while her mind had been racing, she'd been walking fast, and her body felt it now. All around her the woods stretched, dark and vast, and Rose realised she could easily get lost for about forever. She might not have a plan, but she knew a bad one when she saw it.

She turned around to retrace her steps, only to glimpse a flash of white between the trees. A meadow in the distance, with what looked like big tents. Yurts, she realised. This had to be Sam's glamping site. He'd told her a little bit about it, back in Tairua, his voice caught between excitement and dread. Going home was complicated—she got that, even if she didn't understand why it was for Sam.

She hesitated, wondering if she should go check it out, look for him. They could have whatever conversation they needed to, and she'd be able to reassemble her tough, sassy persona, because that was who Sam had fallen for in the first place, and it made her feel strong. She'd show Sam and the whole world that she didn't need anyone, because needing people was dangerous, and it led to heartbreak and hopelessness and worse. No, she and this baby would be fine without Sam, if he chose not to be involved in their lives, which considering all the talk of paternity tests and texting, seemed likely.

And if he did?

Well, she'd cross that unlikely bridge when she came to it.

"THE SHOWER BLOCK is over there and the kitchen tent…"

Sam's voice trailed off as he caught sight of Rose walking across the meadow towards him. She had a stony look on her face even though she was smiling, and it made the words die in his throat.

"The kitchen tent?" One of his first glamping customers, a young woman and her friend, prompted helpfully.

"Er, yes. It's over there." He pointed towards the lean-to he'd built himself, and still smelled of fresh pine. "There's a fridge and a kettle and a stove ring… We're supplied by a generator so there should be ample propane to keep you going, but for environmental reasons we ask everyone to only do what's necessary. Barbecues are allowed, and there is a fire pit…" He trailed off again as Rose came to stand a few feet away, her hands tucked in the pockets of her waxed jacket. Her hair was back in a long French plait, the tip of it touching the small of her back.

"Anyway," Sam finished, "have a look around, go for a wander. I'm here in the on-site office if you need help with anything." He nodded towards the office cum shed he'd also built, at the edge of the meadow, so he could be on site as much as needed. Plus, building things with his hands had kept his brain from reliving too many old memories.

"Thanks," one of the women said, with an uncertain look for Rose. "Are you glamping too?"

"Me?" Rose looked bemused. "Nope, sorry, although if I did camp, I'd definitely be a glamping kind of girl. Gotta have a hairdryer." She smiled, that old, raffish grin he remembered from Tairua, and it gave him a jolt because he realised she hadn't given it since coming to Casterglass. It was like she'd changed outfits, slipped into a second skin.

"I know, right?" The woman grinned. "Well…" Another glance at Sam, and then back at Rose, as if she was trying to work them out, and then she nodded. "Nice meeting you."

When the two women had disappeared into their yurt, Sam turned to face Rose. She was smiling at him, cat's eyes glinting and tilted at the corners, chin tilted too. She seemed much more remote than she had yesterday, even though she looked more approachable.

"Hey." He suppressed the urge to clear his throat. "Did you sleep well?"

"Like a log. Sorry to be so AWOL, but I imagine it was something of a relief, considering?" It wasn't quite a question, and there was a laughing bite to her voice that Sam also remembered. *Are you going to ask me out or what?*

A few raindrops splattered down, almost like an afterthought, or perhaps a warning. At any moment the downpour would start and they would be soaked. "Fancy a cuppa?" he asked, nodding towards his office shed.

Rose shrugged her slender shoulders, as if she really couldn't care either way. "Sure," she said with a nonchalance that bordered on indifference.

Sam remembered this. He remembered how it made him crazy, because he'd been so into her and she'd been light, laughing, always dancing out of reach. Just like she was now.

"Come on, then," he said, and headed over to the hut. It wasn't much, since his main office was back at the castle—a desk, a table with a kettle and mugs and a couple of chairs. There was a propane heater for the chilly days, which were about three hundred and forty a year. He switched on the kettle, and then glanced back at Rose, who was standing in the doorway, looking around with a kind of restrained curiosity, like she didn't want to show much interest.

"You've got a nice set-up here," she remarked as she took a step into the shed and closed the door behind her.

"Yeah, it works pretty well." He was actually quite proud of what he'd accomplished in just a few months—an attractive, functioning glamping site and a ropes course, a doable business model, and the month of August pretty much fully booked. But he still felt restless, wasn't sure how he knew how to stop in one place. Coming back to Casterglass had always made him feel like running.

"So, I thought I'd leave this afternoon," Rose told him

just as the kettle started to boil. "I'll give you my number so you can be in touch if you need to be."

"If I *need* to be?" Sam fumbled for teabags, splattering boiling water as he filled two mugs. "Rose, do you really think I'd be okay with not being involved with my own child? Just letting you saunter off on your merry way, nice knowing you?" He realised as he said the words just how much it stung, to know she thought that way. "Never to see him or her—or you—again? Do you really think that's what I *want*?"

She stared at him for a few moments and he thought he saw a hint of uncertainty beneath her usual bolshie I-can-take-on-the-world expression. "I don't really know what you want, do I?" she finally replied coolly. "Your first question to me was to double-check it was yours, and the second one was why didn't I just text you the news. Considering you never bothered to give me your phone number, I couldn't, but whatever."

Her lips trembled before she pushed them up into a smile, and Sam winced as he handed her a mug of tea. "I'm sorry. That wasn't very sensitive of me. I was just taken aback at how sure you were that I didn't need to be involved. Like you didn't—don't—want me to be involved." He hesitated and then asked baldly, "Do you?"

Rose hunched one shoulder in a shrug. Her gaze was lowered as she blew on her tea. "I just wanted to be clear that I'm not trying to force you into anything. I don't want your money or your title, whatever your sister thinks."

Sam's stomach cramped as she threw him a challenging look. "You heard that?"

"You guys were shouting."

He sighed, raking a hand through his hair. "Look, Althea is suspicious because she's been burned pretty badly by her ex-husband. It's not personal."

"Really?" She let out a laugh that sounded just a little bit bitter. "Because it felt pretty personal." She took a sip of her tea. "Look, I get it. You don't know me, not really, no matter what happened halfway across the world. You have this castle, and a title, and whatever else—none of which I knew, by the way. When someone in the village told me I could find you up at the castle, I assumed you were working there, like a groundsman or something. Then they told me you were the heir." She shook her head as she sipped her tea again.

Sam tensed, because he did not want to think what else some anonymous villagers could have told her. "I don't think you're out for my money, Rose," he said quietly, because that much was true. "And in point of fact, I don't really have that much. Casterglass is run on a shoestring. But..." He hesitated and then, picking his way through the words, knowing it needed to be said, "I have to ask, and I'm not saying this in a judgemental way or anything..." Colour flared in his cheeks while Rose went very pale, but Sam forced himself to continue. "...but don't you think it makes sense to take a paternity test, just in case?" He turned it into a question but Rose was staring at him stonily, refusing to reply. "If the baby is mine, then of course I want to be involved. One hundred per cent. One hundred and *ten* per cent. But—"

"If it's not, buh-bye, it's been nice knowing you?" Rose finished in a hard voice. "Sam, do you actually think I would come all this way if I had any doubts about who the father was?" She shook her head, bitterness twisting her lips and hurt filling her eyes. "Do you think I sleep around that much?"

All right, he felt like a total heel now. A real jerk. Althea had put ideas in his head and the truth was he'd never felt as if he was on solid ground with Rose; she'd been like a will-o'-the-wisp, always out of his reach, even when she was in his arms. But he'd clearly hurt her with his suggestion, even though when Althea had suggested it, it had made sense. Now it just sounded callous. Cruel.

"I'm sorry—" he began, only to have her cut him off with a quick, violent shake of her head.

"The baby is yours, okay? I know that because you're the only possible option for a father." He opened his mouth but she talked over him, her voice rising shrilly. "And I know *that* because you were the first guy I ever slept with, not that you even noticed!"

And then, while Sam gaped at her in complete shock, she shut her mouth, whirled around, and ran out of the shed.

Chapter Five

ROSE RAN FROM the meadow, tearing through the woods, tears streaking her cheeks. They were more angry tears than ones of sorrow, although there was some sadness mixed in there, along with a lot of hurt. But mainly anger. A *lot* of anger. *Jerk. Arse. Thoughtless, arrogant, stupid—*

Her breath came out in a gasp as she dashed at her cheeks and kept running. She could hear Sam calling her, and she definitely didn't want to be found. She'd just blown it. Why had she told him he was the only guy she'd ever been with? It might be the truth, but it completely wrecked her sassy, sexy persona. The armour she'd always needed. She was tough, feisty, carefree, *strong*. She flirted and joked and acted as if she was always up for a laugh. No wonder Sam had asked whether the baby was his.

And yet it had *hurt*. Way, way more than it should have.

For a few seconds, as she ran through the trees, branches slapping her in the face, she let herself remember. She remembered exactly how serious and cute and well, *hot* he'd looked, sitting at the bar back in Tairua. His puppy-dog eyes of piercing blue, such a surprising combination. It was almost as if he hadn't realised how good-looking he was, and yet how could he not, looking the way he did? That mop of blond hair. That powerful body. Those eyes…

He'd kept shooting her looks while she'd been serving drinks, and she'd pretended not to notice, all the while slipping him covert glances she didn't think he'd seen. After half an hour of feeling his interest like a heat lamp, she'd turned to him, hands on hips, eyebrows raised, all flirt and sass.

Are you going to ask me out or what?

He'd looked shocked, and that had almost made her laugh. She'd felt fizzy inside, because while she'd had her fair share of male interest over the years, she'd never had someone look at her the way Sam had. Like she wasn't just sexy or cute, but special. Important.

Stupid.

Their first date had been a walk on the beach while they'd talked about everything but themselves. Rose hadn't wanted to get into her whole, sad history, and Sam had seemed to have his own secrets, or at least reservations, which had been *fine*. Keeping it light suited her perfectly, and so they'd shared travel stories, comparing top destinations and worst horror stories. He'd regaled her with tales of food poisoning in Thailand and she'd told him about getting held up in a bar where she'd been waitressing in Naples.

And yet somehow they'd gone from that to falling into bed the next evening, the kind of enormous leap Rose had obviously never made before, and one that seemed unfamiliar to Sam, as well, judging by the way he'd stammered, as they'd lain among the tangled sheets, *I don't normally do this…*

It had been wonderful and terrifying and frighteningly exposing all at once, to lie in the arms of someone who *got* you at the most fundamental level, but at the same time didn't know you at all. Rose had responded the only way she knew how—by doubling down on her insouciance. *Good thing I couldn't tell,* she'd joked as she'd scrambled up from the futon, already slipping on her sarong, her back to Sam. And obviously he hadn't either, although even in the throes of passion she'd made sure to act like she knew what she was doing.

He'd been silent for a long moment, and then he'd asked if he could see her again. *Maybe,* Rose had replied with such careless nonchalance, and now, as she stopped, panting, at the top of the hill, she wondered why she'd said that instead of what she'd felt—which had been *yes, please! How soon?*

But of course she hadn't said that, because she *never* said that. She survived so much better on her own. She'd learned that the hard way.

Rose looked down the hillside that led right down to a small, winding river snaking its way towards the sea, its steep bank stubbled with the stumps of trees that had been recently cleared. It had started to rain, icy, lashing pellets that stung her cheeks and blurred her vision even though it was late July. The weather here *sucked*. She wanted to go home, except she didn't even know where that was. She never had. It wasn't here, though. It couldn't be.

Why had she come to Casterglass, anyway? She still couldn't untangle the knotted mess of her own feelings, which was incredibly frustrating. Had some secret part of her been hoping Sam would man up and offer to take care of her and their baby? Probably, stupidly, yes, and that made her feel weak and helpless and wrong. Ashamed, too. She'd been so determined to show him she was independent, acting all the while like she wasn't. No wonder he'd been confused. She'd confused herself.

"Rose!"

Her name was a shout through the trees, carried away by the wind. Rose looked behind her and saw Sam striding through the forest, batting away bushes and branches, a thunderously determined look on his face. It was kind of sexy, to see him look so, well *strong*, and she felt a fizzy little thrill in her belly before she forced that stupid feeling away.

She did better by herself, remember? She was trying to be independent. She *was* independent.

Except haring through the forest, especially when she was seventeen weeks pregnant, was really kind of stupid and maybe even dangerous. Where exactly was she running to? Sam's ancestral castle where his scowling sister, not to mention the rest of his family, awaited? In fact, now that she thought about it, fleeing the scene had only made things worse. It had made her look weaker and even more foolish. She should have brazened it out, joked about how her lack of experience just showed how discerning she was, how lucky Sam had been. Instead she'd fled like the proverbial damsel. Hello, distress.

"Rose!"

Sam was coming closer, jogging through the woods, his gaze fastened on her so there was no escape. She would have to brazen it out somehow, although at this point Rose wasn't even sure what that meant. She was tired of acting like she didn't care, and yet the alternative was terrifying. Impossible.

"Rose, please. Let's talk."

Slowly, feeling defeated, Rose turned around to fully face him. Rain streaked down her face and plastered her hair to her head. She probably looked like a drowned rat. As she took a step towards him, her foot started slipping on the muddy bank, and then as she was windmilling her arms to right herself, she tripped on one of those stubbly little stumps and before she could catch herself she started tumbling down the hill, the world blurring by in a way that was completely terrifying while Sam shouted her name, a primal scream of horror; the last thing she saw was him standing at the top, his mouth agape, his eyes wide and panicked.

She rolled over and over, unable to stop herself, jolting and jarring her way down the hillside, one hand instinctively cradling her bump. Then, about halfway down, her head hit a stump and she saw an array of dazzling stars before she finally thudded to a stop at the bottom. The ground beneath her was spongy and soaking wet, and her whole body throbbed and ached. She stared up at the rain-swollen sky for a few dazed moments before the world went slowly black, like a curtain being drawn at the end of the play, and she lost consciousness.

PLEASE DON'T LET her be hurt. Don't let the baby be hurt. Please please please…

The prayer ran on a frantic loop through Sam's mind as he half-slid, half-ran down the hill, dropping to his knees beside Rose. Her face was pale and smeared with mud, and a livid purple bruise was already sprouting on her temple. Even in unconsciousness one hand was cradling her bump in that ancient sight of maternal protectiveness.

Please…

"Rose? Can you hear me?" This felt like the worst kind of déjà vu as he crouched beside her, willing her to wake up. Fainting twice in twenty-four hours! It couldn't be a good sign. "Rose, please, if you can hear me…"

Her eyes fluttered open. Her gaze was dazed and unfocused as she gazed blearily at him. "Oh, heavens…" she croaked. "Everything hurts."

"We need to get you to a hospital," Sam told her. He felt himself thankfully springing into problem-solving action mode, and it felt good. He could handle a crisis. Yesterday he'd been gobsmacked, but today he'd be in charge.

"No…" Rose began, so half-heartedly Sam didn't even bother to respond. Ideally, he would have waited for paramedics to move her, in case of a neck or spinal injury, but that would mean leaving her out in the rain for hours, which was something he couldn't possibly countenance. Slowly he scooped her up in his arms, and something fierce and primal roared within him when she curled her body against him, her damp cheek resting against his chest.

"Thank you," she murmured, and then her eyelids fluttered closed again.

Sam strode up the hill, taking each step with care, conscious that one small stumble could be disastrous for them both…and for the baby. *Their* baby.

The sudden, surprising thrill of it rippled through him, even as the rain lashed down and mud splattered his jeans and jacket. He was going to have a child. A son or a daughter. A family…

Of course, he knew he was getting way ahead of himself. Last time he'd checked, Rose had not seemed to welcome his involvement in any of that. But now that he knew the child was his—and he was sure of that, utterly—he felt as if the scattered pieces inside of himself had shifted, started to settle. He was pretty sure he wanted Rose in his life. He definitely wanted his child in his life.

Not that any of it was going to be easy.

"Sam, what on earth has happened?" Olivia was hurrying towards him from the walled garden as he emerged from the wood, rain sluicing off her waxed jacket as she took in the sight of Rose in his arms. "Is Rose okay?"

"I don't know." The terror of seeing her windmill down that hill slammed into him again. He didn't think he'd ever been so scared, not even on Kilimanjaro in that thunderstorm, or when he'd rowed across the Atlantic with just four other guys, and twenty-foot waves had crashed over their boat. "She fell down the hill in the wood. I'm taking her to hospital."

Olivia's eyes widened. "Oh, my goodness! Poor Rose! Will you go to Barrow or Kendal?"

Sam blinked; he hadn't considered options. "Whichever is closer, I suppose," he said, his arms tightening around Rose who had barely stirred.

"I'd go to Kendal, then," Olivia said. "Oh, poor, poor Rose! Do you want me to go with you?"

"No, you'd better stay here." Despite the downpour, visitors were milling about the garden and filling the tearoom, seemingly happy to make a day of it no matter what the weather. Thank goodness for hardy Cumbrians. He'd have to text his sister Seph and ask her to check on the glamping site, make sure his first campers weren't being rained out.

"Ring me to let me know she's all right," Olivia said, her forehead furrowed with anxiety.

"I will."

Sam marched over to the drive where his battered Land Rover was parked by the kitchen door. Rose opened her eyes.

"I'm fine…" she mumbled as she tried to rouse herself from his grasp.

"You're not. You fell down a hillside and you need to be checked out. And the baby." His throat closed up on the word and he had to swallow before going on. "We need to make sure you're both all right."

Fortunately, Rose didn't protest again, and he helped her into the front seat of the car, his heart lurching when he saw her wince as she adjusted her position. What if she'd sprained or even broken something? And what about the baby?

He ran back to the house to chuck some dry clothes for them both into the back of the Rover and then slid into the driver's seat. The rain lashed the windscreen as Sam drove down the drive towards the village and Kendal beyond. He glanced at Rose; her face was pale, her hair drenched, one hand still cradling her bump.

"I'm sorry," she whispered. "I've been really stupid."

"It was an accident, Rose."

She shook her head, a wet tendril of hair sticking to her cheek as she turned to look out the window. "I've just been really stupid."

"You haven't. If anything, I've been stupid." He grimaced as he thought about all the dumb things he'd said. *Is it mine? Why didn't you text?* And asking her to take a paternity test! He was not only stupid, but a prize arse. And if Rose had meant what she'd said, that he'd been the only one…well, then, he felt even stupider.

She let out a shuddery breath. "I just…the baby needs to be all right. That's all I want."

"I know."

She shook her head again, biting her lip as she stared out the window. Sam had about a million questions to ask, things he wanted to know, and others that he wanted them to figure out together, but he knew now wasn't the time. First things first…they'd make sure the baby—their baby—was okay. And he or she would be okay, because, well, they just had to be.

They didn't talk much as they drove nearly an hour to the hospital in Kendal, and Sam parked before helping Rose into the A&E department, which thankfully wasn't too busy. After half an hour of waiting—both of them miserable, silent, and cold—they were seen by a doctor for the bruise on Rose's head, which fortunately looked worse than it was, with no sign of concussion. After being assured she had no sprains or breaks, just a lot of aching muscles, she was referred to an ultrasound technician who had a reassuringly brisk and cheerful manner.

"Let's see how baby is, then! You'd be amazed how resilient these littles ones are. So very well cushioned, too, so try not to worry, Mum, okay?"

Rose looked a little startled at being called Mum, but she

nodded. The technician turned to Sam. "Are you don't need to worry either, all right, Dad?"

Dad… Sam tried to school his features into something reasonable. All the staff at the hospital so far had acted as if he and Rose were together, and neither of them had corrected the assumption. Sam hadn't because it hardly seemed important at this juncture, and frankly he kind of liked the idea that people thought they were a couple. He certainly didn't want the doctors and nurses thinking that he might be the kind of guy who walked out on the mother of his child.

As for Rose…? The truth was, he had no idea what she'd been thinking since she'd first got in the car. She'd been so quiet, so pale, and he knew she must be aching all over, if the bruise on her forehead was anything to go by. But he wished he had a little more insight into her thought process…something, he acknowledged with a suppressed sigh of resignation, he'd never had.

"So, let's see…" The technician lifted up Rose's shirt, her dungarees already unclasped and rolled down to her hips. Sam had averted his eyes at first, trying to preserve Rose's modesty, but curiosity and something deeper had drawn his gaze back to her bare tummy with its small, proud bump. The technician swathed her bump with clear gel, apologising for how cold it was, while Rose clenched her hands tightly on either side of her. Sam had an urge to hold one of those hands, to lace her fingers with his, but he didn't feel he had the right. They hadn't established anything yet. They'd barely talked.

"Right…" The technician began to prod and poke Rose's stomach—quite forcefully, Sam thought, and he almost said something, especially as Rose was grimacing a little, but then his gaze was caught by the screen, and the fuzzy black-and-white shapes emerging there. Was that a *baby*? It looked like a bunch of blobs, but then the room was filled with a wonderful, whooshing sound, like the hoofbeats of a galloping horse. He found himself grinning, and when he turned to Rose, she looked tremulous, terrified, and near tears.

"Is that the baby's heartbeat?" she asked in a voice full of wonder.

"Well." The technician sounded both smug and secretive, like the proverbial cat licking its whiskers, and Sam tensed instinctively.

"It is, isn't it?" he demanded. Surely now was not the time for guessing games or even being the tiniest bit oblique. The baby's heart had to be beating. That was what that sound was, *surely*.

"It's one of them," the technician replied, and then pointed to the screen. "Look, do you see? There's the head, the stomach, the hands, the feet…" As she pointed out each body part, the blobby shapes started to make sense…and Sam began to realise there were a lot of them. "And there is another head, stomach, hands, feet," the technician continued in a voice that managed to be pitched somewhere between wry and jubilant. "Congratulations, Mummy and Daddy—you're having twins!"

Chapter Six

ROSE STARED AT the ultrasound screen as the blobby shapes of not one, but two babies gained clarity. Yes, she could see two of everything—two stomachs, two beating hearts, two little heads. As well as four tiny hands, four kicking legs. They were curled into one another, like a matched set. *Twins.* She closed her eyes and swallowed down a sudden surge of bile. She hadn't even got a handle on having a baby, not really, and now she was having *two*? Really?

"Twins," Sam said faintly. Rose would have laughed at how gobsmacked he sounded, except she was reeling just as much as he was, if not more. *Twins.* She was going to be *huge*. No wonder she'd started showing early.

"This hasn't been caught before, clearly," the technician said. "So, you should book an appointment with your midwife to discuss your care. Women carrying twins can still have a normal pregnancy and birth, of course, but there can be some added complications, which are good to be aware of."

She handed Rose a scrap of paper towel to wipe the cold, wet gel from her stomach, smiling all the while. Rose had no idea what the expression on her face was. Complications? She couldn't even begin to get her head around the concept of having twins, never mind how difficult it might be. How on earth was she going to cope?

She felt her eyes fill suddenly with tears as she focused on wiping her belly. She tried to blink them back, because she did not want to cry in front of this smiley technician, never mind Sam, and really, most people would probably be thrilled they were having twins. Instant family! Oh heavens...

She sniffed, and Sam reached for her hand. "We'll figure this out," he said quietly, and the technician gave them a curious glance.

"It's a lot to get used to, I know," she said, "but twins are wonderful."

Then you have them, Rose thought, wretchedly. She bobbed her head in the semblance of a nod and kept wiping at the gel.

Neither she nor Sam spoke until they were walking out of the hospital. The rain had finally let up and the sky was a pale, opaque grey, like a blanket had been drawn across the sun. Rose's stomach growled. She realised she hadn't eaten since breakfast that morning, and it was now pushing three o'clock in the afternoon.

"Do you mind if we get something to eat before we head

back?" she asked Sam. "I'd rather not be three for three when it comes to fainting."

"Sure, we'll stop in Kendal." He looked at her with both concern and determination. "It will give us a chance to talk properly."

Oh great, Rose thought, knowing she was not remotely ready for that conversation, just as she knew how much they needed to have it. She had, she was coming to realise, been considering having a baby somewhat like having a handbag, a nice accessory. Pop it in her rucksack and off they went; it would sleep while she worked, they could share a bed, she'd feed it herself. Easy-peasy, although she hadn't even got that far in her thinking, not really, just vague images that had seemed pleasant and easy. *Tell Sam and then…* She'd never had a plan, not anything even *close* to a plan, and now she was having twins.

She really needed to start being sensible. Start *coping*.

They drove in silence to a small café in the centre of Kendal that did toasted sandwiches and jacket potatoes. Rose ordered an enormous potato covered in cheese and beans and a side order of chips, her stomach growling again at the thought of it all.

"I'm eating for three, after all," she told Sam, who looked startled.

"I didn't say anything."

"You looked it," Rose told him as she took a sip of her water. "And I don't blame you. I'm probably going to be the size of a house by the time I'm nine months along." She stared glumly out the rain-spattered window.

"The important thing is that the babies are healthy." He shook his head slowly. "Babies. Wow."

"Yeah, I know."

Sam hesitated, and then, placing his hands flat on the table, studying his spread-out fingers, he asked quietly, "What was your plan, Rose? I mean, what were you thinking you would do when the baby came?"

"I didn't really get that far, to be honest." She couldn't be anything but truthful now, not after this curveball life or fate or providence had thrown at her. Twins, she knew, she could not handle by herself.

"But you were so sure I didn't need to be involved."

She tensed and then forced a shrug. "I just didn't want you to feel cornered."

"Did you want me to be involved?" he asked, looking up. There was a vulnerability lurking in his eyes, but a hardness to his tone. "Do you now?"

Now Rose was the one hesitating. *Honesty, remember?* "I don't know," she admitted. "I've been completely on my own since I was eighteen, so that's what I'm used to."

"I don't actually know anything about your family. Do you…do you have parents?"

Rose rolled her eyes, just another defence mechanism. "Well, I didn't spring from the cabbage patch."

Sam stared at her steadily. "You know what I mean."

Their food arrived then, saving Rose from having to reply right away. She needed to figure out how much to tell Sam, because what she definitely didn't want was him feeling sorry for her. She absolutely refused to let his choices be motivated by either pity or guilt. If he wanted to be involved, fine. They'd figure out a way. But she wouldn't sucker him into manning up as a dad.

"Well?" Sam asked as he bit into his sandwich.

Rose toyed with a bit of potato on her fork. "My mum left when I was four," she finally said. "I barely remember her, so I don't really miss her. She got married again, some millionaire in the south of France. They live there, do the whole party scene."

Sam nodded slowly, absorbing that. "And your dad?"

This one was a bit more difficult. "It was just the two of us for my whole childhood. He travelled for work, and he took me with him. We went everywhere—all the continents save Antarctica. We stayed in hotels, sometimes for a few days, sometimes for a few weeks or even a month. It was amazing." A stupid lump was forming in her throat, because it *had* been amazing. Just her and her dad, against the whole world. And then she'd found out that the whole world had basically been against him...for a reason.

"What about your education?" Sam asked.

Rose shrugged. "If we stayed long enough, I'd go to a local school. If not, I educated myself. When I was sixteen, he put me in a boarding school in Switzerland. One of those fancy finishing schools where half the students get there by private helicopter."

"Wow." Sam smiled wryly. "That sounds even more unconventional than my childhood."

"Oh?" Rose couldn't help but be curious. They'd never talked about their childhoods, in nearly three months of more or less being together. "How so?"

"I was home-educated by my parents until I was ten, although I use the term loosely. It was more like my parents taught us when they remembered we existed; the rest of the time we were practically feral."

Considering her one brief encounter with Violet Penryn, Rose could imagine her forgetting she had children, never mind needing to educate them. "You don't sound bitter," she remarked slowly. "Did you like it like that?"

"Ye-es," Sam said slowly. "I actually did, at the time. The freedom was amazing. Day-long games of hide-and-go-seek or making dens in the woods…the occasional dramatic production when my mum decided to take an interest. I think we performed all five tragedies of Euripides before I was eight."

"I feel like there's a big but coming," Rose told him with a small smile. He was speaking slowly, choosing his words with care just as she had, as if he was deciding just how much to admit.

"When I was ten, I was sent to the local primary for my last two years," Sam said, his tone turning weirdly flat. "The adjustment was difficult. And then after that I went to boarding school, a draughty place in Yorkshire that was run on a shoestring. Cold showers, horrible food, teachers who shouted at you." He gave her a sudden, devastating grin. "I actually loved it."

"Well, we've both had unconventional childhoods, then."

"Yes." Sam was silent, the smile dying from his lips as his gaze turned faraway for a second, before it snapped back to hers. "Yes, we have."

THEY'D SAID ENOUGH about their childhoods, surely. Sam had no desire to talk about those two years of living hell at the primary school in Casterglass, or the ignominious end of his secondary school career and the withdrawn offer from Leeds to study geography. He sensed Rose had things she didn't want to talk about either; she still hadn't explained why she'd been on her own since she was eighteen. Had her father died? Was she completely out of contact with her mother? Either way, he thought he was starting to understand her spikiness a little bit more. They both had their coping mechanisms, perhaps.

"Anyway, perhaps we need to think about the future more than the past," he said, and Rose popped a huge chunk of cheesy potato into her mouth.

"Yes," she said, swallowing. "I suppose we do."

"You said you didn't want me to feel cornered," Sam forced himself to say, even though it felt like opening himself to rejection, "but how do you feel about me being involved? Because I'd like to be. These are my children." The words sounded completely strange, and yet utterly right. "I don't want to walk away from my responsibilities."

Rose had a funny look on her face, which made Sam feel like he'd said the wrong thing. But what was wrong about wanting to care for his own children, for heaven's sake? He was getting tired of feeling like he never put a foot right, but that was his usual mode of operation, at least when it came to his family. It was why he preferred solitude to company, the great outdoors to being cooped inside with people. When he was by himself in nature, he didn't get it wrong. At least, not as much.

"I'm glad you want to be involved," she said after a moment, sounding so neutral Sam felt like gritting his teeth.

"You said you hadn't thought about what you would do when the baby came," he said, trying to sound encouraging rather than judgemental. "What were you going to do after telling me? Where were you going to go?"

Rose looked down at her half-eaten potato as she answered. "I have a friend in Newcastle I was going to look up. She works at a bar. I thought I might get some work there."

That was it? That was her whole plan?

"I know, I know," Rose said, looking up, her mouth twisting. "It wasn't much of a plan, but I thought I had some time to figure things out."

"Have you seen a midwife?"

"I saw one back in Tairua, when I was about twelve weeks. She heard the heartbeat then—but only one. I guess she didn't look for another one. So today really was a surprise."

That had been over a month ago. A sliver of hurt needled him as he realised just how long she'd kept the news of her pregnancy from him—why? "Why didn't you tell me before now?" he asked, trying to keep that sliver of hurt from showing in his voice.

Rose was silent for a long moment, her gaze lowered. Sam decided to wait her out. "I was scared," she finally said, so quietly that Sam sensed this was not an easy admission for her to make. "I thought you'd think I trapped you, that you wouldn't want to be involved." She looked up, her eyes large and luminous, the colour of moss. "I wasn't going to tell you, because I didn't want you to be angry or uninterested or whatever." She took a quick breath and hurried on before Sam could even process that confession. "But then I realised that wasn't fair. That you should know, at least. And I knew I didn't want to stay in Tairua for the winter, so I thought I'd come back to England, have my baby here. I really didn't get much farther than that, which I know sounds massively irresponsible, *is* massively irresponsible..." She trailed off with a shaky laugh. "I was just...taking one day at a time, I suppose."

A new realisation was filtering through Sam's mind. "Rose...I only left New Zealand two months ago. You would have been two months pregnant already, right? Did you know then? Did you know and not tell me, when I was leaving?" He thought of that moment when he'd asked to stay in touch, and she'd laughed and looked away. *It was fun, but...* Had she said that, knowing she was having his child?

Again, Rose was silent for a long moment. "I didn't know for sure," she finally said. "I didn't take a pregnancy test till after you left. I think I was hiding it from myself, never mind you." A pause as she looked down at her plate. "I'm sorry. Saying it all out loud makes me realise how— how selfish I seemed, but I really wasn't thinking that way. I wasn't thinking at all. And...I suppose I just assumed you wouldn't want to be involved. It was only later that I realised you had a right to know, and I had a responsibility to tell you." She looked up at him, her eyes wide and clear. "I'm sorry I didn't tell you before. I should have, I know."

Clearly she had set a very low bar, something else Sam was used to. No matter how many times he climbed a mountain or raised thousands for charity, his father would always regard him with that faintly bewildered look of disappointment. He knew it well. *You had so much potential, Sam. So much promise...*

"Okay," he told Rose. "I mean, I get it." Sort of, but it still hurt. Had she really thought so little of him? Why should he be surprised? "But now you're here, and the situation has changed, so we need to think practically about the future."

"You sound like you're drawing up a development plan." There was a faint note of reproach in Rose's voice that annoyed him.

"Well, that's what we need to do, isn't it?" *What she should have done before.* His tone said the words for him. Rose looked away. "I'm just trying to act responsibly here."

"Right."

Why did she sound so disappointed, when he said that? Sam released a pent-up breath of frustration. "We should probably get back to Casterglass," he told her as he took out his wallet to pay for their meal. "I've got to check in on the glamping site, and you should get some rest."

"But we haven't resolved anything yet."

"We have time." He had another two sets of campers coming tomorrow morning, and there was a hog roast and ceilidh tomorrow night, with all the locals invited, something he was actively dreading. He did not have the emotional space for this, and yet he had to have it, no question, maybe just not right in this moment.

"You're not planning to go anywhere, are you?" he asked her, a hint of challenge in his voice. "I mean, if your big plan was kipping on someone's sofa in Newcastle, you might as well stay at Casterglass, don't you think?"

"With that kind of invitation, how can I resist?" Rose snapped, and they glared at each other for a moment, taking

Sam by surprise.

Okay, he was more than a little bit hurt by the way Rose had handled this, cutting him so completely out of the picture, and it was coming out in the way he spoke to her. He took an even breath. "I'm just saying," he said more levelly, "we have more time. You are, of course, welcome at Casterglass for—well, for as long as you want. Until the baby—babies—come. And after." Concepts that were blowing his mind. Would they try to make a go of it? Get *married*? He felt his heart skip a hectic beat as panic took hold of him. He couldn't think about anything like that just yet. "We don't have to solve everything in one go. The important thing is for you to recover, and see a midwife, and…" He trailed off helplessly. "Get on surer ground."

"Okay," Rose replied after a moment. "Thank you." She reached for her coat, biting her lip as Sam put a twenty-pound note on the table. "I'm sorry, I'll pay you back for lunch."

"That's hardly necessary, Rose."

"I don't want to sponge—"

"You're not *sponging*." Were they going to be constantly arguing about money along with everything else? It seemed absurd, when she so obviously didn't have any. "It's fine, okay? Let's go."

He rose from the table, reaching out a hand to help her up, which she ignored. As she walked out of the café, her small, slender back seemed to bristle with affront. How had he offended her so much? Sam wondered, feeling both frustrated and desolate. He was trying to do the right thing, but just like always, it was never enough. Suppressing a sigh, he followed her out to the car.

Chapter Seven

"H E-*LLO?*"

Rose stirred groggily in her bed, blinking the smiling face of Violet Penryn into focus as she poked her head around her bedroom doorway. It was early evening by the looks of it, and Rose had been asleep since she and Sam had returned from Kendal. She'd avoided all conversation or even so much as a single glance as she'd hurried upstairs and practically flung herself into bed. She hadn't been able to bear thinking about any of it—his sister's hostility, his family's curiosity, his reluctant responsibility. He was doing the right thing, oh yes, but he didn't seem very happy about it, which was exactly the scenario Rose hadn't wanted.

Yet as she'd lain in bed and willed sleep to come, she'd realised she didn't have much, or even any, choice. She had nowhere to go, very little money, and *two* babies in her belly. She was going to have to accept Sam's help.

"Are you awake?" Violet asked as she stepped into the room, closing the door behind her. She was carrying a cup of tea, Rose saw, with a couple of biscuits on the saucer. "I thought you might like a drink," Violet said grandly, and proffered her the cup.

Rose scooted up in bed, wincing as every muscle and sinew ached. She felt as if she'd had a spin in a tumble dryer. "Thank you," she told Violet as she accepted the cup. "That's so very kind of you."

Violet perched on the edge of the bed, clearly settling in for a chat, or at least some information gathering. "Sam said you're going to be staying with us for a while?" she asked, her thin, pencilled eyebrows expectantly raised.

"Er, yes. I suppose so." Realising she sounded ungrateful, Rose continued hurriedly. "Thank you so much for your hospitality."

"Of course, of course." Violet waved this aside with a clank of bangles siding up and down one thin wrist. "We're so very happy to have you, my dear." Her gaze moved with a smiling pointedness to Rose's middle. "Am I correct in believing you to be expecting a child?"

So, Sam hadn't told the rest of his family about her? Rose was surprised, but beneath that surprise was another, more complicated emotion—relief or hurt? Or both? She wanted to be in charge of the narrative but why on earth hadn't he *said*? Was he ashamed of her? Wanting her gone? "Yes, I am," she said, and left it at that.

Violet, however, was clearly too shrewd not to put the rather glaringly obvious two and two together. "And am I correct in also believing that my son is the father?" she asked gently.

Rose stared at her, stricken. Wasn't it for Sam to say? And yet how was she supposed to answer that question, except with the truth?

"Oh, my dear," Violet said, smiling, "there's no need to say anything, for your face says it all." Rose gulped. "I take it the news was a surprise to him?"

"Er, yes."

Violet nodded slowly. "I do think he will make an excellent father," she mused, her gaze turning distant. "He has always taken his responsibilities so seriously. Do you know he spent hours on a project for the village school—a model of the castle, in fact, made of toothpicks and yoghurt pots. It was really quite remarkable. I wonder where that went..." She looked around the room, as if expecting the model to materialise.

Yes, Rose had no doubt that Sam would take his responsibilities seriously indeed, which was a good thing, mostly. But it stuck in her craw only to be someone's responsibility, when she wanted them to *care*.

Although, hold on. Did she really want Sam to care? Why did she have to be such a blasted tangle of contradictions? *Because your parents screwed you up good and proper.* But surely, she was too old to blame them for the way she was. If anyone needed to take responsibility, Rose thought, it was her.

"We're still figuring out how it's all going to work," she

told Violet, her voice coming out in something of a croak.

"Oh, I'm sure it will all work out just fine," Violet said complacently. "It usually does, doesn't it?" This sounded like the life philosophy of someone who had, on occasion, forgotten she had children and it was, Rose knew, very close to her own. She patted Rose's knee. "But you must let us know if you need anything, my dear. I saved some of the baby clothes I knitted for my four… Althea had the most darling Babygro, made out of cheesecloth. Very eco, which is so fashionable these days, isn't it? I must see if I can find it…"

A forty-year-old Babygro made of cheesecloth? Well, Rose supposed, stifling a laugh, it was better than nothing.

Violet rose from the bed. "You will come down to supper, won't you? We're all dying to meet you properly. Olivia's making a sausage casserole. It smells heavenly." She patted Rose's arm. "Do come, my dear."

Rose pictured an inquisition over plates of casserole and her stomach cramped. It sounded awful, and yet… "Thank you. I'd love to."

Violet's smile was a little too knowing for Rose to hope she'd believed that lie. "Excellent," she said, turning to the door. "I think it's in about half an hour, although people do tend to drift in. We don't run a tight ship here, I'm afraid. We never have."

Which did not come as a surprise.

Rose spent the next half hour trying to make herself look

presentable. She took a shower, remembering as she rinsed her hair that Olivia had warned her about the water pressure, which was measured in drips. She shook out her last clean outfit from her rucksack, a loose dress in lavender cotton that was decidedly crumpled. She could hardly ask for an iron, not at this stage anyway, and so she smoothed it out as best as she could, put her damp hair in a French plait, and tried to cover the bruise on her temple with a slick of concealer. To say she'd cleaned up well enough would, unfortunately, be a gross overstatement. She looked barely presentable, but that would have to do.

And yet she was terrified. Heart palpitatingly, hands dampeningly, stomach lurchingly scared out of her *wits*. The thought of heading down those stairs by herself and facing an unknown family, some of them decidedly hostile… How many people had Olivia mentioned? The names were jumbled in her mind—Althea, of course, and Olivia, Violet and Walter, Seph and someone else…quite a few someone elses. She wouldn't even be able to keep their names straight, and they'd all be glaring at her suspiciously.

She'd been alone for a lot of her life, Rose realised, but she'd never *felt* as alone as she did now.

A knock sounded on the door of her bedroom. "Rose?"

It was Sam, and Rose felt an enormous rush of relief as she hurried to the door and opened it. He stood there, hair damp from a recent shower, dressed in a button-down shirt of blue check and a pair of rumpled khakis. His eyes looked very blue, and he smelled like soap and Rose could have kissed him.

"I thought we could go down together," he said, and then she could have cried.

"If you want," she managed in an offhand way, wondering why she always had to ruin it. "Thanks," she added, a half-measure at best.

Sam shrugged. "My family is a bit intimidating, and that's at the best of times."

"Thanks for the warning. Your mother and Althea are both fairly terrifying."

He raised his eyebrows. "You met my mother?"

"Yes, twice. Once this morning and once just a little while ago, when she very kindly brought me a cup of tea." Rose hesitated and then admitted, "She asked me about the baby. Singular, so I'm assuming you didn't tell her about having twins."

"I haven't told anyone yet," Sam replied as he ran a hand through his hair. "I'm still trying to get my head around it first before my family barrages me with questions."

"So am I." They shared a wry smile that heartened Rose, perhaps more than it should. She could fall in love with him, she thought with a sudden jolt, if she let herself. It wouldn't take very much, just a little kindness, to build on what she knew was already there. What she already felt. "I'm sorry," she told him, "if I stole your thunder, but I told her you were the father. She asked me point-blank."

"That's okay." Sam looked surprised. "It's not like we can keep it a secret, Rose. Or that I'd want to. I just haven't had a chance to have a proper discussion with anyone."

"I know, but…information control, you know? Or maybe damage control. Either way…"

"It's fine." He shrugged again, gave her another smile. "It's fine," he said again. "We're going to be telling everyone sooner or later, right? And in about thirty seconds we're going to face my whole family, and trust me, they'll take *point-blank* to a whole new level."

She laughed at that, a soft huff that died away when she realised he was entirely serious. "Okay, well," she said, straightening her shoulders, "we'd better face the music, then."

SAM HAD TO steel himself as he entered the kitchen with Rose at his side. He would have liked to face this evening with more of a sense of what Rose felt, or hell, even what *he* felt. They'd started to talk but it still all felt very new and uncertain. He felt uncertain, anyway. And everyone was going to ask about a million questions, some a bit vague, some basically blunt. He foresaw a lot of awkward moments ahead.

"Well, here they are!" His mother's voice floated through the room as they came together into the kitchen.

Instinctively Sam glanced at his father seated at the head

of the table; he was smiling at him with a look of wry sorrow in his twinkling eyes that Sam knew all too well. He glanced away quickly, taking in the whole scene—Olivia bringing an enormous casserole out of the Aga, Poppy setting glasses, Ben and Toby joshing around. Althea was standing in the corner, her arms folded, her lips pursed as she surveyed both him and Rose. William was wrangling Lally and Jake to the table, and John was chatting with his daughter Alice and Seph, who looked more animated than Sam had seen her in a while. Normally she looked like she was fighting off a sulk, and that only half-heartedly.

All the conversations that had been rumbling through the room broke off, leaving a sudden, appalling silence, as everyone turned to stare at them. Rose's face went red and she tilted her chin up a couple of inches.

"It's so nice to be here," she managed in a voice that didn't quite wobble.

"And it's so nice to have you here," Olivia replied as she placed the casserole in the middle of the table. "Why doesn't everyone grab a seat and then we'll barrage you with all our names?"

"All right," Rose said with a small smile, and Sam sent his sister a grateful look. At least one person was making it easier.

But actually, everyone was, to varying degrees; after they'd all sat down, they went around the table like a Sunday school class and said their names, and Rose laughed and said she'd try to remember everyone's, but probably wouldn't. Althea had lost her thoughtful scowl and even Seph was smiling. Maybe it would be okay.

Sam had just taken his first forkful of casserole when the questions started.

"So, Rose," Will asked with a friendly smile, "what brings you to Casterglass?"

A complete and total silence followed this question, so Will looked around uncertainly. Sam saw Olivia shooting him daggers and realised they must not have had that discussion.

Rose glanced around at all the faces, expressions ranging from mortified to morbidly curious, and Sam saw the gold flash in her eyes and felt the need to brace himself.

"Well, I'm having Sam's baby," she stated baldly. "So, I thought I should tell him about it."

Will's face flushed bright red. "Oh. Er." He tugged at his collar. "Sorry, I didn't realise…"

"Didn't he know?" five-year-old Lally asked, her eyes wide and all too innocent.

Rose bit her lip. "Well, he does now," she said with an attempt at cheerfulness. She shot Will a wry look. "Sorry if that makes things awkward with a birds-and-the-bees discussion—"

"What does this have to do with birds and bees?" Lally demanded in a loud voice, tugging on her father's sleeve.

Rose's face reddened all the more, but Sam saw the exact

moment she decided to ride it out, flashing everyone a laughing look as she tossed her plait over her shoulder. "Well, clearly I've got this parenting thing down," she deadpanned, and a few relieved titters rippled through the room. Sam tried to give Rose an encouraging smile, but she wasn't looking at him.

"So, Althea, what were the day's takings?" Walter asked with a smile, a change of subject he made gallantly enough, but it felt like the screech of conversational tyres. Sam felt Rose sag next to him, just a little, in relief.

"Quite good, I'd have to say," Althea replied, her chest puffing out a little. "We had two hundred adults through the gates today, and at ten pounds a pop…"

The enthusiastic murmurs and cheers that greeted this announcement made her grin. "Of course, we're not going to have these kinds of numbers every day. But it's a good start."

"A very good start," Walter agreed. He beamed at his oldest child in a way he never had at Sam. "Well done, Althea!"

She blushed and ducked her head like a schoolgirl. "Thanks, Daddy."

"And with all the children," Olivia added. "At five pounds a pop…"

"That's some serious money." Ben, having just finished his first year at Durham and who had been helping with the accounts, grinned.

The conversation moved on, as everyone went through

the adventures and mishaps of the day, from a tantrumming child who had found the treasure trail through the garden too difficult, to running out of scones in the tearoom. Seph had sold a round dozen of her woodcarvings, and Poppy was very pleased with the feedback on the Casterglass logo she'd designed.

With the conversation flying all around them, Sam took the opportunity to lean closer to Rose. "How are you feeling?"

"A bit of a headache. Nothing too bad." She gestured to the busy, noisy table. "Is it always like this?"

Sam glanced at everyone in animated conversation. "There are a few more people than usual, I suppose, but essentially yes. Big families."

The smile she gave him was both wry and twisted. "I wouldn't know."

He nodded in understanding, although he knew he didn't, not really. How could he? He'd always been surrounded by family, although, perhaps like Rose, he'd often felt alone.

"Feel free to duck out whenever you need to," he told her. "I do. In fact, I should check on the glamping site. Is that okay—"

"Yeah, sure." She waved him away. "No problem."

Sam couldn't help but feel uneasy as he excused himself from the table. He didn't like leaving Rose alone, and yet in fact she wasn't alone, and she was surely feisty enough to handle his family. And yet…since coming to Casterglass, she'd seemed less and less feisty, more and more vulnerable. What if her sassiness was all an act? Who, then, was the woman he'd fallen so hard for back in Tairua?

The question was still niggling him as he headed out into the night, the bright light of his high-beam torch cutting a powerful swathe through the dark woods. As he came onto the glamping site, he saw the two yurts were lit up from within; everything looked cosy. The kitchen tent had clearly been used, and the shower block, as well. He spent half an hour wiping down the sinks and cleaning loos before he went to his office to check on the camping paperwork—two more camping parties coming the next day, and then another two after that. It looked to be busy all the way through August.

And then what? By September Rose would be nearly six months pregnant. The camping would drop off, and he could go back to the freelance data analysis that paid the bills. As for the charitable ventures that had filled him with purpose, given him a high along with a way to prove himself…well, he couldn't exactly canoe down the Amazon with newborn twins, could he?

Life was going to have to change. Radically. He stared into space for a few minutes, trying to sort through his feelings about that prospect, but he couldn't separate the anxiety of the unknown from the fear of the what-if. Somewhere in there was a flicker of excitement, too, but he was nervous about fanning it into flame. He and Rose needed to talk more; they needed to make sure the babies were okay; they had to figure out the future…

But not tonight.

He walked back to the castle under a sky full of stars; the rain had moved off and the clouds had cleared to leave a night sky like a canvas by Van Gogh, wide and glittering. As he came through the woods he saw the lights of the castle, a welcome glimmer in all the darkness, and then, lit by a swathe of moonlight, a slender figure staring up at the sky. Rose, out here by herself, alone.

Sam walked up to her and slowly she lowered her head to look at him, although in the darkness he wasn't able to gauge her expression. "You survived my family."

"Only just." He thought he saw the glimmer of a smile. "I escaped out here for some peace and quiet."

"Great minds think alike." She nodded, wrapping her arms around herself, and he continued hesitantly, "It's been quite a few days, hasn't it?" Thirty-six hours ago, he hadn't even known he was going to be a father, and now he was having *twins*.

"Yes, it has." She blew out a breath. "Judging from the way everyone was talking after dinner, tomorrow's going to be busy, too."

"Yes, with a ceilidh and a hog roast on the beach."

"All the locals invited?"

"Yes." He heard how taut his voice had gone and he strove to sound more relaxed. "Should be fun."

She shot him an uncertain look and said nothing.

"We can take this slowly, can't we?" he asked quietly. "There's no reason to rush into decisions of any sort." He'd meant to sound reassuring, but he feared he'd managed the opposite.

Rose didn't look at him as she nodded slowly. Then she turned to head back inside. "I should get some sleep," she said, still without looking at him.

"Goodnight—" Sam began, but she'd already gone.

Chapter Eight

THE SKY WAS a pale, washed blue, like faded denim, as Sam poured himself a cup of coffee from the flask he'd brought and gazed out at the glamping site from the doorway of his little office. One set of campers had yet to stir, and the others were doing a fry-up in the kitchen tent, judging from the tantalising smells of bacon and eggs.

He let out a gust of breath and then sipped his coffee, enjoying the early morning sunlight on his face. Last night, after Rose had gone to bed, he'd headed to his broom cupboard cum office in the castle and checked on his schedule—in addition to the glamping, he had a family group of fourteen doing the ropes course this afternoon, and another group of six tomorrow. He also had a shedload of online advertising to be getting on with and a dozen emails to answer; he had not planned for the kind of interruption he'd ended up having. And then of course there was his 'real' job, several freelance gigs he really should agree to do, for the money. *Especially if you're starting a family.*

He started to turn back to the shed when he saw a figure

emerging from the woods. At first, he thought it was Rose, and his heart lurched in panic at the thought of her navigating the muddy trail again, but then he realised with a not-very-pleasant jolt that it was actually his father. Since Walter Penryn rarely left his study or the castle environs, having him come all the way up here must mean, Sam knew, that his father wanted to have a 'serious discussion'.

They'd had a few over the years—from when he'd got in trouble at the village school for skiving, to when he'd been expelled from boarding school, to when his father had asked him if he would ever consider taking on the castle himself. Every single time, Sam knew, his father had both started and finished the conversation disappointed. He had a feeling today would be no different.

"Sam." The smile his father gave him as he huffed and puffed his way over to the shed did not reach his eyes, which drooped sadly, like a basset hound's.

"Hey." Sam nodded a rather terse greeting; he didn't mean to, but somehow he always found his hackles rising instinctively when his father cornered him in this way. They were very different people; he'd always known that, from the time as a little kid he'd knocked over one of his dad's precious orchids, trying to get his attention in the greenhouse, and his father had looked as if he might cry.

It's a flower, Sam had thought then, *and I'm your son.*

He'd never once given voice to that kind of sentiment, though, and he doubted he ever would.

"My goodness." Walter Penryn surveyed the glamping site, one hand to his chest as he caught his breath. "This is all quite extensive, isn't it?"

His father hadn't, as far as Sam knew, visited the glamping site or the ropes course once since he'd started working on them.

"Thanks," he said, although he wasn't sure if 'extensive' was actually a compliment.

Walter turned to him, dropping his hand as his eyes narrowed and he cocked his head to one side. "You've had quite a few interesting developments lately, haven't you?" he remarked in his gently whimsical way. It worked on a treat on Althea and Olivia, Sam knew, who melted into puddles of filial affection when their father gave them that loving, quizzical look, but it just irritated Sam. It felt manipulative somehow, although he suspected it wasn't. It was just the way his father was. He wondered, suddenly, how Seph reacted to it; if like him, she felt a latent anger at their parents for being so, well, *spacey*. Almost as if they didn't care, although Sam knew, deep down, that they did.

"You could say that," he agreed neutrally. A brisk wind was blowing in from the sea, no more than a grey-blue glint into the distance, and he nodded towards his office. "Do you want to come inside?"

"All right."

His father followed him into the shed and Sam pulled out a chair for him. "I have some coffee, if you'd like some," he offered, and his father gave him a surprised smile.

"Do you really! I'd be delighted."

Wordlessly Sam poured the coffee and added a splash of milk, just as he knew his dad liked it. He handed it to him, bracing himself for whatever was coming next.

His father took the cup with murmured thanks, rotating it between his hands as he gazed down into its milky depths. Sam could see the thinning patch on top of his head. The pink skin peeking through the white wispy hair looked pale and somehow fragile. His father was getting old, he thought with a lurch of something like alarm. He was over seventy. He wondered if they would sort out their differences before he died. What a macabre, maudlin thought.

"So," Walter said, looking up with a smile. "Rose."

"Yes…?"

"She is pregnant with your child."

"You know she is." Already he sounded defensive. He just couldn't keep himself from it, it seemed.

"What are your intentions, Sam?" A stern note had entered his father's voice, which Sam recognised from previous conversations. *Now that your university offer has been withdrawn, what do you intend?* He'd stared blankly, shrugged his shoulders, said nothing. Not the best response to make, but he'd been eighteen years old and angry, mainly with himself.

"My intentions," he stared with quiet clarity, "are to support and provide for the mother of my—child." He wasn't ready to explain about it actually being twins. Not yet.

His father nodded slowly. "And what does that mean, exactly? Will she stay at Casterglass? Will I see my grandchild grow up?"

Was he imagining the slightly accusatory note in his father's voice, simply because he felt so sensitive? Sam decided to do his best to ignore it. "I certainly hope so," he replied evenly. "I intend to see my children growing up, and I've told Rose she is welcome to stay at Casterglass for as long as she likes." His father's mouth puckered, and once again Sam felt like he'd said the wrong thing. First Rose, now his father. But what was he supposed to do? March her down the aisle? "We're still working out the details, Dad," he added. "And getting to know each other."

"You knew each other a little before this, I assume," his father replied, smiling slightly, although there was a certain acerbity to his tone.

His parents were far from puritans, Sam knew, but they had their limits. "Yes, a little," he agreed. "Not as much as we should have, perhaps."

"And will you consider marrying?" his father asked quietly. "For the sake of your child?"

So, his father *was* expecting him to march Rose down the aisle. Sam sighed wearily as he raked a hand through his hair. "I'm not ruling it out, but I'm not insisting upon it at this point, either. And anyway, it's not just up to me, Dad."

His father nodded slowly, absorbing what he'd said, accepting it if not approving it, judging by the droopy set of his mouth. "I do hope we'll be able to get to know Rose over the coming weeks and months," he said, seeming to rally a bit. "She seems like quite a lively girl."

"She's great," Sam replied, surprising his father as well as himself. Rose *was* great, but he'd never articulated it quite like that, or realised how much he meant it.

"I look forward to learning more about her," his father said, before rising from his seat. He hadn't taken a single sip of his coffee, Sam saw as he placed it on the desk. "She'll be coming to the ceilidh tonight?"

"I think so."

"Good." His father nodded a couple of times before glancing around the little office. "Quite a set-up you've got here."

"Yes."

"All right, then." Another few nods. "I'll see you later, I suppose."

"Okay."

Sam watched his father head back through the woods, a sigh escaping him as he sat down in his chair with a defeated thud. Once again, he thought, he'd disappointed his father. What a surprise.

ROSE HADN'T BEEN sure how she was going to spend the day; Sam, she knew, was busy at the glamping site, and she had no intention of braving the woods and hillside again. Her whole body was still aching from yesterday's tumble, and she definitely wanted to take it easy. She thought she might explore the garden and, if possible, avoid as many people as she could, because while last night's dinner hadn't been a disaster, it had been a bit full on, and she needed to decompress. Figure out if there was any way she could actually belong here.

Her plans for privacy, however, were not to be. She'd just finished getting dressed when Olivia popped her head round the door.

"Sorry—I don't mean to intrude! I've saved you some breakfast."

"Thank you," Rose said, but if she'd meant it as a friendly dismissal, Olivia didn't get the memo.

She stood in the doorway, her hands knotted together as she looked uncertainly at Rose. "So, you are coming to the ceilidh tonight?"

"Yes, I think so." Even if she wasn't sure she was up for dancing.

"Because I thought perhaps we could find you something to wear. Not that you haven't got anything suitable," she added in a rush. "Sorry, that came out wrong. I just thought it could be fun to go shopping. Will is taking over the garden this morning and I've got some free time…" She trailed off expectantly while Rose scrambled to think how to respond.

"That's very kind of you," she managed after a moment,

"but I'm afraid I can't afford anything new. If I could have access to your washing machine, though—"

"Oh, of course." Olivia waved a hand, her face turning pink. "But what I meant was—it would be our treat. Mine and Althea's."

So, the sisters had decided to gang together to make her presentable? Rose had no desire to be their Cinderella. "That's very kind of you," she said again, "but I couldn't possibly impose on you in such a way. I already feel like a massive freeloader." She smiled to take any sting from the words. "Thank you, though, for all your kindnesses. You've really been most welcoming."

Olivia looked crestfallen, which made Rose feel guilty, but she was adamant that she was not going to accept anything more from the Penryns than she had to. She already felt pretty uncomfortable living off their largesse, and she wasn't willing to sacrifice any more of her independence.

"All right, then," Olivia said, ducking her head. "Well, when you're ready, breakfast is downstairs…" She backed away from the bedroom, a look of apology on her face that made Rose feel equal parts wretched and irritated. She felt as if she'd kicked a puppy, but she was not going to guilt herself into saying yes. She would use the washing machine, though—and make do with her paltry three outfits.

For how long? a sly little voice whispered inside her as she headed downstairs. Right now, she was managing with dungarees and loose dresses, but her bump was going to get bigger—a lot bigger—and she had no maternity clothes. No baby things. Eventually, Rose realised dispiritedly, she was going to have to accept a lot more than a dress…which went deeply against the grain.

As she came into the kitchen, Althea and Olivia were whispering by the Aga, but they sprang apart guiltily as Rose rather pointedly cleared her throat.

"Sorry," she said sunnily, "I hope I'm not interrupting something?"

"We were just talking about how best I can apologise to you," Althea replied.

Surprised by her candour, Rose was startled into a laugh. "An 'I'm sorry' will usually do it," she replied, "but I guess it depends on what you're apologising for."

"It seems I might have misjudged you," Althea said.

Rose couldn't keep from retorting tartly, "Was that the apology?"

Althea let out an abashed laugh. "No, I don't suppose it was. I'm sorry for being so suspicious, Rose. Sam told me you overheard us talking in the kitchen and I realise I probably sounded like a complete cow. I suppose I'm protective of my little brother, and I've also dealt with some shady characters myself."

"Your ex-husband, Jasper," Rose filled in. "I did hear that part." She sat down at the table. "Well, thank you for the apology. I get that coming here has surprised everyone, and not just Sam."

"Have you two talked about…things?" Althea asked, and Rose only just kept from rolling her eyes. What were they expecting, an engagement ring?

"It's a process," she said in the sort of tone to discourage further questions.

"You will be staying, though, won't you?" Olivia asked. "We all want to get to know you."

"For the moment." Considering she had nowhere really to go. She glanced at Althea, and thought she saw her eyes narrow just a tiny bit. Still suspicious? she wondered. Still thought she was a chancer?

Well, maybe she was.

She'd just finished her breakfast, with both sisters watching her rather beadily, when Olivia suggested hesitantly, "Look, if you won't accept a shopping trip to Kendal, what about one upstairs?"

Rose stared at her, nonplussed. "Upstairs?"

"In the attics. There are all sorts up there. Althea and I have helped ourselves plenty of times. We've both learned to be handy with a needle, so we could make any necessary alterations…and wouldn't it be nice to have a new dress?"

Rose hesitated. Yes, it would be nice to have a new dress, but more than that, she felt the need to reach out to these two women, or at least to Olivia. Show them she wasn't as prickly as she seemed. And she wasn't a gold digger, either.

"All right," she said. "Thank you. It's certainly worth a look."

A few minutes later they were trooping upstairs, climbing a stone spiral staircase in the old part of the castle that made Rose feel dizzy. She held on to the wall as she walked, conscious she did not want to faint yet again. Falling down these stairs would be even worse than the hillside.

"This place is amazing," she remarked as they went around and around, ever higher. "Do you ever get used to living in a castle?"

Althea and Olivia exchanged laughing looks before Althea answered dryly, "You get used to the clanking pipes and trickle of water pressure and leaking roof—"

"Hey," Olivia interjected, "we fixed the roof."

"True. But it does have its moments." They'd reached the attic, a soaring space under the eaves, piled with boxes, crates, and steamer trunks circa 1901. It almost looked like the movie set for an attic, Rose couldn't help but think. She was sure to find a magic key or a talking dummy or something amidst all the boxes and trunks.

In point of fact, she didn't find anything magical, save for some dusty dresses packed between layers of tissue paper in ancient trunks, and they were more than magical enough.

"This was our great-grandmother's wedding dress," Althea said, holding up a dress of cobwebby lace that looked tiny. "She wore it around 1915, I think."

"I won't wear it to the ceilidh," Rose joked. In fact, she wasn't sure she should wear any of these dresses. They all looked seriously vintage and like a single breath might have them disintegrating.

"No, but there are plenty of others," Olivia chimed in practically. "Look at this—our mother's muumuu from the seventies."

"She's wearing something similar today," Althea put in dryly. "What about this?" She held up a 1950s-style flocked dress with a full skirt.

"I don't think that will go over my bump."

Althea and Olivia both continued to dig through various trunks, holding up and then discarding dress after dress. Rose wasn't trying to be picky, but the reality was she was over four months pregnant…with twins. Only certain styles were going to work.

Finally, Olivia held up a dress Rose could get behind—or rather, in. It was a deep, mossy green in a clinging, jersey fabric that hugged her bump and hips before flaring out around her calves all the way to her ankles. Big enough to accommodate her bump—in fact, too big, she realised when she wriggled into it. It was tent-sized on her smaller frame.

"We can take it in on the sides," Althea remarked critically. "And the back. Look at those sleeves! Like something royalty would wear."

Rose smiled down at the wide-cuffed sleeves that ended in deep points over her hands. She felt beautiful in this dress, even with it being too big. She felt sexy, which considering her pregnant state was saying something.

"Sam won't believe his eyes," Olivia pronounced. "Just

be careful with the dancing!"

"I will," Rose promised. "Thank you both, for this. You've been so kind."

"It was fun," Althea said with a smile and a quick clap of her hands. "Now let me pin the dress so we'll know where to take it in—I know what my afternoon is going to look like!"

"Thank you," Rose said again, inadequately. She was genuinely touched by their willingness to help her, to care, and for a few second, as she turned around so Althea could pin the dress, she felt as if she had a glimpse of another life, a tantalising peek at a scenario of what could be. To be part of this big, boisterous family. To feel a part of things, included, accepted, and loved. To be married to Sam…

"Ouch!" She flinched away as Althea made a moue of apology.

"I'm so sorry, that was a pin. I haven't done this in ages."

"It's okay." Rose rubbed the sting, and decided it was as good a reminder as any not to let her guard down. Not too much, anyway. She'd take a dress…but that was all.

Chapter Nine

THE BIGGEST BARN had been emptied, swept out, and strung with fairy lights, which was quite an accomplishment considering the amount of junk they'd stored in there. Sam stood in the doorway, running a hand through his damp hair, as he tried not to remember being ten years old and crouching behind some old lumber, trying to hide from his tormentors...some of whom might be kicking up their heels at the ceilidh that very night.

"What do you think?" His seventeen-year-old niece, Poppy, bounced up to him, her face alight with enthusiasm. "My friends are in the band," she said, pointing to a small, makeshift stage where three guys were setting up a sound system. "Josh has been practising calling for ages." She blushed, and Sam guessed she had a crush on the guy who would be the caller, snapping out instructions to the lively beat. Ah, young love. So fraught, and yet so simple.

"It all looks terrific, Poppy," he told her sincerely. "You've done an amazing job with so many things." Poppy had been the main buyer for the gift shop and, judging from the till receipts, she'd done an amazing job indeed. Althea had said something of how miserable Poppy had been when she'd first come to Casterglass, and Sam was glad to see how seven months on she seemed to be flourishing—she'd finished her A levels and was waiting to see if her offer to study marketing at Lancaster would be confirmed. Sam imagined that she'd been itching to get back to the castle during her holidays, to help out with the shop and develop even more ranges of products.

It gave him a pang of envy for the clear, uncomplicated passion she had for this place and this work. He thought he might have a chance of feeling it, as well—if he didn't hate Casterglass so much. Hate the memories that dogged him at nearly every step.

But he was going to do his best not to think about those tonight, not when he might have to deal with the memory-makers in person. People he'd made sure not to see since he was eleven.

"Hey, Sam." Althea's fiancé, John, a local sheep farmer, strolled up to him with an easy smile. Sam had a lot of time for John, and for Olivia's Will, as well. They both seemed like solid, decent guys, men he would be happy to call brothers-in-law.

"Hey."

"How's the glamping?" John asked, and Sam was glad at least one person wasn't going to demand to know more about Rose.

They shot the breeze about business for a while, which felt so much easier than wading through the quagmire of questions about life and marriage and babies and all the rest. Sam was relieved for the break, even as he found himself looking around for Rose. She was coming, right? She'd said she was, although he hadn't actually seen her all day, because he'd been so busy. As partygoers filed into the barn, family members and villagers alike, Sam started to wonder if she was coming at all.

She had a perfectly reasonable excuse not to—everyone here was more or less a stranger, plus she was pregnant, and she'd taken a massive tumble yesterday and was probably still feeling achy. Hell, if it were him, he wouldn't have come.

And yet he wanted her here.

"There she is," John said, the hint of laughter in his voice making Sam realise how obvious he'd been, rubbernecking the whole room for a glimpse of Rose. And yes, there she was, standing in the doorway, dressed in a flowing, medieval-style gown of green, her hair loose and tumbled about her shoulders, and a crown of daisies perched on her head. She looked like Ophelia or *The Princess Bride* or…something. She looked, Sam thought, beautiful.

He started slowly walking towards her, as if in a dream. He no longer heard the chatter of guests, the squeak of the fiddler warming up, a sudden burst of laughter. All he heard was the pounding of his own heart, and all he saw was Rose.

She smiled at him tremulously, touching the daisies in

her hair with a self-conscious grimace. "Is it all a bit too much? Somehow, when we were digging this dress out of the attics, it didn't seem *quite* so dated. Now I feel like I should be at one of those medieval re-enactments, or maybe a jousting tournament."

"I think you look amazing."

She eyed him uncertainly. "Really?"

"Really."

Another beat as she seemed to be deciding whether to believe him, and then with a touch of her old sass, she shook her hair over her shoulders and gave him a flirty look. "If you can't rock a medieval dress at a ceilidh at a castle, then I don't know when you can."

"Actually, I think that dress is from the 1970s," Sam told her with a laugh. "I remember my mother buying it for—" He hesitated. "A medieval festival."

Rose looked at him incredulously for a few seconds before she burst out laughing. The joyous sound it made bubbling up on her lips made Sam start to grin. "That is so *perfect*," she said, still laughing. "I always knew I was a fake."

This was said without a jot of censure or bitterness, and yet it still made Sam pause. What, exactly, did she mean?

"All right, everyone," the caller spoke into his microphone. "Are you ready to dance?"

He'd have to ask her later, he decided. There were so many things they still needed to find out about each other. "Shall we dance?" he asked, and Rose looked sceptical.

"I'm still feeling a bit achy from yesterday, but I think I can manage maybe one turn around the room," she told him.

"Then let's do it."

The caller started shouting out instructions as the band broke into a fast, merry tune. "It's the Flying Scotsman! Men on the right, ladies on the left! All right, lady number one, let's dance across, behind your man, and back to your place—"

Sam had been to a few ceilidhs in his time, especially when he'd been younger, but he'd forgotten how fast and furious they were, whirling and spinning across the room as they tried to follow the caller's cheerful, fast-paced instructions, only to come together with Rose again, both of them breathless and laughing.

By the time the dance ended, Rose was good-naturedly wilting. "That's it for me, I think! I'll spend the rest of the evening sitting in a chair along the wall like someone's maiden auntie."

"A pregnant maiden auntie," Sam replied with a smile, and she rolled her eyes.

"Even more scandal!"

Were they flirting—or merely having a bit of banter? Either way Sam found he was enjoying himself quite a lot. Then he glanced across the room, and he felt as if he'd been sucker punched in the stomach when he saw a familiar face by the refreshments table. Rob Lamb. He wasn't looking at him, thank goodness, but even so in an instant the music and laughter drained away, and he was ten years old, running for his life.

Wait until we get you…

He could hear the ragged pants of his breathing, his feet hitting the dirt hard as he tore up the road. Just a little farther…

"Sam?" Rose put her hand on his sleeve. He blinked, the room suddenly coming into hyper focus—the music too loud, the conversation too jarring, the memories still there, lapping at the edges of his consciousness. "Is everything all right? You went really pale all of a sudden." She gave a small smile. "I thought you were going to faint."

"Sorry. Just a bit breathless from dancing." The words came automatically and made him sound like a robot.

"You, breathless? Didn't you hike up Kilimanjaro with a fridge on your back?"

"Mount Rainier, actually." And why had he done something so stupid? It had been for some eco-friendly charity, but Sam could think of plenty more useful things than hiking up a hill while hefting a major appliance. He glanced again, unwillingly, at the refreshments table; Jake was still there. He'd been the smallest of the group, the most reluctant, yet he'd still joined in. The sight of his leering face pushed into Sam's was burned onto his retinas forever.

"Come on," he told Rose. "Let's go outside."

ROSE FOLLOWED SAM outside, breathing in the cool, fresh air as he led her a little bit away from the barn's entrance. The band was starting up again, the caller merrily shouting out his instructions. Sam let out an unsteady breath as he wiped his hand over his face.

"Whew. Tough stuff."

Rose had the feeling he wasn't talking about the dancing, even if he thought he was, but she wasn't sure whether to press. "Is it hard being home?" she asked uncertainly. "After travelling for so long?"

Sam shrugged and dug his hands into the pockets of his khakis. "Yeah, kind of."

"Will you go back to it again, do you think?" When she'd met him in New Zealand, he'd just finished some big charity run. From what he'd told her then it sounded as if he did a lot of that sort of thing—hikes and rows and runs to raise thousands for a cause du jour.

"I don't know." He glanced at her bump. "With two babies on the way, I can't see myself zipping off to Africa or somewhere, can you?"

She tensed instinctively. "I wouldn't keep you from—"

He held up a hand to pacify her bristling response. "I mean, I wouldn't want to. I don't want to miss my kids growing up. I want to get it right."

A reel of images suddenly blazed through Rose's mind— Sam holding a baby, the hands of two chubby toddlers, the back of a six-year-old's bike. Being there in a way her father never had, even when they'd been travelling together. She could hardly imagine it was possible, and yet Sam spoke of it like a certainty. "That would be nice," she said quietly.

He gave her a crooked smile. "Weird to think about, huh? But I'm starting to get used to the whole idea. Fatherhood, I mean. Children."

"Are you?" She rested a hand on her bump. "When are we going to tell everyone we're having twins?"

He shrugged and glanced up at the sky. "I don't know. Soon, I guess. I'm still giving them time to process the first shock, before I level them with another."

"Sensible, I suppose." She glanced upwards, enjoying the sight of the star-scattered sky. Before she even knew what she was saying, she found herself remarking softly, "I haven't seen so many stars since Tairua."

Realisation scorched through her, along with embarrassment and a memory of them lying tangled on the beach, gazing up at the Southern Lights. With all the talk of bumps and babies, it was bizarrely easy to forget they'd had a rather passionate fling.

"Me neither," Sam said after a moment. They both continued to look at the sky, mainly, Rose suspected, because they didn't dare risk looking at each other. Remembering how lying on that beach had felt. Sam's arms around her, his leg slipped between hers, her cheek on his chest so she could hear the steady thud of his heart. She'd never been as close to another person as she had Sam, not just physically but emotionally, even though they'd both agreed to keep it light. The emotional, Rose had discovered, had followed the physical, even though she hadn't wanted it to. It was something she didn't think Sam had ever realised, and she was in no rush to enlighten him. *I was halfway to falling in love with you, when you left.* Nope, she definitely wasn't in a hurry to admit that.

"It was pretty good between us, wasn't it?" Sam said, still staring at the sky. Rose tensed as she kept her own gaze on all those stars. "Back in Tairua?"

"Yes…" She sounded hesitant, and with good reason. Where was he going with this? Where did she want him to go?

"I know it's been a long time and things have changed, but…" He hesitated, and Rose held her breath. "Considering what's happening now, that you're pregnant, that we're in this together…is there any reason why we shouldn't think about that again? Being a couple, I mean?" Rose's mind spun as he finally lowered his gaze to look at her. "I don't mean right now or even next week or whatever. Just…as a possibility…perhaps. Something we could think about, for the future. For our children. Maybe."

Wow, he had just added a *lot* of caveats there. Rose had a feeling the starry night had made him lose his head for a second and now he was dialling it back as quickly as he could.

"One day?" she clarified. "Maybe?"

"Yeah." He nodded, clearly relieved. "One day. Maybe."

Hardly words to build a life upon, and yet Rose knew she would have backed away from anything more. She was commitment-shy, had good reason to be, even as part of her craved that intimacy. That security. Too bad she couldn't trust Sam Penryn to give it to her. Not yet, anyway. But one day, maybe…?

"I suppose it's something we could think about," she said finally, offering no promises even as she fought a ridiculous sense of disappointment that he wasn't, either. "But we've got more pressing matters to deal with now, surely."

"Yeah. Right."

He nodded, and so did she, and that seemed to be the end of the conversation. *One day we might think about dating, but meanwhile let's have some children.* Yeah, that worked. It would have to.

"I suppose I should find a midwife," Rose said hesitantly. "And figure out a more permanent arrangement."

"What do you mean, a more permanent arrangement?" Sam asked, frowning.

"A place to stay. A job." She'd been thinking, vaguely, of seeing if there was a job going in the village, maybe even renting a room in a house there. Obviously, there was loads of space at Casterglass, but she felt a deep-seated reluctance at just moving in there, being the freeloader Althea had suspected she was, and maybe still did.

"You have a place to stay," Sam pointed out. He sounded

like he was trying for a reasonable tone, but there was definitely an edge to his voice. "You can have your pick of rooms. And as for a job…there's plenty to do at Casterglass. We can use all the help we can get."

"Yes, but I need to earn some money," Rose said as gently as she could. She did not want to just fall in with everyone else's plans. She knew how that could go pear-shaped *very* quickly.

"You don't need to earn money," Sam said, his lower lip pushed out a little. "I mean, I understand why you feel you do, but…I can provide for you."

Rose shook her head, doing her best to be firm although part of her was tempted to simply say *yes please*. She'd been fending for herself for so long… How good would it feel, to have someone else do the heavy lifting, even if just for a little while? But, no. That wasn't how this could work. "Sam, I need to be independent. At least a little bit."

He didn't look particularly pleased by that notion. "So what job are you going to get? I mean, Rose, you're four and a half months pregnant with twins." He tempered his words with a rueful smile. "You're not exactly an employer's dream, are you?"

"No." Something she hadn't thought through, along with a million other things. "There has to be something, though."

"I wish you didn't feel you had to do this."

She shrugged, because what could she say? She did.

"I want to be supportive, Rose," Sam continued, his expression both earnest and uncertain. "I know I was surprised at first—hell, I'm still surprised, but I want to be involved. Whatever that means. Whatever it takes."

She nodded slowly, grateful for his words, yet also knowing that's just what they were. Words. *Call me anytime, darling.* Her mother had promised her that, in a syrupy-sweet voice, but when Rose had actually picked up the phone, well…that had been a different story.

"I mean it, Rose," Sam said, as if he'd just guessed her entire thought process. He reached for the hand she had resting on her bump, and at the same time she felt a sudden, fluttering kick.

"Oh!"

He drew his hand back, alarmed. "What—"

"The baby. One of them, anyway. I think I just felt it move. Kick." She laughed, a sound of wonder, as she felt the same sensation again. "There's actually a baby inside of me!" she said, knowing how stupid she sounded, and yet… A baby! Inside of her! actually. She realised she must have been feeling these flutters for a while, but hadn't acknowledged them as what they were—proper kicks.

"Two, actually," Sam said. He hesitated and then asked, almost shyly, "Can I…?"

"Oh, yes. *Yes.*" She grabbed his hand, overcome by the moment, forgetting all her careful reticence as she placed his hand on her bump, her fingers resting on top of his. "I don't know if it's strong enough for you to feel yet. Maybe a little…"

They both stood there, hands clasped, breath held. The baby had to move again. It just had to…

And then it did, a cross between a flutter and a kick, and Sam let out a surprised laugh. "Oh gosh, wow," he said, shaking his head. "*Wow.* I actually felt that. Amazing."

"I know, right?" Rose still couldn't believe it. "That is an actual human."

She glanced up at him, smiling, and found he was smiling back, and their faces were actually kind of close. Suddenly she was experiencing flutters of a completely different kind.

"Rose," Sam said, and stepped closer to her.

Rose could feel her heart beating rather wildly. She remained where she was, staring up at him, wondering if he was actually going to kiss her, and what that would mean—for her, for him, for the babies still kicking away. Would it be a humungous mistake or the best thing ever?

She really didn't know, and she didn't get to find out, because just as Sam was getting a sleepy, heavy-lidded look about him, leaning forward a little while Rose held her breath, he saw someone or something behind her, and the expression dropped away, to be replaced by a tense alertness.

"Hey," he said, his voice a husky croak, and he raised one hand.

Rose twisted around to see a guy about Sam's age standing by the barn's doors, staring at him quizzically. "Do I know you?" he asked, and Sam's mouth tightened.

"No, maybe not," he said, and the guy shrugged and turned away. Rose glanced back at Sam; he wasn't looking at her, and the moment, if there had even been one, was well and truly broken.

Chapter Ten

ROSE WOKE UP to bright sunshine even though it was only a little after seven o'clock in the morning. She'd set her alarm to get up early, all too aware that she'd been living like a guest at Casterglass, waking up late and having breakfast made for her, and she needed to start acting more like a tenant.

Last night's discussion with Sam about working had woke her up to the realisation that she needed to get her act together on several fronts. No more coasting through life, waiting to see what happened, hoping something would turn up, which was, more or less, how she'd lived the last five years. Why make a plan when plans could be ruined? But she couldn't be quite so lackadaisical now, not when there was a baby involved. Two, in fact.

And so she'd decided today, Monday, would be a day of new beginnings, of starting as she meant to go on. She'd be downstairs in time for breakfast, she'd help with the washing up, she'd call the midwife, she'd figure things out. Finally.

And she would do her best not to think about the kiss

that hadn't happened, because, well, there really wasn't any point, was there? *One day. Maybe.* Whatever.

The kitchen was bustling with activity when she headed downstairs, conversation flying as people passed jam or butter, sipped coffee or scrawled on notepads. There seemed to be a million things that needed to be done to keep Casterglass running, and Rose didn't know how to do a single one of them.

"Poppy, how are we on our logo stock? Do we need to put another order in?" Althea sat at the head of the table, a pair of glasses forgotten on her forehead as she frowned down at a long to-do list.

"The dish towels are flying off the shelves," Poppy replied promptly, sounding more like a CEO than a seventeen-year-old. "We can definitely order more of those. The tea cosies aren't so big a hit."

"Does anyone even use a tea cosy anymore?" Olivia wondered aloud. "I think of that as something a granny might use."

"I've never used a tea cosy in my life," Violet put in, sounding almost affronted by the very idea. "And I'm a granny."

"We had a tea cosy, though, do you remember?" Althea looked up, a small smile curving her mouth and making her look a lot less stern. "We used it as a Roman helmet in one of our plays."

"Why use a tea cosy when we had an actual Roman helmet?" Violet asked, sounding even more affronted. *"Honest-ly."*

"We have an actual Roman helmet?" Olivia's voice was full of interest. "Mummy, that must be worth a mint."

"We had it valued and sadly it was a Victorian replica," Walter told her with a wistful smile. "But never mind."

The conversation flowed on, now talking about the workshops housed in the barns. Seph, sitting at the end of the table, said she was thinking about running classes, as was Ellie, the woman who ran the pottery place. Rose knew Seph was around her age, maybe a little younger, but she seemed positively intimidating, with her pink dreadlocks and perma-scowl. The only time she looked remotely approachable was when she was talking about her woodcarving.

"All right, then," Althea said, slapping the table with both of her hands. "Everyone know what they're doing, then? Good. Who's on the rota for kitchen clean—"

"I can clean the kitchen," Rose offered, and was met with a split second of deafening silence. "I'm not sure about any of those other jobs," she continued, trying to smile, "but I can definitely wash dishes."

Althea glanced at Sam, as if seeking his permission, which annoyed Rose somehow. Was she here in her own right or just as Sam's bit on the side? Admittedly, she wouldn't be here if it wasn't for Sam, but…

She was here now.

"Please," she said, and wondered why she practically had

to beg.

"Are you sure, Rose?" Olivia's voice was kind, too kind, making Rose feel fragile. "You had a big tumble the other day and you're probably still jet-lagged, plus you've already done the washing up once—"

"I can do it again, and I'm fine," Rose said firmly. She hated just moping around, and she wanted to feel useful. She'd realised last night that finding a job in the village was going to be hard, if not impossible, but she could at least do this.

"All right," Althea relented, and Rose wondered who had made her the ultimate decision-maker. "That would be helpful. Thank you."

A few minutes later everyone started filing out, and Rose was left with an enormous pile of washing up. She would definitely be earning her keep.

Sam lingered in the doorway, and the look he gave her stupidly reminded her about last night, when he'd almost kissed her. Stupidly, because he wasn't looking at all like he wanted to kiss her now.

"Are you sure about this?"

"Washing up? Yes. It's not rocket science, Sam."

"I know, but you should rest—"

"Oh my goodness, don't be one of those men who treats a pregnant woman like a wilting lily. I'm fine. I'll let you know if I'm not."

"Will you?" he asked seriously, and Rose hesitated,

knowing he had the right to wonder.

"Yes, I promise," she said firmly. "Now go glamp or whatever it is you're doing."

"Ropes assault course this morning," he told her with a rather devastating grin. Rose almost wished he wasn't quite so ridiculously good-looking. It was very distracting. "But we can talk later?"

"Talk talk or *talk* talk?" she asked, and he looked at her, nonplussed. "Have a nice chat or a discussion with a capital D?" she clarified, and he gave a little laugh.

"Why don't we start with a chat?"

"Sounds good." She smiled, and he smiled back, and there was her stomach going fizzy again. Strange, how they were having a child—*children*—together and yet it felt like a first date. The three months in Tairua were a blur; they'd never truly been real, an on-again, off-again carousel of casual. *This* was real...whatever this was. Not much, obviously, but still.

Just as before, Rose enjoyed the peaceful solitude of the big kitchen. Sunlight streamed through the windows, and she had a lovely view of the walled garden, looking like something out of a children's story, as she scrubbed pots and pans in the sink.

Maybe she could become the unofficial housekeeper of Casterglass, she mused. She wouldn't mind making meals and keeping things tidy. Turning this behemoth of a place into something close to a home. It would be a way to earn her keep and feel useful, and she'd actually enjoy doing it. She'd always gone in for jobs in cleaning, cooking, or waitressing; she'd much prefer working in a home to a bar. Perhaps she'd suggest it to Sam, or even to Althea.

Assuming, of course, that she was staying here, which she was beginning to realise she was. She had to, more or less, because she had nowhere else to go and there was no point haring off just because she could. Sam wanted her here...at least she thought he did. She hoped so.

When the kitchen was clean, she turned her mind to the matter of finding a midwife. A few phone calls later she was feeling pleased, having registered with the Duddon Valley practice in nearby Broughton-in-Furness.

"We have a cancellation today, actually," the receptionist told her. "If you could make it here in the next hour?"

"Oh, er..." She was reluctant to ask anyone to drive her, when she knew how busy they all were, on only the third day of being fully open. Was there a bus from Casterglass?

"Otherwise," the receptionist continued in an apologetic tone, "I'm afraid it will be another four weeks."

Four weeks! She couldn't wait that long. "I'll take the appointment," Rose said firmly. Somehow she'd figure out a way to get there.

"WHERE'S ROSE?"

Sam came into the kitchen, frowning when he'd been

expecting to see Rose and she clearly wasn't there. Althea was at the counter, making a cup of tea, looking bemused.

"I have no idea. She could be anywhere, I suppose. I must say, she did a very good job cleaning the kitchen. I've never seen it look so sparkling! I think she even dusted the leaves of that ficus." She nodded towards a tired-looking houseplant on the windowsill.

"I thought she'd be around," Sam said, realising how silly he sounded. Althea was right; Rose could be anywhere. Up in her room, taking a walk, exploring the castle. He didn't need to keep tabs on her. He'd just been hoping to see her, that was all.

"How is all going?" Althea asked in what Sam suspected was a deceptively mild tone. "Three days in?"

"Fine."

He didn't know how it was going, really. Last night he'd almost kissed her, and they'd agreed that one day, maybe, they might try a relationship. At the time he'd felt ridiculously pleased; now he wondered what that even meant. Still, it had been nice, having her by his side all evening. After the ceilidh they'd gone down to the beach for the hog roast, and Sam had spent his time with Rose, glad to avoid the few familiar faces he saw from the village, even if Jake Lamb hadn't recognised him. No one spared him a passing glance, which was both a relief and kind of annoying, considering.

"So, are you guys a thing?" Althea asked. "A couple?"

"We're still figuring it out, Althea. We need to get to

know each other properly first." Why did he feel like he had to keep saying the same thing, over and over?

"And what you know of her so far, you like?" Althea pressed.

"Obviously, or I wouldn't be in this situation in the first place."

"I just don't want you to feel trapped, Sam."

Althea had always had a somewhat irritating protective streak, he acknowledged with an inward sigh. "I don't feel trapped," he told her. If anything, he was worried Rose felt trapped. Trapped into staying at Casterglass, in the middle of nowhere, because he'd hitched his wagon to this uncertain star. Trapped into a life with him because she didn't have a lot of options, especially with twins on the way. *Twins.* He really needed to tell his family about that.

Just then Rose and Seph walked into the kitchen together. Before he could keep himself from it, Sam found himself demanding rather severely, "Where were you?"

Rose's eyebrows rose as she met his challenging stare with a cool one of her own. "I had a midwife appointment in Broughton-in-Furness. Seph kindly drove me there."

"What!" He stared at her in dismay, trying to mask the hurt he felt that she hadn't bothered to tell him, never mind ask him to drive her. "You couldn't even tell me?"

"It all happened very quickly." She glanced at Althea and Seph, who both decided to make themselves scarce.

"Back to the office for me," Althea said, hefting her mug

aloft, and Seph muttered something about her workshop.

Alone in the kitchen Rose stared at him for several seconds before asking levelly, "Why are you sounding so angry?"

"I'm not angry." He scrubbed his hands over his face. "Just surprised you arranged it so quickly, and you didn't even tell me." *And it feels like you keep trying to cut me out of things,* he added mentally, but decided not to say. Yet.

"A cancellation came up and the next appointment was in four weeks. I decided to jump on it. I didn't really have time to hike up to the glamping site to let you know. Besides, I knew you were busy."

"You could have called me."

"I still don't have your number, as it happens." Her voice came out cool, and Sam flinched. He'd forgotten to give her his number, he recalled. How could he have forgotten something like that?

"Did you really never in Tairua—" he began, rather feebly.

"No. You never offered it."

She'd never offered hers back then, either, but Sam decided this was not the time to argue the point. Clearly Rose remembered that he hadn't; perhaps she'd even been hurt by it, which almost felt like an encouragement. "Well, I'll give it to you now," he told her. "If you give me your phone, I'll type in my contact."

"All right." She gave a little shrug, as if it didn't matter either way to her, and handed him her phone.

Sam opened the contacts and typed his details in before handing the phone back to her. She took it, glancing down, and a small smile curved her mouth.

"Name of contact—'Sam Penryn, the father of your children?'" she read out, and then looked up, eyes dancing.

"Yes," he stated firmly, "because that is what I am."

Her smile deepened. "You're not going all caveman on me, are you?"

"No." He hesitated, then admitted with a small smile, "Maybe a *bit* caveman. It's just...sometimes it feels like you're trying to cut me out of things, Rose. Like you really don't want me to be involved, no matter what you've said." It took a lot to admit that much, to show her how, well, *vulnerable* he felt. And he had no idea from her expression what she made of it.

She gave a little sigh as she slid her phone back in her pocket. "I'm sorry. I don't actually mean to—it's more of an instinct. And today it really was just a matter of timing. The appointment came up quickly and I needed someone to drive me. Seph came into the kitchen at the right moment, and I asked."

Fair enough, he supposed, even if he still felt a little sting of hurt. "How was the appointment?"

"Fine. Two heartbeats, everything seeming to progress normally. I have a scan booked in at Kendal in a few weeks' time. You can definitely come to that."

"Okay." He remembered seeing those blobby shapes on the screen and realised he couldn't wait to see them again. "This is kind of exciting, isn't it?" he stated slowly, feeling the truth of the words as he spoke them.

"Is it?" She eyed him closely. "I know you didn't ask for any of this, Sam."

"Neither did you."

"No, but I made the decision to keep the baby—babies—when I found out I was pregnant."

"I'm glad you did."

"Are you? Truly?"

"Yes, Rose. I admit, the timing could be better, and it's a little awkward that we don't actually know each other that well, but…I'm happy. I want to be involved. And I'll keep saying that until you involve me. Completely."

"Eventually I might even believe you." The smile she gave him was mischievous and a little bit sexy. His heart flipped and he remembered how they had almost kissed. "About the knowing each other thing," she continued. "How about we go out, when you've got a spare hour or two? Get to know each other a bit better. I'd love to have a tour of the village."

The smile that had been spreading across his face started to curl in at the edges. "There's not much in the village, actually," he told her, his voice turning a tiny bit brusque. "A pub and a post office shop, that's pretty much it."

"Still—"

"I could show you the castle, if you like? Or if you want to get offsite we could go somewhere a little further afield…Santon Bridge or even Ambleside?"

He'd thought he'd spoke nonchalantly enough, but Rose was looking at him with a troubled gleam in her eyes, her head cocked to one side, as if she didn't quite know what to make of him.

"Okay," she said at last, with a little shrug. "Whatever you prefer."

Sam didn't miss the irony that they were making plans to get to know each other better, and yet he was keeping from her one of the most important things that had shaped so much of his life. And he wasn't in any hurry to talk about it, either.

"Great," he said, managing a smile. "Ambleside it is."

Chapter Eleven

I T WAS A week before Sam and Rose managed to make it to Ambleside, but in the meantime, Rose set about being quietly, unobtrusively useful. She took to cleaning the kitchen after meals without making a fuss about it, and while sometimes people chipped in to help, including a companionable half hour rinsing plates while Sam dried, she generally just got on with it by herself.

She also found other ways to be helpful to all those around who seemed inclined to run around like a bunch of chickens with their collective heads cut off, always halfway to a panic or at least a tizz about something as the tourists continued to roll, or sometimes trickle, in.

"It's because we're operating on such a tight budget," Olivia told her when Rose made remarks to that effect. "An absolute shoestring, and we were right down to the wire in terms of being ready to open. I'm not sure we've actually managed to tick every single box in terms of red tape and health and safety, but *hopefully* we have." She made a face. "The important ones, anyway. But it still feels like we're teetering on the edge of disaster—I wonder if it will always feel like that?"

"It always has for me," Rose told her with a laugh, and Olivia gave her one of those troubled, thoughtful looks that made her inwardly cringe.

"Has it? I really don't know much about your background."

Rose shrugged, determined to make light of her past, just as she had with Sam. "My father sold software to businesses around the world, and he took me with him. I travelled everywhere—really, it was amazing."

Olivia gazed at her with a soft look of sympathy. "It sounds lonely."

A lump started to form in Rose's throat, which was horrifying. Her hormones were clearly all over the place, because she didn't cry. Not about this. Not anymore. "I learned to make do with my own company, it's true, but that's no bad thing. But it was a bit chaotic, at times."

"I imagine it must have been," Olivia agreed slowly. "What about your mum?"

"She left when I was four and has barely kept in touch since." Rose gave a little what-can-you-do kind of shrug. "You can't really miss what you never had, can you?"

"Oh, I think you can," Olivia replied seriously. "I certainly have. Growing up, part of me longed for some boring little box of a house with parents who were…" She blew out a breath. "Normal. I know no one is truly normal—

everyone's got their quirks—but you must have realised by now my parents are a bit quirkier than average."

"Yes," Rose admitted with a ready smile. "I think they're brilliant." She hadn't spent too much time with either Walter or Violet Penryn, but she'd seen Walter's whimsical gentleness and been the recipient of Violet's shrewd yet baffling leaps in conversation.

"They are brilliant," Olivia agreed. "And I love them to bits and wouldn't have them any other way now. But when I was a child or a teenager, I felt differently."

"Do you think you've all been like that?" Rose asked curiously. "Do you think Sam was?" She felt a flicker of remorse for digging for information so shamelessly from Sam's sister, but they still hadn't had that get-to-know-you conversation and she *was* curious. Perhaps Olivia could shed some light on Sam that he wouldn't be able to himself.

Olivia pursed her lips thoughtfully. "I think we were, to greater or lesser degrees. Sam loved Casterglass as a boy. He was always tearing through the countryside, building dens and swimming in the river. I remember him constantly having muddy knees and looking as if he'd been dragged backwards through a hedge."

"I can imagine that," Rose replied, and she could. A little Sam, with the same blue eyes and tousled hair—if they had a boy, or even *two* boys, would they be like that? It was a prospect that made her feel a ripple of excitement, a shiver of incredulous apprehension.

"But when he was older," Olivia continued, "he certainly couldn't wait to leave Casterglass...and not come back."

"You mean all the charity stuff he did?"

"Yes, but even before that. He blew off his A levels and then took off backpacking when he was eighteen." Rose felt a jolt of surprise as well as recognition, because wasn't that exactly what she had done? Had had to do. What had been Sam's reason? And why had they never discovered this similarity before?

Well, they'd never actually tried to get to know each other before. Not really. Not *that* way.

"So, he went backpacking, and then what?" Rose asked.

Olivia hesitated. "Are you sure you don't want to hear this from Sam?"

"Is there something to hear?"

Olivia wrinkled her nose as she considered the question. "I suppose there isn't, not really, not from my perspective, at least. It's just, Sam hardly ever came home after that. He was always on some adventure or other, doing something fairly ridiculous for charity."

"Climbing up a mountain with a fridge on his back."

Olivia nodded, laughing. "Yes, exactly. And with a job that allowed him to travel anywhere, I can see why he didn't want to stay put in Casterglass. We all left home, in one way or another, save Seph, but Sam seemed happy to stay away."

"And yet you all came back."

Olivia gave a little laugh. "Yes, it's amazing, isn't it? I

suppose you can take the castle out of the Penryn, but not the Penryn out of the castle. Or is it the other way round?"

Laughing too, Rose replied, "Both, I think now. Thanks for telling me all that." She was glad she'd talked to Olivia. She felt she knew Sam a little bit more now, enough to ask some relevant questions, at least.

She was getting to know *all* the Penryns, to greater or lesser degrees. When Seph had offered, quite unexpectedly, to drive her to her midwife appointment, Rose had been more than a little intimidated by her surly manner and tough exterior, but Seph had been surprisingly chatty…well, chatty might be overegging it a *bit*, but she'd talked. Some. And Rose had wondered if the other woman's take-no-prisoners persona was just that—a persona. Just as she'd adopted a flirty, feisty sass, had Seph found a way to face the world and feel strong? There were times, when her expression had softened or her gaze had turned distant, that Rose had wondered.

As for Violet and Walter…well, she hadn't got to know them, precisely, but she wasn't scared of them anymore, and she didn't think they disapproved of her, at least not entirely. Olivia had always been lovely, and Althea…well, Althea was still a tough nut to crack. She was friendly, it was true, in a bossy sort of way, and she'd apologised for jumping to conclusions, but Rose didn't get the feeling that Althea really trusted her. Yet.

Olivia and Althea's significant others, Will and John,

were both kind, and Althea's children were all, considering how reserved their mother could be, surprisingly friendly and down to earth. Ben treated her like a mate—there was only five years' difference between them—and Poppy was keen to be her personal stylist. She'd already asked if she could go shopping with her to help her select her 'maternity wardrobe' and Rose had laughed and said her maternity wardrobe was going to consist of charity shops finds, and that was if she was lucky.

Poppy had squealed that she loved charity shops—'properly vintage'—and told her she'd take her to Ulverston, where apparently there were a selection of charity shops that were 'actually decent'.

All in all, when she didn't let herself worry too much, Rose felt she was actually starting to settle in. She just hadn't seen Sam very much. He spent ten to twelve hours a day at the glamping sites or ropes course, and after her spectacular tumble Rose wasn't enthused about the prospect of hiking up there again. Besides, she had both a loathing and fear of appearing needy to him. It suited her fine if Sam had other stuff to do, because she did, too. She would.

But in moments when she let it, it still felt a little lonely.

Overall, though, she told herself, she was doing okay. She'd made herself useful, no one was looking at her askance, and she felt like she had a plan. Sort of. She'd stay at Casterglass until the babies were due, and then…

Well, it wasn't a very *specific* plan, but she'd moved on a little from *tell Sam and then…* Hadn't she? Enough for now, anyway. She wasn't ready for yet another 'serious discussion'.

When Sam was finally able to take an afternoon to go to Ambleside, Rose told herself they'd converse rather than 'discuss'. They'd learn about each other, so they could start to decide whether 'one day maybe' could become something a little more definite. Even if that possibility terrified her more than a little.

THE DAY DID not start out well. Sam had been intending to knock off work at noon, but the group of eight who had booked the ropes course were snail-paced slow, and Sam had to help through most of it, so it was already half one before he managed to head back to the castle. He was uncomfortably aware that he hadn't seen much of Rose since they'd agreed to go out; a quick chat here and there, a half hour washing dishes and exchanging movie trivia, and a quick check-in to see if this afternoon would suit for what was, ostensibly, meant to be their big date.

He felt like a lot was riding on a single afternoon in Ambleside, but maybe he was looking at it wrong. Instead of being some sort of deciding moment with an alarming air of finality, he could see this as a beginning. He didn't need to impress Rose or convince her that he was dad material, and dare he think it, even husband material; he just had to be himself. Let her get to know him, and try to get to know her, as well. Knowing how prickly and private they could both be, that was hard enough, surely?

After grabbing the quickest shower he'd ever had, he dressed and hurried downstairs, to find Rose in the library, absorbed in a book that looked about two hundred years old.

"Sorry I'm late—"

"It's all right." She looked up from the fragile, faded pages, her expression dreamy. "I was reading *The Picture of Dorian Gray*. I think this might actually be a first edition."

"Oh?" He wasn't well versed on books, never had been. That had been part of his struggle with his father; unlike both his parents, Sam had never been an academic. He'd worked hard, yes, but essay writing and exam taking hadn't come easily to him.

"Have you read it?" she asked, and he shook his head. "Well, it's fascinating, to think about how we seem to the world versus how we really are." Sam looked at her blankly and Rose quickly filled him in on the plot, how Dorian Gray was a dissolute rake who had committed all sorts of crimes; the evidence of which was in his portrait, rather than on his face. "So here's this young, beautiful man, who hid an absolutely blackened heart. We're all a bit like that, don't you think?" She swung her legs over the sofa as she stood up. "We're all hiding something."

He knew he was, but it felt like an uncomfortably perceptive way to start off what he'd thought was meant to be a fun and light-hearted date. "What are you hiding, then?" he asked with an attempt at joviality, and she gave him a teasing, flirty look back.

"Wouldn't you like to know."

They headed outside for the car, with Sam still wondering what it was she wasn't telling him. He hadn't yet figured out what was real and what was just an act—at times she seemed so tough, and other times achingly vulnerable.

But perhaps everyone was a bit like that. Wasn't he? He liked to be the tough outdoorsy guy who could row across the ocean or climb a mountain, but all too often inside he felt like that little boy, running for his life.

We're going to get you, Penryn...

And he couldn't bear to admit it to Rose, to have her see him as anything other than a strong, capable guy. A hero. Even if he doubted that she really did look at him like that in the first place. Or that he really was at all.

"So where are we going in Ambleside?" Rose asked when they'd reached his Rover, reminding him that today was about having fun, not feeling lost in either worry or regret.

"I thought we could stroll through the town, maybe go for a row?"

"A row?"

"Yes, you can hire a rowboat at Brockhole, which is between Ambleside and Windermere. It's a nice way to see the lake."

"Ah, so Windermere is a lake," Rose said, and Sam couldn't tell if she was teasing.

"You knew that, right?" he asked uncertainly, and she burst out laughing.

"Sort of? I mean, I've heard of Windermere, but I'd never been to the Lake District before, and I suppose I sort of assumed that in the *Lake* District, the bodies of water would be called…lakes."

Her eyes were dancing with bits of gold, and the smile she gave him was infectious. Sam felt his whole self start to lighten. "A fair point," he acknowledged, "but in point of fact, only one of the district's lakes is called a lake— Bassenthwaite Lake. The rest are waters, tarns, or meres."

"Mere District doesn't have *quite* the same ring, I suppose?"

He let out a deep-throated laugh that opened something up inside him, loosened the tightly held parts of himself. "I suppose not."

"Or Tarn District… Water District sounds like a plumbing company."

"I think they named it right," he agreed.

"It *is* beautiful," Rose remarked as they drove inland, through deeply cut hills, or fells, to use the Cumbrian word, under a sky that was part sweet aching blue, and part swollen storm cloud; the weather, as it so often did in Cumbria, could go either way. "Rugged and desolate and awe-inspiring."

"Indeed."

She turned to him with an impish smile. "Did you love

it, when you were little? Having all sorts of adventures here?"

He tensed instinctively then forced himself to relax. "How did you guess?"

"Olivia said something about it," Rose replied honestly. "But not much more than that. She said you went around with muddy knees and hair that looked like you'd been dragged backwards through a hedge."

"I suppose I did." Olivia didn't know much more than that, Sam acknowledged to himself. She and Althea had been away at boarding school by the time he'd gone to the primary and his life had become one long, torturous endurance test. He'd never told them, or anyone else, about any of it. He'd never dared.

"So why did you leave and never look back?" Rose asked quietly. "Until recently, that is."

"I suppose I wanted to see more of the world. And you never appreciate home so much until you leave it, do you?"

"I wouldn't really know," she replied after a pause. "I never really had a home."

He was surprised, even though she'd intimated as much before. "There wasn't a place you could return to, from your travels? A house or a flat somewhere?"

She shrugged. "Whenever we came back, we stayed in one of those soulless corporate flats in the suburb of some city—London, Birmingham, Manchester. They all blurred together, to be honest. I don't remember any of them very well."

"Did you go to school during those times?"

She wrinkled her nose. "Not that I can remember. I think my father wanted to fly under the radar. I'm not sure what social services would have thought of my rather unorthodox upbringing."

"But you liked it, didn't you?" Sam asked, and he heard a note of anxiety in his voice. He didn't like thinking about her as a child, being miserable, stuck in a situation she could barely endure…the way he had been.

Rose turned to look out the window, the glint of Windermere in the distance. "I loved it," she said quietly, the words heartfelt. "But you don't always know what's best for you, when you're a child, do you?"

Which sounded as if she had some pretty big regrets. They were driving into Ambleside, and Sam decided to shelve the serious talk for now. "So, there's a bakery on the high street that does the best flapjacks in all the lakes. If you like flapjacks?"

"I'm partial to the occasional flapjack," Rose returned, sounding so serious that Sam felt himself grinning.

"Glad to hear it. I thought we could grab something to eat, maybe a coffee, and then have a stroll around before we head for the lake."

Rose nodded her agreement and, after parking, they went to the bakery for the promised flapjacks—gooey with golden syrup, and meltingly sweet. They ate and sipped their coffees as they strolled the quaint, cobblestone streets with their terraced houses of Lakeland stone.

Sam felt himself start to relax properly—away from Casterglass, not needing to have one of their serious discussions, had loosened him up, and Rose too perhaps, so they could just chat and laugh. He'd forgotten from Tairua how fun Rose could be, with her sharp sense of humour, her ready smile, the deep belly laugh she gave when she was genuinely amused.

He supposed she hadn't much reason to laugh since coming to Casterglass, what with his lukewarm response, his sister's suspicion, and then a tumble down a hillside and the shock of expecting twins. He was glad to see her laugh today. He was grateful to laugh with her.

And who knew? He thought as they headed to the lake to rent a rowboat. Maybe this was the beginning of their future. The start of 'one day, maybe', not as some hazy prospect on the horizon, but happening now. Or, he amended as he helped Rose into the boat, starting to.

Chapter Twelve

A WEEK PASSED in a blur of work, as Sam spent most of his time up at the glamping site and Rose continued to make herself useful. She'd become used to the rather chaotic rhythms of Casterglass, taking people's sudden tizzes and tempers in her stride, as she learned to live, not as a solitary being as she'd been most of her life, but part of a large, rambunctious household.

There were times—quite a few of them—when she craved quiet and solitude and so she retreated to her room or the peacefulness of the walled garden for a little alone time. At other times, though, she was happy enough to muck in—or sit back, as the case often was, and let the conversation, banter, and arguments fly around her.

One morning while she was washing up, Poppy announced that they simply had to go shopping, because Rose clearly needed some decent maternity clothes. Rose acquiesced mainly because Poppy was right—she'd been making do with her three outfits but the dungarees were starting to strain against her ever-growing bump, and the lavender sundress wasn't the sort of thing she'd wear while doing housework.

"I'm afraid I don't drive," she told Poppy, "but I'm up for a trip to Ulverston if you are."

"I drive," Poppy assured her. "I got my licence a couple of months ago." She perked up, her eyes alight. "I could teach you—"

"I think I've got enough to be getting on with," Rose told her hurriedly. She'd never stayed anywhere long enough to need to know how to drive, and she had never really needed to anyway, but when the time came, she thought she'd want a slightly more experienced driver than almost eighteen-year-old Poppy.

"All right," Poppy said with a sigh. "I'm not sure it would be legal, anyway."

Rose realised she was grateful to be getting away from Casterglass for a little while, as much as she was coming to like the place. She hadn't been off the property since her and Sam's afternoon in Ambleside a week ago, and what a surprisingly pleasant time that had been. They'd wandered the quaint streets and then rowed around the lake, engaging in a brief splashing war before subsiding into laughter. She'd had fun, and she'd felt as if she'd gained part of herself back, the part she'd shown to the world that was carefree and easy and light.

Sometimes it had been an act, it was true, but part of it was real and she was glad to be that person again, even if just for a little bit. She didn't want to feel fragile and needy all the time, which was pretty much how she'd been feeling since coming to Casterglass.

"Right, so Ulverston," Rose said as she and Poppy climbed into Althea's black Range Rover—exactly the kind of car Rose thought Althea would drive. While Sam's older sister had definitely thawed towards her, Rose didn't feel she was all that warm still. Perhaps that was just Althea's personality—brisk and capable, decidedly no-nonsense—but Rose still felt the need to tiptoe around her a bit. "There are some good charity shops there?"

"Decent," Poppy allowed, eyes narrowed against the sun's surprising glare—for once it wasn't raining. "I mean, they're nothing on Notting Hill or anything, but we should be able to find something."

"I don't know that I actually want to wear maternity clothes," Rose confessed. The words summoned images of loose smocks and fussy bows.

"Maternity clothes are really trendy now," Poppy told her, an unlikely voice of authority. "Not like they used to be. There's a photo of my mum in a dress when she was pregnant with Toby—ugh!" She grimaced and laughed at the same time. "So ugly. The dress, I mean, not Mum. It was a corduroy smock—right there you know you're in trouble."

"Too true," Rose agreed. She could not imagine wearing such a thing, but perhaps she'd have to.

"We'll find something, don't worry," Poppy told her

confidently.

Ulverston was a small town, not as quaint as Ambleside, but still possessing its own unique charm, with its narrow streets and scattering of shops, the distant fells rising steeply in every direction.

As they entered the first charity shop, Poppy flicked her long, blonde hair behind her shoulders and marched up to a rack, fingers flying expertly through the clothes as if she were looking for something in particular.

"Ah, here we go." She took out a hanger on which a simple black top in stretchy jersey hung. "A basic layering piece. The material is stretchy enough it should cover your bump, especially as it's a large. Let's find something to pair it with." And off she went, fingers flying yet again, while Rose ambled over to the small children's section.

She took a white Babygro from its hanger, running her fingers along the nubby velveteen material, amazed at how tiny it was. She would need enough of these for *two* babies. Even though she'd been feeling the babies' kicks more and more, and her bump was definitely getting bigger, the reality of what was coming in just four months was more than a little daunting. It was surreal, incredible, impossible. Even with Sam, how was she going to do this? And what about all the baby stuff she was going to need?

"Okay." Poppy marched over to her, several items of clothing draped over one arm. "Why don't you try these on?"

"Umm, okay." Rose had to smile at the teenager's take-charge attitude. "Thanks, Poppy."

In the changing room, Rose made a face at her reflection in the full-length mirror; she hadn't seen her full, undressed body in a while as there was no such mirror in her bedroom, and the sight of her belly popping out of her body was more than a little alarming. She rested one hand on the taut skin of her bump. There were *babies* in there. She imagined Sam saying such a thing and it made her smile.

"Well?" Poppy demanded, from the other side of the curtain, sounding a lot like her mother. "Does anything fit?"

"Just putting them on now," Rose replied, and hurriedly, or as hurriedly as she could, considering her cumbersome state, put on the black jersey top and a brown suede skirt with a stretchy waist. Maternity clothes had come on, she decided, as she ran her hands over her bump and hips, smoothing the material and admiring her curvy silhouette. Maybe pregnant could be beautiful…and sexy.

"This is the first outfit," she told Poppy as she pulled aside the curtain.

"Wow." Poppy grinned her affirmation before whistling under her breath. "You look *hot*. We could totally Instagram that." Already she was reaching for her phone.

"No thanks," Rose said quickly. "I don't want to be on social media. But thanks for the compliment."

Poppy's face fell but she nodded resignedly and put her phone back in her pocket. "All right, fine. Can you try the other outfits on?"

Rose did a little impromptu fashion show for each one; besides the suede skirt and black top, there was a pair of flowy trousers in deep green, a loose jumper in soft cream wool that flowed over her bump, and a floral dress they both agreed was not the look Rose was going for.

"Way too mumsy," Poppy pronounced. "I mean, I know you're going to be a mum, but you don't have to look it, you know?"

"Yes, I know," Rose agreed in heartfelt tones. She'd never been a proper fashionista, but in her more carefree days she'd rocked an easy, bohemian style and she didn't want to lose it now.

They hit a few more charity shops, buying a couple of select pieces at each one, before Rose insisted she treat Poppy to lunch at a small café near the town's market hall.

"So, you like living at Casterglass?" she asked as she dug into her jacket potato with cheese and beans—she'd been having a craving for them lately, and she couldn't get enough.

"Yeah, it's pretty good." Poppy was very carefully picking out all the pieces of cucumber from her salad and laying them rather disdainfully on the side of her plate, which made Rose smile. "I didn't like it at the beginning, though," she added as she dug into her cucumber-less salad. "I found it really hard. I mean, it is so remote, you know? And I'd left all my friends back in Cobham…"

"That must have been difficult."

"Yeah, it was. Mainly because they totally forgot me as soon as I'd left. They weren't great friends, actually. Not like Alice."

Alice, Rose knew, was Althea's fiancé John's daughter, in the same year as Poppy. "How fun that you guys are going to be sisters," she remarked. "Have your mum and John set a date for the wedding?"

"Christmas, I think, when we're home from uni." She gave Rose a rather keen look. "You'll have had the baby by then."

Startled, Rose nodded. "Yes, I suppose I will have. It still feels so hard to imagine."

"Will you stay at Casterglass? Will you and Sam get married?" Poppy fired off the questions in a matter-of-fact way that had Rose holding up one hand.

"Whoa. That's a lot."

"Well, everyone is wondering."

"Everyone?"

Poppy shrugged. "Pretty much, yeah."

Rose knew she shouldn't be surprised, but she still didn't like the idea she was being talked about. "I don't know what's going to happen, Poppy. Sam and I are taking it one day at a time. But I will stay at Casterglass until the babies are born. That seems the most sensible."

"Whoa—*babies*?" Poppy's eyes rounded and Rose bit her lip. She hadn't meant to let that slip.

"Yes, babies. We found out we're having twins, but we haven't told anyone yet. One shock at a time, I guess."

"Wow, that is so cool." Poppy speared a piece of lettuce and popped it into her mouth. "*Twins.* That's unreal."

"Yes," Rose replied with both a laugh and a sigh. "My thoughts exactly."

AFTER LUNCH ROSE had thought they would head home, but Poppy insisted they visit a baby boutique, complete with fancy-looking pram, all chrome and black plastic, in the shop window.

"Oh my goodness," Rose whispered when she dared to glance at the price tag. "Eight hundred pounds for a pram."

"It's one of those fancy ones, isn't it?" Poppy replied sagely. "All the mums have them in London, but you can get one for much cheaper on eBay."

"Still…" Once again Rose was overwhelmed by how much she'd need. How on earth was she going to afford it? Yes, she knew Sam would want to buy some stuff, but she hated having to depend on him for absolutely everything. She needed to stand on her own two feet at least a little.

"There's a Silver Cross pram in the attic at Casterglass, I think. Proper old-fashioned, with big white rubber wheels. You could use that."

"Yes…" But she was as reluctant to depend on the largesse of Casterglass as she was on Sam. No matter what way she looked at it, she simply couldn't fend for herself, and it was both aggravating and terrifying.

"Look at these!" Poppy held up matching boy and girl sleepsuits, one pink and one blue, with piping in the opposite colour along the sleeves and collar. "These would be perfect."

"We don't know whether we're having boys or girls or both," Rose told her, fingering one of the sleepsuits. It was impossibly soft.

"Will you find out?"

"Maybe." Her scan was next month. Rose felt a thrill of wonder at finding out more about these babies. Maybe then it would feel more real.

"I'm going to buy them anyway," Poppy decided as she draped the two sleepsuits over her arm.

"Poppy...they're thirty pounds each!"

"So?" Poppy sounded blithe. "I'm earning proper money now, thanks to the gift shop. Mum pays me minimum wage for all my work. She pays everyone else, too," she added quickly. "No one's working for free."

Except me, Rose couldn't help but think. Was there a way for her to earn her own money at Casterglass? She was not brave enough to ask Althea, who definitely seemed to be the one in charge. And, she acknowledged, Althea certainly hadn't offered such a thing.

Poppy was already heading towards the till, and Rose decided to let her. She was clearly a very determined young lady.

After Poppy had bought the sleepsuits and handed them to Rose in their own luxury gift bag, Rose insisted they head back to Casterglass, before Poppy decided to buy her even more extravagant gifts.

Her heart lightened a little as they came up the drive, the sun shining down on the terraced lawns, the grass glinting jewel green. The castle had been doing a pleasingly brisk business since it had opened over two weeks ago, and Rose was glad to see the car park on the side lawn was three-quarters full.

"I'd better get back to the gift shop," Poppy said as she hopped out of the car. "Ben and Toby were in charge, but they don't know the meaning of a hard sell."

"And you do, definitely," Rose replied with a laugh.

Poppy gave her a pert look. "Of course I do."

She watched as Poppy loped off to the converted dairy that was now a gift shop, half a dozen people browsing inside. She saw Seph and Ellie were busy in their workshops, and Olivia and Will were chatting to some visitors by the gate to the walled garden. Violet and Walter were no doubt similarly occupied, Rose thought. Walter gave tours of his orchids in their glasshouse and Violet was hoping to stage a play in the natural amphitheatre by the beach. Everyone had fulfilling and interesting work, and she was…cleaning dishes. Doing the laundry. Wrestling the Hoover upstairs.

Well, it could be worse, she told herself pragmatically as

she headed inside. She had a roof over her head, and plenty of food, and people who were keen to support her. She was determined to count her blessings, even as she fought a persistent sense of unease about being so dependent on other people, some of them basically strangers.

It wasn't in her nature to do so; at least, it hadn't been since her life had imploded at eighteen, her future falling about her in fragments, and the people who were supposed to love her, care for her, had let her down spectacularly. Rose had relinquished her bitterness a long time ago, but the scars still remained. Relying on herself had become her creed, and yet here she was, utterly dependent. She just didn't know how to do anything about it.

As she headed into the kitchen, she felt the strained atmosphere before she saw Sam and Althea hunched over the kitchen table, just as Olivia and Althea had been that first morning. Sam looked unhappy, his mouth turned down, his expression troubled, while Althea looked...*angry*, Rose realised, with a ripple of foreboding. As she glanced between the two of them, she knew instinctively they'd been talking about her.

"Sam?" she asked uncertainly, and he raked a hand through his hair and blew out a breath. "What's going on?"

"Sam and I have been talking," Althea said before Sam could reply, her voice loud and pointed, making Rose feel both tense and itch to slap her. She sounded so...*censorious*.

"Yes, I got that part," she replied coolly, because Althea

seemed to want some sort of response, and already she was feeling very prickly.

"About your *father*," Althea finished, sounding even more pointed. She raised her eyebrows in challenge while Rose simply stared.

Then, without saying a word, Rose turned around and walked out of the kitchen. She didn't know where she was going, only that she needed to get away. She wasn't about to make the same mistake twice and run into the wood, so she headed across the meadow instead, towards the sea, a grey-blue glimmer in the distance. She walked blindly, putting one foot in front of another, trying not to stumble on the tufty grass, tears smarting her eyes.

Drat Althea and her nosiness! Despite her overtures of friendship, she obviously had remained suspicious and decided to go digging. And what she'd found had probably confirmed every dark thought she'd had about Rose since she'd got here.

Well, that was fine, Rose told herself, even as she tried not to tremble. *Fine.* She hadn't wanted to depend on these people anyway. She'd known it was foolhardy, even danger-ous, and now she wouldn't have to anymore. Starting today, she'd find a job. A new place to live. She'd manage perfectly well on her own, as she always had before, even with two babies on the way. She'd do it because she had no choice, because Althea and Sam and everyone else had shown her she'd been right not to trust them. Not to depend on them.

A choked sob escaped her, and she kept walking, right onto the beach, the sand damp and hard beneath her feet. She was, she realised, still clutching that designer gift bag with the two sleepsuits in it. She had a reckless urge to toss the whole thing into the sea, but she refrained from such an impulse because frankly she needed all the baby clothes she could get, now that she wouldn't be asking Sam or any of the other Penryns for anything.

Rose rested a hand on her bump as she gazed out at the sea, watching the rolling waves crashing onto the shore and then retreating again, with a spray of seafoam.

No, she wouldn't be trusting anyone anymore. Lesson learned. Again.

"It's just us three from now on," she told her babies softly, and bit her lip to keep any more tears from coming.

Chapter Thirteen

"WELL," ALTHEA SAID, as if Rose storming out had just proved something.

Sam put both hands to his head, his mind spinning. *What the hell had just happened?*

He dropped his hands as he glared at his sister. "Why did you do that, Althea?" he demanded.

She reared back, looking affronted. "Do what?"

"Talk to Rose like that, like she'd committed some crime."

"Well, maybe she—"

"It's her father who did, not her," Sam snapped. "And I'll thank you to stop interfering in my life!" He rose from the table, his heart starting to thud. He needed to find Rose. Immediately.

Althea's face crumpled. "Sam, you know I'm just looking out for you—"

"I am thirty-three years old. I don't need you looking out for me," Sam told her in a hard voice. "Because, frankly, Althea, you've just been messing things up."

Althea bit her lip, her eyes starting to look glassy. "I'm sorry if I seem harsh, but Sam, I know what it's like to be taken in by someone—"

"Rose is not Jasper!" Sam exclaimed, his voice rising to a near-roar. "How many times do I have to tell you that?"

"She's hiding something, though," Althea persisted, a distinct wobble in her voice now, along with an irritatingly stubborn note. "I know she is. You said as much, before she came in."

"That doesn't mean I think she's a *criminal.*" He whirled away from the table, too frustrated to keep arguing with Althea. She seemed determined not to see sense—and not to leave him and Rose alone. "Please, just…butt out, okay? I mean that in the nicest way possible. As well-intentioned as your concern might be, I don't need it. I don't want it."

"Sam—" She sounded anguished, but Sam was un-moved. Althea had meddled enough.

Not trusting himself to say anything more, he stalked out of the kitchen.

Of course, by the time he made it outside, Rose was long gone. Sam let out a frustrated groan as he swung his gaze around the property—the walled garden, the barns with their courtyard, the drive, a glimpse of the front terrace. Where was she?

He didn't think she'd brave heading up into the wood again, not after her tumble. He strode towards Olivia, who was standing by the entrance to the walled garden, chatting with what looked like a lovely, happy family.

"Olivia," he said tersely, "have you seen Rose?"

"Oh, er…" Olivia glanced at the family in apology. "Um, yes, I think so. I think I saw her heading towards the meadow."

Sam glanced at the meadow that ran along the side of the castle, now full of wildflowers and tufty grass, leading all the way to the sea.

"Thanks," he said to Olivia, and then he glanced at the family, who were looking a bit confused by his brusque interruption. "Sorry." Then he started striding through the long grass, towards the sea, and hopefully, Rose.

It took ten minutes before he reached the beach, and his heart lurched with both relief and fear when he saw Rose perched on a twisted piece of driftwood, her shoulders hunched, her long, reddish-blonde hair blowing wild in the wind.

"Rose," he said as he came towards her, and she stiffened. Sam realised he hadn't actually thought through what he was going to say. "Rose, you didn't have to run away like that."

"I thought I'd go before Althea or anyone else asked me to." Her voice was brittle and she wasn't looking at him. "You don't have to worry. I'll be out of here by tonight."

"Wait—what?" Sam stared at her in confused incredulity. He'd expected her to be upset, based on how she'd run out of the kitchen, and also on what he'd learned from Althea, but he hadn't expected *this*. "You're just…leaving?"

"It's better that way." Rose stood up, slipping her phone into her pocket. There was a bag at her feet, one of those luxury gift bags with gold cord handles. She picked it up, clutching it to her. "I've got a job, doing telemarketing. At least, I think I do. They're going to confirm tomorrow. And there's a possibility of a room in Barrow, so that's all good." She still wasn't looking at him, even though she was facing him, that stupid bag clutched to her chest like a shield, her gaze averted.

"Why are you doing this?" he asked, caught between irritation, hurt, and total confusion. It had been only about ten minutes since she'd left the kitchen, and she already had a job and a room? *What the hell?*

Rose's chin lifted. "Don't you want me to?"

"No." Sam raked a hand through his hair. "No," he said again, even more vehemently. "Rose, please. Can we just…press pause on all this? The room and the job? And talk properly?"

She pressed her lips together, eyes flashing. "What do you want to talk about?"

"Why you're going so haywire." He shook his head slowly as realisation started to trickle through him. "Did you think I was going to kick you out or something?"

Again with that chin, the flash of her eyes. "Weren't you?"

"No, of course not."

"Even though my father is in prison?"

He flinched a little, he couldn't help it, and of course Rose saw. She nodded, as if that tiny flinch had confirmed every bad thing she'd ever thought about him. Damn it, he *wasn't* going to fail. Not this time. Not with this. "I don't care about your father," he said. "At least, I only care about him in how he's affected you. And if you want to tell me what happened—"

"Didn't Althea tell you?" She flung the words at him, her voice vibrating with hurt.

"She said he'd been convicted of fraud, and that he was serving a jail sentence of seven years."

She gave a quick nod. "That's about the size of it."

She was trembling, Sam realised, and he longed to hold her. To comfort her. To make all this go away, but of course he couldn't. Still, he could try. "Althea gave me the bare bones of it," he told her quietly. "And I don't want to hear that kind of thing from her—"

"Well, no one wants to hear that kind of thing, I imagine!" Rose burst out, her voice turning shrill.

"What I meant," Sam replied steadily, "was that I want to hear it from you. I want you to tell me what happened. Nothing your father did will change how I feel about you." Although he wasn't entirely sure *how* he felt about her. And if what Althea had intimated—that Rose might have been involved in her father's long-running scam—was true, then that did change things.

But he didn't really think she was involved in some scam,

of course he didn't, not even for a second. But he thought he might have trouble getting Rose to believe that.

"There's nothing to tell," Rose stated flatly. "Besides what Althea told you—and I can guess what she told you. She decided to do a deep dive on Google and found out about my father. Well, he is in prison. He's been there for five years, and he's probably going to get out soon." She shrugged defiantly. "What of it?"

"That must have been hard for you," Sam remarked slowly. Five years… Rose would only have been nineteen, right around the time she'd started travelling. Did those two things relate? Had she been trying to escape her father's long shadow?

"It was what it was."

She was so prickly, barely looking at him, clutching that stupid bag, everything about her angry and defensive. Sam wished he knew how to reach her, but everything he said just seemed to bounce off her hardened shell.

"I don't want you to leave," he told her finally. "At all. And I don't think you were involved in what your father did—"

Rose let out a hard, hollow laugh. "Oh, but Althea does? Typical."

"I don't care what my sister thinks."

"Well, maybe I do," she flashed back. "Maybe I don't feel like staying in a place where everyone's giving me the side-eye, thinking I'm some sort of criminal."

"Althea was out of order," Sam said, a bit desperately now. "And I told her so. And I think everyone else in my family would, as well. She had a tough time with her ex-husband—"

"Yeah, so she said. Back when she was apologising to me for being suspicious at the start, but nothing seems to have changed."

"I'll talk to her—"

"Don't bother." Rose started to walk past him, and Sam reached for her shoulder.

"Rose, please. Don't stomp away from me—"

She shrugged his hand away. "I'm not stomping!"

"I just mean, don't go. I want you here. We have a future together. We're having *children* together. Don't run off the first time things get hard—"

"You think that's what I'm doing? Running away?"

For once he didn't seek to placate her. "Aren't you?" He met her gaze levelly, and she fell silent, surprised. "You didn't even ask me what I thought. What I believed. I gave Althea a proper telling-off, let me tell you."

"She seems determined to believe the worst of me."

"Maybe, but she can change. She'll have to. And anyway, she's not important. You are. We are. We can get through this, Rose. Together."

She stared at him uncertainly, confusion clouding her hazel eyes. "Sam, you barely know me."

"I know you more and more every day, and what I know

I like. We're working towards that 'one day, maybe'—let's keep working."

She bit her lip, her expression still so unhappy. He longed to see her smile, to hear her laugh like he had in Ambleside. "How?"

"Let's set aside some time, proper time, to talk about these things."

Her mouth twisted. "Another serious discussion?"

"But about the past, not the future. I need to understand why you are the way you are, and you—you need to understand the same about me." Because heaven knew he'd been keeping some secrets, too. "Please, Rose. We can...go away somewhere, where we won't be interrupted. Where we can talk about the past, our childhoods, our parents, whatever it is we need to. I want to know. I want to understand...if you want to tell me."

She sighed, her shoulders sagging, like the weight of the world she'd been carrying was slipping, just a little. "I don't know if I do."

"I understand that. Sharing this stuff is hard." He hesitated and then added with raw honesty, "There's stuff I've never told anyone in my family. Stuff that kept me from coming back to Casterglass."

A mingled look of curiosity and sympathy gleamed in her eyes. "And you'll tell me?"

"If you want to listen."

"I do." She shook her head. "I'm sorry, Sam. I know I

probably overreacted. I just...I really have a hard time trusting people. Depending on them. And since I've come here, I've felt so...vulnerable. Depending on you, on Casterglass, for everything. And even if you're happy to give it, it's really hard."

"I can understand that," he said quietly.

She searched his face, her expression still troubled, her lower lip caught between her teeth. "Can you?" she asked at last, sounding doubtful.

"I think I can, Rose. I'm trying." He didn't know what more he could say to convince her.

After a long moment, as the wind off the sea blew her hair into tangles around her face, she finally nodded. "Okay."

"Okay...?"

"Let's do this. Plan an evening or afternoon or whatever, just the two of us. And we'll talk." She gave him a small, fragile smile. "Thank you for...being willing to believe in me."

Relief coursed through him, along with something both fierier and sweeter. Excitement. The two of them...alone. Learning about each other. Was it wrong for the prospect to make his blood heat?

"Okay, let's do it," he said, and she let out a little huff of laughter.

"I'm sorry for freaking out. I seem to have a tendency to do that."

"It's okay." He smiled back, and then they were grinning at each other, rather foolishly, and it felt good. It felt *really* good. "I need to get back to the glamping site," Sam finally said, his voice filled with reluctance because part of him wanted to simply stay here with Rose, smiling. "Are you going to head back to the house?"

Rose understandably did not look thrilled by that prospect. "I suppose so."

He didn't blame her for sounding uncertain; if he were her, he wouldn't want to face Althea again. He hoped his older sister had got the message. He was already determined to talk to her again, just to make it *very* clear. He believed Rose, and he wanted everyone else to as well, including Althea. "Please don't worry about my sister," he told her. "She knows she was in the wrong."

Rose pursed her lips. "But she's still suspicious."

He couldn't deny that. "Less so, I think," Sam said, and she sighed.

"All right. I'll do my best."

She turned to go, and without even thinking about what he was doing, he reached for her shoulder again, drawing her into a clumsy hug that somehow surprised not just Rose, but him as well. He hadn't realised he'd been intending to hug her, but as he felt her slender body against his, her bump pressing into him, he was glad he had. "Thank you, Rose," he said, and he felt her soften against him, her hair tickling his cheek. She smelled like roses, which was, Sam thought wryly, apt.

Then she laughed a little and moved away, and Sam realised the bag she'd been carrying had been squashed between their bodies.

"What is this, anyway?" he asked ruefully, and to his surprise Rose blushed, looking uncertain.

"It's some baby clothes. Poppy bought them for me. For—for us."

His heart leapt, turned over. *Baby clothes.* "Can I see them?"

She nodded and drew two tiny sleepsuits out of the bag—one pink, one blue. After flipping, his heart now seemed to still in his chest. He reached for the pink sleepsuit with a thrill of incredulous wonder. "It's so *small.*"

She let out a soft huff of laughter. "I know, right?"

"I can't believe we'll have *babies* filling these out in just a few months." Children. Actual children. His children. *Their* children.

She nodded in agreement. "Scary, huh?"

He glanced up at her. "And exciting," he said softly, and she smiled.

"Yes, that too."

They stood there together for another moment, gazing down at the sleepsuits, filled with wonder, brought together by the miracle—*miracles*—they'd made. Sam imagined the solid little body of a baby in one of those sleepsuits, hefted against his shoulder, cradled in his arms. They'd be a *family.* It created a pressure in his chest, a burst of something like joy in his heart.

As frightening and shocking as this all had been, he knew he'd meant what he said. This was exciting. *He* was excited. He wanted to say something of that to Rose, tell her how excited and happy he was, even if he was terrified too, but before he could untangle the words, she gave him a quick smile and stepped away. Sam couldn't help but feel just a little bereft.

"You should get up there." She nodded towards the woods. "I'm sure there are some glampers who need you."

He let out a shaky laugh, more affected by that brief moment than he'd realised. "They do seem to need quite a lot." Although many of the campers had been friendly and relaxed, a few had had some rather specific demands—including the use of hair straighteners and a wok. The fact that Sam had provided a hair dryer and a normal saucepan had not appeased them in the slightest.

"I'm sorry I have to go," he said, meaning it utterly. Unable to keep himself from it, he reached for her hand. "You'll tell me if anything…if anything happens that upsets you, okay? I want to know."

She nodded, a funny look on her face, a cross between uncertainty and tenderness. "Okay," she said and then, sliding her hand from his, she started walking back to the castle.

Sam stood there on the sand, watching her go, until she'd topped the crest of a small hill and then slipped out of view.

Chapter Fourteen

ROSE LAY IN bed and stared at the ceiling, straining to hear the various Penryns troop out of the kitchen. Even though she'd been awake for an hour, she'd decided to give breakfast a miss—she'd managed to avoid seeing any Penryn since she came back from the beach yesterday, and she wasn't ready to break her streak.

She'd been both grateful and touched by Sam's concern and sincerity—they'd moved and frightened her in just about equal measure. Did she really want to talk properly about the past in the way he'd suggested? Part of her craved such honesty, such intimacy, while another part felt like backing away. Quickly.

As for all the other Penryns...well, she wasn't ready to look any of them in the eye just yet. Not because she had anything to be afraid of, but because she couldn't bear to see their suspicion and judgement. And as for Althea...Rose didn't yet trust herself to be civil to her. She'd give it another fifteen minutes, she decided, and then when everyone was out working, she'd eat some breakfast and tackle the dishes, because she suspected they'd be waiting for her. Two weeks on and she'd become, if not indispensable, then at least useful, which was just as she wanted.

Rose swung her legs over the side of the bed and ran a hand through her tangled hair. She'd take a quick shower and then dress in some of the clothes she'd bought yesterday, to make herself feel good, and then she'd go downstairs.

Twenty minutes later she was creeping downstairs, dressed in the stretchy black top and a loose, ankle-skimming skirt, tiptoeing and skulking around corners like she was a spy. She breathed a loud, gusty sigh of relief when she saw the kitchen was empty. And yes, there was a stack of dirty dishes in the sink, waiting for her. Well, fine. She could handle a crusty pan much better than one of Althea's sharp-eyed looks.

She was halfway through the pile when she heard someone come into the kitchen and she tensed instinctively before turning around. Violet stood in the doorway, wearing what looked a dozen voluminous scarves, eyeing her narrowly. Not Violet too, Rose thought, her heart sinking. She'd half-hoped the eccentric older lady might be a semi-ally.

"You know, my dear," she said gently, "you don't need to make yourself so *useful.*"

Rose simply stared at her, not really sure what she meant. "I like being useful," she replied uncertainly, after a moment.

"Oh, I know," Violet assured her with a warm smile. "And we are lazy enough to let you be so. But it isn't necessary." She paused, her lips pursed thoughtfully as she adjusted one of her many scarves. "What I'm saying, my dear, is you don't need to earn your keep."

Rose opened her mouth, closed it. "I…" she began and then shook her head. She felt her eyes filling with tears and blinked them back. Darn those pregnancy hormones yet again. That had to be all it was, and not that Violet—this funny, strange, charming, and more than a little batty woman—seemed to see right through her.

"You've all done so much for me," she finally managed, turning back to the dishes to hide her suspiciously bright eyes. "I want to repay you in some way."

"That's understandable," Violet replied. "But I think it's a little more than that, don't you?"

Her voice was so gentle, and yet so knowing, that Rose had to close her eyes. "I don't…" she began, and then had to stop.

"I understand, my dear, because I was the same way, once. Of course I've made up for it since—I'm completely useless now." She let out a guffaw of genuine laughter that had Rose smiling and turning around. The threat of tears had thankfully passed.

"What do you mean?"

"When I was young, I was always trying to make myself useful. My mother died when I was little more than a baby, and my father was an archaeologist who dragged me all around the world." She smiled faintly. "I loved it, I must confess, but I was always terrified he'd put me in boarding school, so I made myself as useful as I could—cooking, cleaning, washing, mending. Whatever it took."

"And did it work?" Rose asked, fascinated by this glimpse into Violet's surprisingly similar life. They'd both been child nomads—had Violet, like her, clung to a father who had been charming and affectionate when he chose, and then forgotten her when it was convenient?

"Yes," she answered, "until I was sixteen, and then he decided I needed to do Sixth Form properly, which I did, and I actually loved it. I was very good at hockey—can you imagine?" She let out a little snort and Rose gave a small smile. "I adored boarding school, and university was even better."

So they weren't all that similar after all, Rose thought, turning back to the dishes.

"In any case," Violet continued, "that's neither here nor there. My point is, well...you're here for a reason. And it's not because you are so terribly good at ironing, which, my dear, you are. I am really most impressed."

"I'm here because I'm pregnant," Rose stated baldly as she turned around again, folding her arms and giving the older woman a look of challenge. "That's the only reason."

Violet raised her eyebrows. "Is that a bad thing?"

"No...but it means nobody chose it." Chose her. Which, she realised, rankled, even if that wasn't fair or reasonable, which she knew it wasn't.

"You chose to have this baby, though," Violet replied.

"Yes." She wasn't making much sense, Rose realised. Of course the baby—babies—were the only reason she was here. *She* wouldn't have chosen to come here if she hadn't been pregnant. But she still hated feeling unwanted, an interloper. "Did Althea tell you about my father?" she asked, deciding to grasp that nettle once and for all.

"That he's in prison for fraud?" Violet replied without missing a beat. "Yes, she said something about it, and I imagine it must have been very difficult for you, but, my dear, how *delicious*. He sounds like an absolute scoundrel. I wish I'd met him."

Rose let out a surprised laugh. "I suppose he was. Is." She had no idea if her father had reformed or not; they had not had any contact since he'd gone to prison. She'd sent a postcard, back at the beginning, just to let him know where she was, but he hadn't replied, and she had told herself she didn't care. She wouldn't.

"I so wish we had a black sheep in our family tree," Violet mused mistily. "A swashbuckling pirate or a nefarious highwayman. As far as I know, the only proper scandal was a great-great-aunt who came to church tipsy. She had a fondness for cooking sherry. *So* shocking." She let out a little laugh before subsiding into more musing, leaving Rose feeling a bit bemused. Violet's wisdom came with a hefty side helping of strange, she thought with affection. Not a bad way to be, all things considered.

As Violet wandered out of the kitchen, Rose turned back to the dishes. No, she wasn't earning her keep, she thought with a tiny spurt of bitterness. She doubted Althea would ever let her. But as she continued to scrub and soak, her gaze moving over the walled garden in all of its artful wildness, she wondered if there was something else she could do at Casterglass, something that was a little more interesting than housework, a little more *her*. Although what really was *her*? she wondered. She wasn't sure she'd ever got the chance to find out.

But everyone else here had found a passion—Olivia with her garden, Poppy with the shop, Seph with her woodcarving, and Sam with his outdoorsy stuff. Even Althea with her bossy business sense. Could she do the same? Would they let her?

Don't be stupid. The voice inside her head was quick and waspish. *You aren't going to be treated like a Penryn, like you belong. You're only here on sufferance.*

That wasn't true, Rose told herself stoutly. Not entirely, anyway. But it was hard to silence that mocking inner voice.

She managed to avoid Althea for the rest of the morning, busying herself with household tasks and grateful that Olivia, Poppy and Seph, when she saw them, had all treated her normally. Maybe Althea hadn't spread the story about her father, or maybe they just didn't care. Rose was glad, anyway, that not everyone at Casterglass was giving her the side-eye.

Then, that afternoon, after she'd gone for a walk outside, she came into the kitchen to make a pot of tea to find Althea standing there looking resolute. Rose faltered in the doorway, wanting to turn tail and run, but deciding not to because she knew she had to face Althea down at some point. It might as well be now.

"Don't go," Althea said, something of a command, and Rose pressed her lips together.

"I wasn't going to, but I thought that was what you wanted?"

Althea sighed. "We need to talk. Would you like a cup of tea?"

"I was just going to make a pot for everyone." It had become her habit to brew a cuppa for Seph, Poppy, and Ellie and bring it to them in their respective workplaces; if Olivia or Will or anyone else was around, she brought them one, as well.

"I'll make it," Althea said, going to the sink to fill the kettle. "Why don't you sit down?"

Was that an order? Rose wondered as she took a seat at the table and laced her hands together in front of her. She had no idea what Althea was going to say, but she felt the need to brace herself.

"I imagine you're quite angry with me," Althea remarked, her back to Rose as she filled the kettle. "I would be, if I were you."

Rose took a deep breath and let it out evenly. "I was,"

she admitted after a moment. "And I still am, I suppose." Although weirdly she suddenly didn't feel that angry now. More wary, and tired.

"Fair enough." Althea plonked the kettle on top of the Aga and then turned around to face Rose, her arms folded, her face set. "Look, I might as well say it. I acted like a—like a real bitch." She grimaced. "I'm sorry. I was wrong. Completely wrong, and out of order, which Sam told me in no uncertain terms."

Rose hadn't expected such a blatant, blanket apology. She'd been waiting for excuses, explanations. *I'm just looking out for my little brother. You must realise how strange it looked; we didn't know you at all...* "Yes," she said, surprising herself because it hadn't been what she'd been going to say. "You were."

"I jumped to conclusions," Althea continued. "Because I've been burned before."

Ah, there was the excuse and explanation. "By your ex-husband. Yes, I know."

"All right, it does sound like an excuse," Althea said, startling Rose. She hadn't said that out loud, had she? "I know it does. But he was a serial liar and I've learned to be able to tell when someone isn't giving me the truth."

The kettle began to boil, and Rose waited until Althea had whisked it off the stove and poured water into the teapot before saying carefully, "And you think I'm not telling the truth?"

"I think you're hiding something," Althea replied. "Aren't you? I don't just mean about your father. Something else."

Rose stared at her looking back at her so levelly, and felt a sudden, hot flare of anger. "And what right do you have to demand anything from me?" she asked in a low voice. "Do I need to give you my whole personal history, tell you my secrets? Because anything like that, I should imagine, is between me and Sam, not his sister."

Althea lifted her chin a notch. "But you haven't told Sam, have you? Whatever it is."

"And I'm sure there are things Sam hasn't told me! Do you reveal everything about yourself all at once? I don't think so. Besides, that's none of your business, Althea. Sam and I are working through things just fine." And they were going to talk about their pasts soon. Besides, it wasn't as if she was keeping some massive secret. All right, maybe she could have told him her father was in prison, but what did that really matter? It had nothing to do with *them*. As for the other stuff…that was just part of who she was. It wasn't a secret. Not exactly.

"You had no right," she told Althea, her voice shaking a little. "And if you were concerned, you could have come to me. Not gone behind my back to try to poison Sam against me, make me leave."

"It wasn't like that," Althea protested. "Rose, I actually like you—"

"Yeah, right," Rose scoffed. She had thought she wasn't angry, and maybe she wasn't. Maybe she was just hurt, and this was the way she was showing it.

Althea shook her head, pouring the tea out into cups. "I suppose your situation with Sam has brought up a lot of complicated feelings for me. I got pregnant young—I didn't feel trapped, but I think my husband did."

"Your lousy liar of an ex-husband—yes, I get that," Rose filled in, her voice still trembling. She really was hurt. She'd hoped Althea was starting to like her, but everything she had said so far confirmed that she didn't, even if she'd claimed the opposite.

"I just didn't want Sam to feel trapped in the same way," Althea persisted.

"So, what? He should just walk away from his responsibilities?"

"No. No, of course not." Althea rubbed her face. "I don't know. I've clearly handled this really wrong. I'm sorry. I guess that's all I can say. There are no excuses, no reasonable explanations. I reacted on a visceral level and didn't think through things. I really am sorry." Rose took a steadying breath, unsure how to respond. Althea hung her head humbly. "Can you forgive me?"

"This isn't the first time you've had to apologise," Rose said after a moment. She still felt shaky. "And yes, I can forgive you, of course I can. But I need to know that you aren't going to pull something like this again. Sam and I are talking things through, Althea, like I said. We don't need your interference, even if it is well intentioned." Which Rose wasn't wholly convinced it was.

Althea gave her the glimmer of a smile. "Sam basically said the same thing to me."

"So…?"

"Okay. No more cyberstalking. Or talking behind your back." She made a face. "Wow, I really sound like a charmer, don't I? I really am sorry. I don't know what came over me. I just…got scared, I suppose. For Sam."

Because she was clearly such a monster. Rose forced the unhelpful thought back. Now was the time for new beginnings. "Okay, then." She took the cup of tea Althea handed her with a small smile. "Maybe we can call this a clean slate."

"Yes. Speaking of clean, actually…"

Rose tensed. Was Althea going to hire her as a housekeeper or something? Or tell her she needed to dust a little better? She didn't think she could handle that right now. In fact, she knew she couldn't. If Althea criticised *anything* right now, Rose might slap her.

"You don't need to keep doing the housework," she said, "especially in your condition."

Surprised, Rose simply stared for a second. "I'm pregnant, not ill," she protested finally.

"Yes, but we've all always chipped in before and I think that's the better way to do it, with everyone helping. We'll make a rota. You don't need to be our maid."

Rose gazed down at her cup. "I like being useful, and regardless of what you may have thought, I do appreciate the hospitality you've all shown me. I don't want to take advantage by freeloading—"

"I understand, and I'm not asking you to lie around on your backside all day." Althea gave her another glimmering smile. "But there must be some way to utilise your gifts and abilities better than by pushing a mop. Everyone here is doing something they love—Olivia in the garden, Seph in her workshop, Poppy in the gift shop, Sam up at the glamping site." Just as she had been thinking herself, Rose thought, with a rush of surprised gratitude towards Althea. She'd never expected her to suggest something like this. "Is there something you'd be interested in doing?" she continued. "We've been wanting to get the café going a bit more. It's pretty basic at the moment, because we don't have the staff or really the skill. We all take turns making teas and coffees and doling out ice creams, but if we had a proper kitchen, offering meals and cakes and things…" Althea shrugged. "Anyway, it's just an idea."

Rose recognised an olive branch when she saw one, and she appreciated the gesture. Would she want to take over the café? She had the experience, after six years working her way around the world by bartending, cooking, and cleaning. A small flare of excitement leapt within her. It would be a way to be useful and maybe feel fulfilled, just as she'd been wondering before.

"Thank you," she said sincerely. "I'll definitely think about it."

"Good. And I really hope we can put—well, everything else behind us." Althea gave a grimacing smile. "Really."

"I already have," Rose assured her. Well, sort of. Mostly. It would no doubt be a process, but she did feel they'd both taken some small steps as Althea flashed her a grateful smile before heading back to her office.

Having finished her tea, Rose decided to have a little wander around the courtyard and café space, such as it was. The courtyard was framed on three sides by various barns and outbuildings that had been turned into retail spaces and workshops, with the café adjoining the gift shop. It was, as Althea had said, very basic at the moment; there were a dozen tables with pretty checked tablecloths, as well as a few outside in the courtyard, and a coffee bar with the basic sink and kettle—not even an espresso machine. There were also ice cream tubs provided by a local creamery, kept in a chest freezer, and some snack packs of crisps and Hula Hoops for sale by the till. And that was it.

Really, Rose thought as she walked around the café, now empty at four o'clock, so much more could be done with it. They could offer toasted sandwiches and jacket potatoes, as well as proper cappuccinos and lattes, at a bare minimum. They could also get a local baker to provide scrummy cakes and traybakes. Rose already could picture them dusted with icing sugar underneath domed glass lids. There was room too, she thought, for a few squashy armchairs, maybe even a sofa, if visitors wanted to relax a bit more. Maybe even a few bookshelves offering a do-it-yourself library, or a curated selection of books for sale, some about the local area... The café could become a destination in itself, she thought with a thrill, never mind the actual castle. Why not?

"Althea said I might find you in here," Sam said as he poked his head through the door.

"Did she?" The woman was cannier than Rose gave her credit for. She hadn't said anything to her about having a nose around, but clearly Althea had anticipated it. "I was just thinking about doing some work in the café, turning it into a bit more of a going concern."

"A bit more?" Sam asked, stepping into the room.

Feeling shy, Rose gave a little shrug. "Just, you know, a bit comfier and more welcoming. A few more food offerings."

"That sounds like a great idea, as long as you're up for it. I don't want you to exhaust yourself."

"I won't." She appreciated his concern, but she realised she was properly excited about this. It felt both good and strange, and new in a way that was invigorating.

"Good." He reached for her hand, the touch of his warm, dry palm sliding across hers making her insides jolt, just like that hug last night had. She wasn't used to being touched, but it felt nice. Really nice. "I have things ready for tonight," he told her.

Rose eyed him uncertainly.

"Tonight?"

"A chance to talk properly. Get to know one another. I've got it all arranged."

She felt a flicker of unease, a flare of excitement. This sounded, well, serious. "What do you mean exactly, arranged?"

The smile he gave her was mysterious, with the impish mischief of a little boy dancing in his bright blue eyes. "You'll see. Meet me outside the kitchen at eight o'clock."

"Okay," Rose said, wondering just what he had planned—and if she was ready for it.

"It's a date," Sam said, squeezing her hand, and then he was gone, leaving Rose to wonder—was it really a date? Or had he just used that as a turn of phrase?

And which one of those possibilities, she wondered, did she actually want it to be?

Chapter Fifteen

EVERYTHING WAS PERFECT. At least, Sam had done his best. He'd tried.

But that hasn't been good enough before, has it?

He did his best to silence that inner sceptic, the voice from his childhood that kept reminding him of his shortcomings. He didn't know when that voice had started with its mocking comments; he remembered being happy as a little kid, racing through the woods, building dens, wild and free. He'd always known he wasn't going to be an academic like either of his parents, but he didn't think he'd really minded, not until he'd got a bit older, maybe nine or so. His father had made an offhand remark to someone—a relative, maybe?—about Althea being the 'brainy' one, and Olivia loving to read.

"And Sam?" the person had asked, a smile in their voice.

Sam remembered how his father's gaze had moved from Althea and Olivia to Sam, his expression turning a bit perplexed. "Sam loves being outside," he finally said, like a man at a loss. "Don't you, Sam?"

And Sam had said yes, because he did, but he'd felt, from his father's tone, that he'd disappointed him somehow. That being outdoorsy wasn't quite the same as being brainy or loving to read.

Of course, it was absurd to take such a small thing to heart. His father wouldn't even remember the conversation; it had been a throwaway remark, made in a moment. Sam knew it didn't actually mean or prove anything, not really, but there had been dozens of such moments, remarks and looks and suppressed sighs, that had solidified the feeling inside him that he didn't quite measure up. And *that* had been further cemented when he'd been expelled from boarding school and lost his place at university. His father hadn't even hidden his disappointment then.

But why, Sam? How could you be so foolish? So wrong?

Yeah, well, he'd never really come up with an answer to that one, although he'd been trying to make it up ever since, in one way or another. Make it up to his father—and make it up to himself.

With a sigh Sam pushed such thoughts out of his mind. Admittedly, he was going to have to think about it all over again tonight, when he and Rose finally levelled with each other. He'd promised himself he'd be honest, and he hoped she would be, as well. Already just thinking about saying all that stuff to her made the old emotions bubble up—the hurt, the fear, the insecurity. He hated feeling so weak. He especially hated showing that weakness to anyone, and worst of all Rose.

But he'd made a promise and he intended to keep it.

Rose was waiting by the kitchen door, looking both beautiful and bemused. She was wearing the patchwork maxi skirt she'd worn the first day she'd arrived, and she'd paired it with a white flowing top with a pretty pattern of broderie anglaise on the front. Her hair was back in a loose plait, a few wispy tendrils framing her face.

"So where are we going, exactly?" she asked.

"You'll see."

Maybe it was silly to make it a surprise, but Sam enjoyed the sense of expectation. As he headed towards the meadow, he took Rose's hand. She gave him a funny look, but didn't comment, and he found he enjoyed walking hand in hand with her across the tufty grass, towards the sea. He enjoyed it a lot.

"Are we going to the beach?" she asked as they headed across the meadow.

"Yep."

She shot him a narrowed look. "Did you *do* something?"

"Maybe."

She gave a little laugh and shook her head. "Okay, I guess I'll be surprised."

As they rounded the little hill that led down to the beach, she gave a small gasp. "Oh, Sam…"

"Do you like it?"

"It's lovely."

It wasn't much, but it had taken him the better part of the afternoon to set up one of the unused glamping tents right there on the beach, its flaps drawn back so they could see the sea from the comfortable chairs inside. He'd dug a fire pit out in front and laid the wood and kindling for a fire, and there was a cooler of picnic items that he hoped weren't too cringey while still being romantic—strawberries and cold chicken, elderflower cordial and jam tarts and a salad of couscous and bell peppers.

"This is all amazing," Rose said, shaking her head in wonder as she glanced around. He'd brought some big pillows and a blanket, as well, which he'd set up outside the tent so they could lie there and watch the stars…just as they'd done in Tairua.

Was she thinking about that night, when they'd lain together, limbs tangled, and the Southern Lights had shot off fireworks in the sky above them?

Not that he was intending to replicate that evening. "This isn't meant to be…" he blurted, wanting to make it clear. "I'm not expecting anything," he half-mumbled, and she laughed even as she blushed.

"Okay, good to know." Her cheeks had turned fiery.

Laughing a little, he shook his head. "Anyway. Moving on."

"Yeah."

How could they feel so new to each other, he wondered, when they'd already had a fling lasting several months? But

Tairua, he knew, had been out of time; he suspected that neither of them had been revealing their true selves. It had never been about that.

This was.

He helped her over to the blanket and then crouched down to get the bonfire going while Rose settled herself against the cushions.

"This is amazing," she said as she gazed at the sea lapping the shore just a few metres from them. "And it's not even raining."

"Don't jinx it," he joked. "Why do you think I brought the tent?"

"The sky is perfectly clear," Rose protested.

"You do know it rains three hundred days a year here?" Sam replied seriously. "A perfectly blue sky can morph into a thunderstorm within minutes."

"That's kind of like life, isn't it?" Rose replied as he scooted back to sit next to her while the fire started to emit a cheerful, crackling warmth.

"That was a very smooth segue," he told her, "into talking about all this stuff."

"All this stuff," she mused, scooping a handful of sand and letting the grains trickle through her fingers. "Can we eat first? Because I am actually kind of starving. Eating for three and all that, you know."

"Yes, of course we can." He didn't mind the reprieve, either. He fixed her a plate and poured her a glass of elderflower before doing the same for himself.

As they sat back with their plates of food, she looked at him seriously. "Thank you, Sam. This really is amazing." He shrugged, both embarrassed and touched by her sincerity. "I mean it. I know I've been prickly and difficult sometimes, and you really have been patient. And kind. And just…well, wonderful, really. So thank you."

"I've had my moments, as well," Sam couldn't help but say. He thought of how he'd asked if the baby was his, just minutes after she'd arrived. Not his finest moment, for sure, but he hoped he'd made it up to her since then.

"Well, we're both new to this, I guess," she said with a soft laugh. "Pregnancy. Parenthood." She paused. "Relationships. At least, I am." She glanced at him from under her lashes, waiting for more.

Sam cleared his throat. "Yeah, you could say I'm kind of new to all those too," he said, his gaze on his plate as he toyed with his fork. "Pregnancy and parenthood, definitely. As for relationships…I've had a few girlfriends, it's true, but it was never that serious. I never…" He let that trail off, wondering just how he'd been thinking he'd finish it. *Felt this way before? This much?* Did he even mean that?

"Yeah, same here," Rose said, and they shared a brief, relieved smile before she burst out laughing. "What are we like! You'd think we were a couple of teenagers on a first date."

"It feels that way, a bit."

"Yeah," she agreed, smiling, "I suppose it does."

They gazed at each other for a long moment, the only sound the crackling of the logs in the fire and the gentle *shooshing* of the waves on the sand. Rose's eyes were a warm golden green, steady on him. Her lips were slightly parted, and a strand of hair brushed her cheek. Sam felt his heart flip. His body tingled all over. He leaned forward, just a little, not even sure what he intended, not *entirely*, when Rose suddenly put her plate aside and sat up straight, her gaze turning intent. Intense.

"Okay, look," she said. "I think I might as well just say it."

Sam stared at her, wondering if he had just completely misread that moment. He'd been about to kiss her, and she was about to say—what? "Say it?" he repeated warily.

"Everything," Rose replied.

Wow, dramatic much? Rose let out shaky laugh. "Sorry, that was needless melodrama," she told Sam, who had leaned back against the cushions, his gaze alert, a little cautious. For a few seconds there she'd thought he might kiss her, and while part of her—quite a large part, actually—had been very much ready for that, wanting it, another part had backed away because they'd come here to talk, and that was what she needed to do. The kissing—maybe—could come later.

"So. My father is in prison," she stated, rubbing her

hands down the length of her skirt, feeling an urge to move. "About that. Remember when I told you he took me all over the world?"

"Yes…"

"What I didn't realise as a kid—I mean, why would I?— was that he was perpetuating this massive scam, selling companies this cutting-edge IT software that didn't actually work." She let out a shaky laugh. "Which I suppose was part of the reason we never stayed anywhere that long. He was a proper con artist—I looked up his stuff, later, you know, when he was being prosecuted. He had a fancy website, customer testimonials, a whole slick operation that made it look like he was representing this well-respected corporation, when it was only him. At least I think it was. Even now I don't know all the details, and I'm not sure I want to. I don't even know what the software was supposed to do—stop a virus or something?—but he was great at selling stuff. A proper salesman. Charming, smooth."

She ran out of breath, the words having come out on a rush, leaving her a little flat as she stared down at the sand.

They'd had a lot of fun, her father and her. A lot of laughter, a lot of fancy meals and interesting days out— strolling through museums, exploring narrow, twisting streets or city parks, always wondering what was around the next corner. They'd also had a lot of leaving places quickly, and she'd had a lot of time on her own—nights in anony-mous hotel rooms while her father chatted up some company or other, days kicking around a strange city, sometimes accompanied by a babysitter her father had hired on the fly. No one stayed for long, and she'd had literally no friends. Adventures, yes, but not much of a life, in the end.

"How did it all fall apart?" Sam asked quietly.

"His past caught up with him eventually, I guess. I don't know all the details, only that he was arrested when I was eighteen. I was at boarding school when I got the news." She hesitated. "I actually haven't spoken to my father since he was convicted."

Sam's eyes widened a little. "You've never visited him in prison?"

"No. I sent him a postcard, right at the beginning, to let him know I was okay, not that he was even wondering." She shook her head, unable to keep that old bitterness from rising up. "He never replied, so we've had zero contact. And I haven't had contact with my mother, either, since that time, so in a way I'm like an orphan." She tried to laugh but it came out sounding strangled, and she had to blink rapidly a few times. Goodness, but this was hard. Harder than she'd thought, and she'd *known* it would be tough. There was a reason she didn't talk about all this stuff. Think about it.

Sam reached for her hand, threading her fingers through his "I'm sorry, Rose. That all had to have been so hard."

"Yeah, it was." She gazed down at their twined fingers—his brown and strong, hers slender and pale. They were so different, and yet she sensed their similarities. Was it enough to draw them together? Keep them together?

"I can understand why you have trouble trusting people," Sam continued. "Depending on them, when your father let you down so much."

"Well, it wasn't just that." She stared down at their fingers. "It was more what *didn't* happen."

"What do you mean?"

She kept staring down at their fingers as she explained slowly, "It was my dad and me against the world for so long. Always just us two, nobody else. I loved him. I trusted him." She felt her throat thicken and she had to stop to swallow, breathe. "I know my childhood was unorthodox—no formal education, no friends. It didn't actually bother me, at least not that much, until my dad insisted I go to boarding school for Sixth Form."

"In Switzerland."

"Yes, a very fancy place. Too fancy for me. I didn't fit in—I was too weird, I suppose. I'd never been around gaggles of girls, I had no idea what field hockey even *was*, I had no interest in make-up or pop songs or boys." She sighed. "So I was an oddball, and that was okay. I didn't actually mind, because I was used to my own company. I worked hard—I wanted to go to university, get a proper degree, do something with my life." She paused. "Make my dad proud of me."

Gently he squeezed her hand, encouraging her to continue. "And?" he asked softly.

"And, amazingly, I was offered a place at Oxford. St John's College, to study English. I was *so* chuffed."

"But…you didn't go to Oxford," Sam said slowly. "Did you?"

Finally, she looked up at him, trying to smile. "Nope. Because in February of that year, right when I was about to sit my mock exams, the headmistress called me into her study. Told me that she regretted this very deeply, but as my father hadn't paid my fees for the last two terms, I could no longer continue at the school."

"Oh, Rose…"

"I was shocked. At first, I thought it was just an oversight. I called and texted him, but he didn't even respond. The headmistress told me to arrange my travel, as I couldn't stay at the school any longer. She was sorry, but very firm. I felt…lost." She swallowed hard, the memory of those days— the confusion, the terror, the sense of disbelief that had morphed into a terrible, soul-deep betrayal, as she realised just how alone she was.

"Eventually I got in touch with my dad. He was sorry, but there was no money. At that time he was actually on the run from the police, would you believe." She managed a huff of laughter. "They caught up with him a short while later, but he had no interest in having me tag along with him. He told me to use my credit card and find somewhere to stay. No question about continuing school, or going to uni, or anything. Just…you're eighteen, sort yourself out."

"I'm sorry." The words were quietly heartfelt.

"Yeah, well, I shouldn't complain really, because plenty of people have it much worse. I mean, boohoo, I had to leave my expensive Swiss boarding school, right? With a tuition of thirty grand a year? Cry me a river." She shook her head, her mouth twisting. "It's not even that, you know. I mean, I could have got over *that*. At least I think I could have. What really hurt was…the sense of being abandoned. Forgotten. Like he'd never really cared." She sniffed, trying to keep the tears that were pooling in her eyes at bay. "Not to mention my whole future down the drain." Goodness, but she was sounding sorry for herself. "I know it's not that bad—"

"Rose, you don't need to make excuses. It sounds—well, terrible, frankly." Sam's eyes were crinkled with concern. "What about your mum? Could she help?"

"No." There was her throat, going all thick again. Her voice sounded thick, as well. Clogged. "I rang her, too. She'd remarried, was living in the south of France with her second husband, whom I'd never even met. She'd always said I could ask her for help if I needed it, but when I actually did…" A tear fell and almost angrily she dashed it away. "Well, it turned out she didn't mean it, after all. I asked her for enough to cover the last term of my fees, just so I could finish and get my degree, and she refused. I know they had the money, but she said she really couldn't impose on her husband for such an amount. And you know, I got that. Thirty grand isn't nothing, which is what it would have been, with the two terms in arrears to pay, as well." She sighed. "But then I asked her if I could live with her and go to school somewhere else. Just so I could *finish*. And she said no to that, too. Apparently, it would be 'awkward' for her husband, or something like that."

Sam's eyes had rounded, and now they flashed with anger. "Seriously? So what did you do?"

"I was stupid, really. Looking back, I think I could have handled it all so much better. I'm sure there are programs and grants and things for people who were in my situation. But as it was…" She shook her head slowly. "I felt sort of numb inside. Frozen. The school didn't want to have anything to do with me, my father was basically AWOL, my mother didn't want to know. I didn't have any friends or relatives that I knew of; I didn't even have a place I could call home. And I just didn't know what to do. When I tried to use my credit card to book a flight to London, so I'd at least be in my home country, it was declined. I had about fifty pounds in my bank account—my father had been putting money in there for me, for little things, but he hadn't done it for ages, and I hadn't noticed because I hardly spent any money, anyway." She sighed, the sound a long, low quaver. "So there I was, in Switzerland, way up in the mountains, with fifty pounds to my name and nowhere to go, no one who cared."

"The school, surely," Sam exclaimed. "It would have been a safeguarding issue…?"

Rose shrugged. "I was eighteen. I was no longer a pupil. I wasn't their responsibility."

Sam shook his head slowly, his lips pressed together, his eyes glinting with anger on her behalf, which made her feel a little better. "So what *did* you do?"

"A teacher at the school gave me the money to get to London. She was really kind—she was worried about what I'd do, if I had a place to stay, and I told her I did. I couldn't bear to be the object of anyone's pity, and yet I needed someone to help me. I wish I'd been a little more honest, really." She sniffed. "Maybe she could have arranged for me to have classes at a local school or given me a contact of someone who could help me finish the year. I could have contacted Oxford, explained the situation. Who knows what they would have said? Maybe it could have all worked out somehow."

"But you didn't do that," Sam stated quietly.

Rose shook her head. "No, I didn't do any of those sensible things. I didn't even consider them. I—I couldn't. I just…shut down, I suppose. I think I was in shock, or maybe grieving. Both, really. In any case, back in London I found a job waiting tables and a grotty bedsit that I could just about afford. And I said goodbye to dreams of finishing school or going to uni. I worked all hours and when I'd saved up enough, I bought a ticket to Rome and started working my way around the world, making money bartending or cleaning or whatever other work I could pick up. It was the life I'd always known—a carefree, fly-by-night existence, and there was some comfort in that, I think. It felt familiar, which made it feel safe, in a strange way." She pursed her lips. "And that's what I'd been doing, until I met you."

There. That was her story, or at least the majority of it. There was no point going into the details of her travels—the nights she'd curled up in bed, alone in some grotty hostel, while a drunk guy hammered on her door. The dodging of groping hands and ignoring lustful looks that was the unfortunate, unjust part and parcel of waitressing. The unending, bone-deep loneliness of knowing she was utterly alone in the world, drifting from place to place.

There had been good parts too, she reminded herself. Sunrises alone on a beach, sipping a cappuccino in a café, daydreaming. She'd seen some amazing things. She'd been to wonderful places. And she'd felt strong, because she'd been able to take care of herself.

And yet…

"Rose, I'm so sorry," Sam said. "I can't imagine how hard that must have been. How lonely."

He squeezed her hand, his face full of sympathy and tenderness, and that was Rose's undoing. The tears she'd been doing her best to hold back finally fell. And as Sam drew her gently into his arms, she let herself do the one thing she hadn't since she'd first walked out of that school in Switzerland six years ago. She wept.

Chapter Sixteen

S AM HELD ROSE in his arms and stroked her hair and let her cry. How much sorrow had she stored up, during all those lonely years? She wept as if her heart would break, or perhaps it already had. If so, Sam was determined to help her bind it back together, piece by piece. He wouldn't fail at this, he thought fiercely. He wouldn't let himself.

After a few minutes where her shoulders shook silently and she burrowed into his chest, her tears dampening his shirt, she tried to pull away, wiping her wet cheeks as she let out a shaky laugh. "Goodness, I don't know where all that came from. It was a long time ago—I don't normally fall apart like this…"

Sam resisted the urge to pull her back into his arms, knowing she needed a little space, understanding why. He'd feel the same. It was hard, so hard, to show the broken pieces of yourself, offer them up for inspection. "Maybe you needed to," he told her quietly. "You can't hold it all in forever."

"Maybe not, but I still wasn't expecting to blubber." She grimaced, and he knew she had to find such vulnerability just as difficult as he did. Just as exposing and scary. What a pair they were, he thought, both of them trying to hide even as they were desperate to be known and understood. And he did feel as if he understood her so much more now, the how and why she'd constructed that tough, sassy shell to hide the hurt and softness underneath. He'd done the same thing, in a different way.

"Anyway." She cleared her throat and pushed the damp strands of her hair away from her flushed face. "That's my story, such as it is." She lifted her chin, met his gaze with a hint of challenge. "Now you can tell me yours."

Now Sam was the one to grimace. As much as he appreciated that vulnerability had to go both ways for the whole thing to work, he was still reluctant to share his sad little story. It was all going to sound rather pathetic compared to hers, wasn't it? No major tragedies. No huge betrayals. Just a little boy who'd got his feelings hurt. Like Rose had said: *Cry me a river.*

"Sam." She wagged a finger at him, tears still glinting in her eyes although she was blinking them away with determination. "You promised."

"I know. I want to tell you." Sort of. "It's just…my story is going to seem rather small and, well, pathetic compared to yours."

She shook her head, smiling now. "It's not a competition."

"I know that." But he still felt kind of pathetic. What

could he say? *I was teased as a kid, and I felt like my dad didn't like me.* Wow, really tragic stuff. Get the violins out right now, a whole orchestra of them.

She raised her eyebrows, waiting, and he nodded.

"Okay." He blew out a breath, his hands braced on his thighs as Rose sat back, curled up against the cushions, composed once more, or almost, her golden-green gaze steady on him, everything about her attentive, interested. "I suppose…part of the reason I've been reluctant to come back to Casterglass is…because I'm not close to my father." Her eyes widened in surprise, and he continued quickly, "I mean, we're not estranged or anything like that. We're perfectly polite to one another. I don't even know if he'd think anything was really wrong between us. But I've always felt like I disappointed him somehow. I haven't been the son he wanted."

"Him, and not your mother?" Rose asked, with her usual perceptiveness.

Sam raised his eyebrows, managed a joke. "Have you met my mother?"

She laughed softly. "Yes, and I can't imagine her focusing on something or someone long enough to be disappointed by it—or them. But that had to have been hard to grow up with, too. To live with someone so…distracted."

His mother's scattiness actually hadn't bothered him that much. She'd always been loving, in her rather abstracted way. It was his father's smiling, confused disappointment, never articulated but always felt, that had rubbed him raw again and again. "Maybe, but the thing with my dad…" He blew out a breath. "I don't know. Maybe it's because I'm the only boy and I'll inherit his title one day—"

Rose's eyes widened further. "I'd nearly forgotten about that. A baron, right?"

"Right. I try not to think about it, either." He sighed before continuing slowly, "I just always had the feeling that I wasn't quite what he wanted. Not academic or serious enough, maybe." He really was sounding as if he were throwing his own personal pity party. "We were never close, even though I wanted to be, but I just…I don't know. I never felt like I got it right with him."

"Surely that's not a child's responsibility?"

"Maybe, but…" He felt the need to explain, to excuse. He didn't want to be the kind of grown man who blamed his father for all his woes. "I've probably read too much into it all," he told her. "Been too sensitive about some throwaway comments, a few befuddled looks. There wasn't anything actually…*bad*."

"You don't have to make excuses to me," Rose told him with a small smile. "Just like I didn't with you."

"I guess what I'm saying is, it was okay, more or less. I could deal with it." He raked a hand through his hair. "That isn't what…made me stay away. Not really. It just…made other things worse." He took a deep breath and then made himself continue, "When I was ten my parents sent me to the local primary in Casterglass village, to get some proper learning before boarding school. Althea and Olivia had both gone before me for the last year or two of primary school, although they were away at boarding school by the time I went. I started in Year Five and…" He blew out another breath. "It was tough." His gut tightened as the memories flashed through his mind, each one more devastating than the last. "I was bullied." And now he really sounded like a whinger. "I mean, properly bullied. Badly bullied."

He felt the need to explain. "They used to chase me back to the castle after school every day—there were three of them who did it." Mark Adams, Stephen Barwise, and Jake Lamb. He'd seen Jake at the ceilidh, but he had looked at Sam as if he hadn't even recognised him, something that had brought equal measures of relief and indignation. *After the hell you put me through, you don't even remember me?* Not that he wanted to be remembered.

"Anyway," Sam resumed, "if they caught me…well, it wasn't nice." Talk about understatement. He swallowed, aware his heart had started to thud, a visceral reaction to the memories, the terror he'd felt. "They'd kick or punch me, although they made sure not to leave bruises anyone could see. There were a lot of nasty threats. One time they dragged me to the river and kept my head underwater until I thought I was going to drown." He shook his head slowly as he recalled how the water had filled his mouth, his lungs, until he hadn't even been able to choke and stars had burst through his head as he'd started to black out, before they'd hauled him up, left him coughing and spluttering on the grass as they ran away. That had been one of the worst times. "I really thought they meant to kill me."

"Oh, Sam." Rose's eyes were wide and one hand fluttered out to rest on his arm. "I'm so sorry. I can't even imagine… Did you tell your parents? Or a teacher?"

"No." He set his jaw. "In retrospect, I probably should have, but I didn't. I was…ashamed, I suppose." He cringed to admit it. "I felt like I'd already let my dad down in some way; I wasn't even sure how. I didn't want to do it again. I felt like I should have been able to handle it, like it would reflect badly on me. I thought it must."

"Oh, Sam." Her slender fingers tightened on his wrist, her lovely face full of compassion.

"It was two years of pretty much hell. They always knew not to leave marks—they wouldn't punch me in the face or anything like that, but they'd terrify me. Once they locked me in an old, abandoned barn far from anywhere—I thought I'd never get out. A farmer let me out after about six hours— by that time it was dark, well past supper, but my parents hadn't really noticed. They assumed I'd just been playing out. I couldn't bear to tell them the truth. Anyway." He shrugged, all too conscious he was really sounding a bit too woe-is-me. Yes, it had been awful, truly awful, but it had been twenty years ago and he was a grown man now.

"I survived. I went to boarding school in Year Seven, and

things were a lot better there. I wasn't bullied, and I also discovered I was good at sports." The first time he'd scored a try in rugby he'd been exultant. He'd felt so powerful, compared to his years at Casterglass Primary. "I felt…appreciated, I guess. Useful. But the academics still didn't come easily to me—they never have, really."

He gave an abashed smile, aware he was talking to someone who had been offered a place at Oxford, while he'd struggled through his GCSEs and not even managed his A levels. Book learning had always been harder than the physical stuff. He'd always preferred *doing* to reading or writing. "But I was foolish," he told her, "very foolish, and I messed it all up." Regret burned like acid through him as he remembered how it had all played out. "I was struggling to make my A-level grades. I'd been offered a place at Leeds to study geography. I needed an A and two B's, and I knew I wasn't going to get them. My teachers had told me the same." He took a deep breath. "And I couldn't bear to disappoint my dad again, especially about something academic when that was so important to him, although of course that's not an excuse."

He took another breath and then said baldly, "And so I cheated. I wrote some notes on my arm, very basic and stupid. I mean, if you're going to cheat…" He shook his head, trying for wry, but he couldn't quite manage it. Remembering that stupid mistake made him feel so damned low. "I was caught. And expelled immediately. And my offer from Leeds was rescinded. So, in some ways, it was a similar experience to you—the rug pulled out from under my feet right as I was making all my future plans. But while you were a victim, I was the architect of my own fate. I had absolutely no one to blame but myself."

"I'm sorry, Sam." There was no judgement in her lovely face, just sorrow. "You were only eighteen. We make a lot of stupid mistakes at that age."

"Most people manage not to make that one." He shook his head. "I take full responsibility. I knew it was wrong. I just felt so desperate, I guess. But that is no excuse, I know."

"I know you do."

"Anyway, my father came to collect me. The look on his face…it was awful. I knew I'd let him down worse than ever before. And we never even spoke about it, not really. He asked me why I'd done something so wrong, and I didn't answer, because I don't think I even knew how to. After that I couldn't wait to get out of Casterglass. I got an apprenticeship in data analysis, worked my way up, and came back as rarely as I could."

"And you did all your charity runs and hikes and things—why?" Rose asked quietly. "For absolution?"

He jerked his head in the semblance of a nod, humbled by her perception. "Maybe. I mean, I enjoyed the challenges. I liked feeling as if I was accomplishing something." He rolled his eyes, tried to smile. "A psychiatrist would have a field day with me."

"With both of us. With anyone, perhaps." Rose's lips were pursed, her expression thoughtful. "Everyone has baggage, don't they? Scars and wounds and hurts. No one is exempt, not in this life."

"Maybe not."

"It's how you deal with all of those things that matter," Rose continued, her voice growing stronger. "And I know I haven't dealt with them all that well. I ran away at the start, and then I more or less kept running for five years. I didn't let people close. I didn't let myself trust them."

Sam's breath caught at how intently she was looking at him. "And now...?" he asked softly.

"And now...maybe I can be different. Maybe we both can. If we want to." Her hand was still on his arm, her fingers fluttering like the wings of a butterfly. The logs crackled and settled, the fire's flames dancing up towards the darkening sky. The sun had begun to set, long rays of pink and gold streaking the horizon, casting their light onto the shimmering surface of the sea.

Rose was looking at him with her eyes wide, full of both hope and uncertainty. She was so beautiful, with her hair in a golden tangle about her heart-shaped face, her slender body bending towards him like a bough in the wind. Her fingers tightened on his arm.

Slowly, so slowly that at any moment she could pull away or tell him to stop, he put his hand on hers and drew her towards him. She came with a little unsteady rush of breath, a tremble of her lips. Their bodies brushed.

"Rose…" Sam whispered, something of a question.

Her lips, still trembling, curved into a smile. He moved his other hand to the dip of her waist, amazed at how new this all felt. They'd once known each other's bodies intimately, but this felt completely different, completely new. Completely right.

"Are you going to kiss me," she whispered, "or what?"

He laughed, because it was an echo of what she'd said when he'd first met her, and it seemed fitting and right, and yet so much more than that had ever been. Smiling, he bent his head and did exactly what she'd asked him to, his lips brushing against her smiling mouth before settling there.

She let out a soft sigh as her body relaxed against his and his other arm came around her. As if in slow motion, they eased back against the cushions. He kissed her mouth, and then her cheeks, and then her eyelids while she laughed softly and submitted to his butterfly caresses, her eyes closed, her lips curved into a soft smile. He felt as if he were memorising her with his lips, his heart.

She placed one hand against his cheek, her leg slipping between his. What had started out as tender suddenly, in a moment, roared into something else, a desire that felt primal and overwhelming. He took an unsteady breath as he eased back a little, his heated blood still rushing through him.

"No need to hurry things," he told her, because he didn't quite trust himself and he wanted to do it properly this time.

For real. *For keeps.*

"No," she agreed, her voice a little shaky, her face flushed. Gently she traced the line of his eyebrow and then his jaw with the tips of her fingers, and he closed his eyes, fighting a shudder that her simple touch caused to go through him. How could he feel even more for her now? Back in Tairua it had all been about the physical, but this felt emotional. Soul-changing. And they'd only kissed.

He captured her hand in his own and drew it down because he didn't know how much more he could bear, and then he wrapped his arms around her and rolled onto his back, fitting her head into the crook of his shoulder.

"Look at the stars."

She craned her neck to gaze up at the sky, the first pale glimmers coming out against the indigo canvas. "It's not as spectacular as the Southern Lights," she said softly, "but I think I like this view better."

"Me too."

They lay in silence as the last of the sun's light faded from the sky and the stars came out like diamond pinpricks, little glittering bits of promise. Sam couldn't remember when he had last felt so happy—and so at peace.

Chapter Seventeen

ROSE WALKED AROUND the café, humming. It was a week after her and Sam's evening on the beach, sharing secrets as well as kisses, and she felt as if she couldn't stop smiling. Every time she looked at him, she felt a silly, sloppy grin come over her face. It was almost embarrassing. It was also wonderful, and a tiny bit frightening, because she'd never felt this way about anyone before, not even Sam himself, back in Tairua. This was entirely new. She was mapping the uncharted territory of her own heart along with Sam's, and it was exhilarating. *Scary.* But mostly exhilarating.

Not much had actually happened since that night, nothing earth-shattering anyway, so there was no real reason to feel quite so, well, *happy* about everything. Life had gone on as normal. Sam spent a lot of time up at the glamping site or running the ropes course, and Rose split her time between tidying up—it was like a compulsion; she couldn't quite stop—and sketching plans for the café.

Two days ago she'd braved Althea in the den of her office and told her she had some ideas for the café. Over cups of tea, she'd laid out her plans—the squashy sofas, the really decent coffee, local cakes, maybe even some kind of informal lending library since, Poppy had told her, Casterglass had lost its mobile library several months ago.

"I love it," Althea had exclaimed. "So much better than what we had been able to envision—a few small tables with plastic flowers in vases and a pot of lukewarm tea, Twinings if you're lucky. So where do you start? And how much will you need?"

Rose had already figured out that Althea was pretty tight-fisted when it came to money, which was something she could appreciate, having operated on the stringiest of shoestring budgets for the last six years. "Not that much," she'd told her with a tad more confidence than she felt. "The bookshelves we can probably find around somewhere in the castle, and I already contacted the library in Millom and they're willing to donate a whole bunch of books they don't have room for. Plus, I imagine there are already a fair number of books on site that we could use. The espresso machine is a bit pricier, of course, but I've found one that can be rented for fifteen pounds a week. There's a lady in Bootle who runs a bakery out of her house—she'd love to supply the cakes, which we could sell at a thirty per cent profit. The only other things we'd need are the sofas…but I imagine we could source those from somewhere in the castle, as well."

She'd stopped, having run out of breath, and looked

nervously at Althea for her response, her fingers pleated together in front of her, her heart beginning to thud.

Althea had sat back in her chair, her arms folded. Rose had had no idea what she was thinking. "Rose," she'd said after an endless few seconds, "you are a woman after my own heart. This all sounds amazing—and within budget, which is even more amazing. How soon can you get it up and running?"

Rose's jaw had dropped, because she hadn't expected quite so much approbation, not to mention a great big green light to keep working. Her mind had raced, and her heart had fluttered with excitement. "Give me three days," she'd said, and Althea had whistled, impressed.

"Done."

Fortunately, all the paperwork and red tape with hygiene certificates and such had already been dealt with, so all Rose had to do was order the coffee machine, which was being delivered tomorrow, and enlist Ben and Sam to find some bookshelves and two decent sofas and bring them into the café. Seph had offered to pick up the library books from Millom, and Violet had, in one of her bursts of bonhomie, offered Rose free rein of the attics because apparently there was 'all kinds' of china up there.

"Walter's aunt collected teacups," Violet had confided in her. "It was something of an obsession. I'm sure they could be put to good use."

Rose had spent a happy hour sorting through boxes of

china tea sets, collecting a motley assortment of teacups that she wanted to use in the café. She liked the idea that instead of the usual bog-standard chunky white porcelain, they'd have something special and quirky. Of course, there was the danger of breakages, but she'd googled some of the teacups and none of them were very rare or valuable. She figured it was worth the risk.

It was all coming together, she thought happily as she wandered around the café. The sofas were in, the bookshelves were full if not quite organised, and a huge sack of premium coffee beans had been delivered that morning.

She was hoping to open officially tomorrow, with offerings of coffees and cakes; hopefully, if things went well and the café made a good profit, they could put in a proper kitchen soon and offer some sandwiches and soups, quiches and jacket potatoes. Who knew, one day they'd do dinners, fancy food, candlelight and steak…

"Hey." Rose turned to see Sam standing in the doorway. "I thought I'd find you here," he said as he came into the café. "I feel like you've been spending a lot of time in this place."

"I'm trying to get a feel for it." She'd also cleaned it from top to bottom, added some eclectic artwork that she'd found in the attics, as well as some old Turkish carpets for the floor. The result was the place was a lot cosier, with a funky, welcoming look.

"I think you've done an amazing job," Sam said, reaching for her.

Rose came into his arms with a silly little smile; this still felt so new. Strange, too, but in a good way. They were a *couple*. At least, she assumed they were. They hadn't had one of those 'serious discussions', but maybe they didn't need one this time. He kissed her softly, and her smile deepened.

"You remember your scan is today, in Kendal?"

"Oh, yeah." She grimaced sheepishly. How could she have forgotten something so important? And yet she had, because she'd been so taken up with the café—and with Sam. A few days ago, they'd told everyone she was having twins, and the delight and excitement had been overwhelming. Rose had wondered if half the Penryns would insist on coming along to the scan, but fortunately it was just Sam. "Do we need to get going now?" she asked.

"You have time to wash your face," he told her with a smile. "You've got dust on your nose."

"I've been cleaning," she protested laughingly, and she glanced in the antique mirror by the coffee machine, grimacing at her reflection. A little dust on her nose was Sam being nice. She was positively grimy.

"I'm amazed you kissed me, when I look like this," she said, and Sam's smile deepened.

"Didn't even cross my mind not to."

"I need a quick shower," she proclaimed. "Three minutes tops."

"I'll meet you in the car."

Rose was still smiling as she hurried inside, took the quickest shower ever, and then dressed in one of her new maternity outfits—this one a sweeping skirt in pale pink and cream, paired with a loose blouse. Poppy had taken her shopping again, this time to hit the charity shops in Broughton-in-Furness. They'd scored quite a few finds.

She quickly plaited her damp hair, put on a slick of lip gloss, and hurried downstairs to where Sam was waiting in the car as promised.

"Seven minutes," he informed her severely, and then laughed.

"Sorry," Rose told him meekly, and then grinned. They were both a couple of loons, she thought as he drove out the castle drive. So happy they probably annoyed everyone they came across. She didn't care. She wanted to feel this happy, to revel in it, like a warm bath or a sunny summer's day. She was frolicking in the field, she was swimming in the sea, she was staring up at a sky full of stars. She was, she thought, finally living, in a way she never had before…because of Sam. It felt so surprising, and yet so right.

They talked about everything and nothing on the way to Kendal, easy in each other's company, and then spent half an hour in the ultrasound waiting room while Rose chugged nearly a quart of water, as she'd forgotten she needed a full bladder for the scan.

Ten minutes later she was fidgeting and shifting on her seat, while Sam looked on in amusement.

"You try it," she hissed, and he stifled a laugh before pulling a sympathetic face. Rose rolled her eyes.

"Rose Lacey?"

Rose lumbered up, Sam hurrying to support her elbow. She hadn't quite realised until that moment just how huge she was starting to feel. She was only twenty-three weeks along, but she looked at least six months pregnant. And to think she had another seventeen to go, if she made it to full term. She'd already read that most women expecting twins didn't, which meant these babies might be coming even sooner.

"So, you're expecting twins?" the technician said with a smile as she looked through her notes and Rose eased herself back on the examining table, feeling more and more like a beached whale.

"Yes, we are." Sam's voice rang with pride, making her smile. "Quite a surprise for us, actually."

"Do twins run in your family?"

Rose exchanged an uncertain glance with Sam. "Not in my family," she said, while Sam, she noticed, had started to blush.

"Actually, I have cousins who are twins," he confessed.

Rose couldn't keep from bursting out, "So it's *your* fault!"

They both laughed as the technician looked on, amused. "Right, well let's see how these two little ones are doing. Everything's been fine so far?"

"Yes, I had a scan at seventeen weeks, when we found out about the twins, and things looked fine." Rose glanced at Sam, and he gave her a tender smile. How things had changed in just over a month, she thought. They'd been uncertain allies then, and she'd felt so prickly and suspicious. She'd softened, and so had Sam. They'd changed each other.

A few minutes later, her bump was slathered in cold, clear gel, and the technician started with her poking and prodding while Rose tried not to wince—or wet herself. The blobby forms on the screen began to take shape—yes, there they were, two babies nestled together likes pea in a pod, complete with legs and arms, fingers and toes.

"They're *real*," Sam said wonderingly, and Rose let out another laugh.

"I've felt them move enough to know they are." Sometimes she felt as if she had a nest of snakes writhing inside her.

"Let's just take some measurements," the technician said, frowning slightly in concentration, and Sam reached out to hold Rose's hand. She was smiling as she looked at those shapes on the screen, wondering if they'd be able to find out the sex—boys? Girls? One of each? She didn't care which, but it would be exciting to know.

The technician had fallen silent, her gaze focused on the screen as she clicked and pressed, measuring various things—Rose couldn't tell what. Size of the head? Length of the spine? She was still smiling, holding Sam's hand, feeling excited and thankful and just a little bit scared, but in a good way, when the technician rose from her chair.

"Please excuse me for a moment," she said, and walked quickly out of the room. Rose's smile slipped off her face as she glanced at Sam.

"Is that normal?" she asked in a low voice. "For her to just leave like that?"

Sam shrugged, looking troubled. "I don't know."

"Nothing's...*wrong*, is it?" Rose heard the anxiety creeping into her voice, the fear winding its icy tendrils around her heart. "Nothing can be wrong," she said, a statement more than a plea, and Sam squeezed her hand.

"I'm sure it's fine. She would have said if it wasn't."

"What is she doing, then?"

"I don't know. Maybe she needs to consult an obstetrician or something."

"About *what*?"

"Rose." Sam turned to take her face in his hands, his voice gentle yet strong. "I know it's hard not to, but there's no point in panicking right now. We don't know anything, except what we saw on the screen. Two babies kicking away, looking pretty healthy to me. Okay?"

She nodded, grateful for his steady reassurance. "Okay," she whispered.

He kissed her softly and then eased back just as the technician returned, followed by a doctor in a white lab coat.

"I'm Heather White, an obstetrics consultant here at the

hospital," the woman introduced herself with a quick smile. "Kerry just wanted me to check on some of the measurements she's taken of your twins."

"Is everything okay?" The words burst out of Rose, her voice thin and high and trembling.

"That's what we're here to find out," Heather replied cheerfully. "Try not to worry." She turned to the screen, clicking and pressing just as the technician had, while they talked in low voices and Rose tried not to scream. Didn't they realise what *torture* this was, not knowing? She'd been shocked and frightened by the prospect of having twins, it was true, but the prospect of *not* having them, of something, *anything*, going wrong, was worse by far.

Sam held her hand again as they waited several endless minutes before the doctor finally turned back to them. "So, everything looks pretty much fine," she said, and Rose let out a trembling sigh of relief. "Babies are active, growing well, heart and lungs what they should be at this point. But...one of the babies is a little small."

"Small?" Rose clung to Sam's hand, her rush of relief replaced by yet more fear. How bad was it, to be small?

"Yes, and let me stress this is perfectly normal with twins." Heather gave her a reassuring smile. "They very rarely develop at exactly the same size and pace. Often this happens because, with identical twins, they are sharing one placenta and their umbilical cords can implant at different places, which causes unequal sharing of the placenta and therefore different rates of growth."

Rose simply stared, struggling to make sense of that info dump. Her brain felt as if it had stuck in one gear, and all she could hear was the static buzz of her frightened thoughts.

"So is the smaller twin's size a cause for concern?" Sam asked levelly, and she was so grateful he wasn't frozen by fear, the way she was.

"Not necessarily," Heather replied, which Rose recognised was not the *absolutely not* she craved. "In most cases, what happens is simply that the smaller twin catches up, or they might remain smaller through birth. He or she might continue to be a bit smaller as they develop and grow, or they might catch up in a few years' time. In most cases, it's all absolutely fine and just a case of how people come in all shapes and sizes."

"But in the other cases?" Sam asked, because it had to be said. Rose's whole body felt as if it were vibrating with tension.

"In a small number of cases," the doctor said slowly, "the twin that doesn't have the same access to the placenta can have their growth restricted in a way that causes problems with development. It's something we monitor very closely, and while I don't see a problem now, I think it would be wise to come back in two weeks for another scan, just to make sure both twins are continuing to progress."

"And if that twin hasn't progressed?" Sam asked after a moment when they'd both been silent, simply absorbing all that she'd said.

"Then we'd monitor the situation even more closely," she replied, "possibly with an extended stay in hospital for Mum. If it looks as if the twins might be in danger, we'd consider an early delivery, assuming their chances would be better outside the womb than in it." She turned to Rose, her expression soft with sympathy. "I know this all sounds really scary, and there is always more risk associated with a twin pregnancy, but there are some positives here. I don't see any sign of twin-to-twin transfusion syndrome, which would be a potentially dangerous condition. Both babies look active and happy, moving freely, kicking away, and besides measuring just six days smaller, your littlest one appears to be developing normally. So I really don't think there is any cause to worry right now, but we'll schedule a scan, just in case, and most likely continue with scans every two weeks, or potentially every week, until you deliver."

Slowly Rose nodded. "Thank you," she said after a moment, not quite trusting her voice. Despite the doctor's reassurances, she still felt dazed and frightened. She'd been so sure everything would be fine, mainly, she knew, because she'd been so happy. As if nothing could pierce the bubble of the joy she'd found with Sam. As if bad things couldn't happen now, when really she should have known, had always known, that that was *exactly* when bad things happened. How could she have been so naïve? So stupid?

She wiped the gel from her bump and pulled her shirt

down, still feeling as if she were sleepwalking, or walking under water, distant from everything, her mind a blur of fear and worry. Back in the reception area, they scheduled another scan for the beginning of September, and then they were heading outside to the car park, to a day that had grown chilly and grey; summer was almost over. Rose had been staying as Casterglass for five weeks, which felt now as if they'd flown by, and yet what would the next five weeks hold? The whole future, *their* future? Their babies'?

"We don't need to worry," Sam told her as he opened the passenger door. "Not yet, anyway. I know it is scary, Rose, but try to see the positives."

"Right." Rose tried to smile but she felt as if her lips weren't working properly. Nothing was. Where was her carefree insouciance, her laughing certainty that nothing would go wrong? It wasn't anywhere to be found, because it had never been real, just part of the persona she'd worn like armour. She couldn't assemble it now, couldn't even begin to.

"Rose?" Sam said gently, and she realised she was simply standing there, staring into space.

She blinked him into focus, her mind still spinning. "Right."

"Are you okay?"

"I…I don't know."

Wordlessly he pulled her into a quick hug; she breathed in the scent of him—the clean freshness of the outdoors with the spicy tang of his aftershave—before she got in the car, stared straight ahead. Sam climbed into the driver's seat. They drove in silence, both of them seeming lost in their thoughts until they'd reached Casterglass village, and then Rose felt a sudden wave of dread crash over her. She wasn't ready to go back to the castle and face everyone there, see their excitement and curiosity morph into worry and concern. Olivia would worry, Althea would boss her around, Seph would scowl, Violet would pull out some ancient anecdote about a distant relative who had had triplets, and one was the size of an apple, and it was all fine. *Really, most extraordinary, I wouldn't worry, my dear, not at all…*

She couldn't face any of it, not yet. "Can we just…pause for a second?" she asked Sam. "Stop somewhere and get our thoughts together before we face your family and all their questions?"

He glanced at her warily. "Where?"

She gestured to the pub across from the village green that they were just driving by. "Here? We could get a coffee or a cold drink. Just…have a moment."

He hesitated, looking tense, and then with a quick nod he pulled into the car park behind the building.

Chapter Eighteen

THE LAST THING he should be thinking about was seeing someone he knew, but Sam couldn't keep the worry from skirting his mind as he put his arm around Rose and they walked into Casterglass pub. He knew her mind was taken up entirely with the babies, and his was too, *mostly*. But he also had that creeping feeling along the back of his neck, like he was being watched, like he needed to brace himself for a blow. He hadn't actually been in this pub in years. Decades.

He hadn't gone for the celebratory drink on his eighteenth birthday, had avoided the occasional evenings out when they'd all been home for a holiday, and in any case, he'd rarely come back for those. Because he knew Mark Adams, Stephen Barwise, and Jake Lamb frequented this pub, and had since their Sixth Form days. On a few occasions he'd seen them swagger out of it, half-cut and spoiling for a fight. He'd almost wanted to give it to them, because he was stronger then, and he knew how to use his fists. But he never did, because he might look tougher but inside, when it came to those three, he still felt like a frightened Year Five. Pathetic, but true.

Fortunately, the pub was empty save for a couple of farmers in flat caps by the bar, nursing their pints. They took a table in the back and Sam went to the bar to order their drinks.

"How are things up at the castle?" the woman behind the bar asked. She was about his age, and he supposed they'd gone to school together, but those days were such a blur of misery he couldn't place her at all.

"Pretty good."

"It's given us more custom, for sure," she said, with a laughing look for the near-empty room. "Not that you'd know it now."

"I'm glad."

Her smile turned a bit cat-like, knowing. "You don't remember me, do you?"

He hefted the two glasses of lemonade he'd ordered, his body tensing even as he kept his smile in place. "Sorry, no."

"Louise Adler. We went to school together, when you came in Year Five. Although I'm Louise Barwise now. I married Stephen two years ago."

Sam's knuckles whitened as he clenched the two glasses. Was that a sly look she gave him, because she knew about the bullying? No, he realised, it wasn't. She was looking confused, because he was glaring at her in a way that was weird.

"Congratulations," he forced out. "That's great."

"Do you remember Stephen?"

He felt as if he could choke. "No, sorry. I don't think I do," he said, and then he turned around and walked back to Rose.

"What's wrong?" she asked immediately. Sam knew he was acting strangely; he placed the glasses on the table with enough force to send the lemonade splashing out. Rose grabbed a napkin and mopped up the spill. "Sam, seriously, what?"

He shook his head, sat down, and took a sip of his drink, willing the sudden rage he'd felt to recede. He hadn't expected to feel it, never mind have it overtake him like that, like a wave crashing over him, pulling him under. For the last twenty years he'd done his best not to think about Stephen Barwise, or the other two. Seeing Jake at the ceilidh had been bad enough, but Jake had always been the least willing one, who had come along for the ride reluctantly. Stephen had been the ringleader. He'd been the one to hold Sam's head underwater. He'd locked the barn door and run away, laughing. He'd punched Sam in the stomach as hard as he could, and then grinned when Sam had doubled over, wheezing, trying not to cry.

He'd been waiting for Sam one morning, he recalled, when he'd walked to school with a stupid model of a castle he'd built from toothpicks and yoghurt pots, all part of a misguided hope to make his father proud of him, and

Stephen Barwise had knocked it out of his arms and stamped on it until it was nothing but a mess of broken bits. His father had asked his teacher at some parents' night about it, and she'd looked perplexed. *Sam didn't make a model, Lord Casterglass. He drew a picture of the castle. To be honest, it looked a bit rushed.*

His father had looked confused, and then disappointed. He'd never asked Sam about it, and Sam had never told. And now Stephen Barwise, who had made his life such absolute *hell*, was here, working at the pub, married, maybe with a child or even two. He should put it behind him; Sam knew he should. It was years ago, and he was a grown man. None of it mattered anymore, as he'd told himself so many times before. And yet he was finding it hard not to shake with rage—or old, remembered fear.

"Sam." Rose laid a hand on his arm, her golden brows drawn together, her expression both solemn and concerned. "What is it? Have you seen someone you—you knew?"

"No. Sorry." He passed a hand over his face. "Just some old memories. It doesn't matter. Let's focus on the future."

"Are you sure?" Her concerned gaze was scanning his face. "Is one of those guys…?"

"No." He couldn't bear for her to know how affected he was, *still*. Over something so…childish. And yet it hadn't felt childish, not when they'd been holding his head underwater. Not when he'd been locked in that barn, wondering if he would ever get out. "No, it's fine." He managed a smile even though his face felt funny, the skin tight. "Let's think about our babies."

Her expression softened even as worry clouded her eyes. "I did a quick internet search while you were getting our drinks—"

He put his hand over hers. "Never a good idea, Rose. The internet is a worst-case-scenario world."

"I know, but it can also give you the facts, if you filter out all the hysteria." She gave him a rallying sort of smile. "And the good news is that what the consultant said is right. One twin often is smaller than the other, and it's absolutely fine."

"Okay. Good." He would have felt more relieved if she didn't still look so worried.

"But sometimes, if the twin's growth continues to be restricted, it can cause problems. Like, major problems with development. Or even…viability."

Sam felt as if a giant fist was clenching around his heart. "But that's not likely here," he said steadily. "You're already at twenty-three weeks, and the baby is only six days behind. Which means their heart and lungs and everything has been growing pretty much okay." He stopped suddenly and slapped a hand to his forehead. "We forgot to ask what we're having! Boys or girls."

"What *we're* having?" Rose replied tartly, but she was smiling. "We can ask in two weeks, I suppose."

"You do want to find out?"

"Yes, I think so." She shook her head slowly. "It's so strange. It all feels both more and less real at the same time."

"I know."

She scanned his face, her expression turning serious, even anxious. "Are you sure you're ready for this, Sam?"

"I don't think anyone is ready for twins," he replied, not even half-joking.

"I know, but what I mean is, five weeks ago you had no idea you'd even see me again, much less be a father to our children. It's a lot to take in."

"I know, and I've taken it in. Mostly. It's a process, but...I'm happy about it." He frowned. "Why are you asking me all this stuff now? Are *you* having doubts?"

She rested one hand on her ever-growing bumping with a small, wry smile. "It's a little late for that."

"I don't mean doubts about the babies." He spoke directly, feeling compelled to it by her own questioning of him, by the insecurity remembering his childhood had caused to rear up again. "I mean about me."

She was quiet for a long moment, too long. Clearly the answer wasn't cut and dried. Sam tried to school his face into some sort of an expression that wasn't hurt. "N-o-o," she said at last, the word coming so drawn out it sounded more like *well, actually, yes.*

"Really?" His expression might be placid enough, but his voice sounded spiky.

"I just don't want you to feel trapped, Sam." She leaned

forward, moving her hand from her bump to his arm. "You didn't choose this."

"Neither did you," he felt compelled to point out.

"Maybe not at first," she allowed quietly, "but I chose to continue with the pregnancy."

Sam was silent as he realised he'd never even considered an alternative. "Did you think about getting an abortion?" he asked in a low voice, hating even the thought.

"No," Rose replied simply. "Not even for a second. I think I delayed taking a pregnancy test because as long as I didn't know, I didn't have to think about it. But once I knew, I realised I didn't have to think about it then, either—not in that way, at least. I was always going to keep the baby. Or babies, as it happens. There was never any decision to make."

He reached for her hand again. "I'm glad."

She was silent for a moment, gazing down at their clasped hands. "I wanted a family," she said in a low voice, her gaze still on their hands. "Sometimes I think that's all I've ever wanted."

"We'll be a family, Rose."

She looked up at him, her eyes wide and luminous. "But I don't want you to feel forced into it. Or for me to feel like I forced you into it."

"I'd say you did the opposite," Sam remarked dryly. "Trying to leave as quickly as you could."

She gave a quick, bashful grin. "We have come a long

way from that, haven't we?"

"Definitely." Sam kept her hand in his as he smiled at her, wanting to imbue her with his own certainty. Because he *was* certain, wasn't he? He wasn't having doubts or second thoughts…and yet he was scared. Scared of messing up, of making a mistake, of getting something spectacularly wrong, as he so often felt he had.

She stared at him, her expression so serious and yet so hopeful that Sam felt a clutch of emotion grab his chest—happiness, thankfulness, and yes, that fear. Because they had come a long way…and they still had a long way to go.

"This is real," he said, because he knew that's what she was wondering.

"Real, but new."

"Yes. But that doesn't make it any less real."

Rose nodded slowly. "And what if something is wrong with one of the twins? Something serious?"

"Then we'll cross that bridge when we come to it." She didn't reply and he continued, not wanting to sound so glib. "I mean, I have no idea what will happen, or how we'll handle it, because it's completely out of the realm of my experience. And it'll be tough and scary, yes; but we'll handle it, Rose. Together."

"You sound so sure."

"I am sure."

She nodded again, but she didn't look convinced, and Sam felt that needling of hurt again. *Was* she having doubts…about him? Could he even blame her, considering how flaky he'd been at the start?

"Sam?"

The voice, low and gravelly with a decided Cumbrian accent, wasn't familiar, and yet Sam knew it all the same. He turned from Rose to see Stephen Barwise staring down at him. He had the same pale blue eyes, the blond buzz cut, the blunt face with a nose that had been broken once or twice since primary school. Sam slid his hand from Rose's as his whole body went tense, like he was bracing himself for a punch.

"Stephen."

"Steve, now." Steve rubbed the back of his neck. "How are you, man? It's been a while."

Why was he talking to him? To taunt him? Sam couldn't gauge Steve's expression, could barely figure out how to make his brain function properly. He was remembering Steve's hand on the back of his head, holding him underwater. His fist ploughing into his stomach. His sneering face as he slammed the barn door. So many painful memories, coursing through in a hot rush of both rage and shame.

"Yeah," he finally forced out. "It's been a while."

"Louise told you we're together now?" He nodded towards the bar, where Louise was watching them. "We got married three years ago."

"Congratulations."

"Got a little one, another one on the way."

Somehow Sam managed to bare his teeth in a smile. "Congratulations again."

"You too, huh?" Steve nodded towards Rose, who was looking at him with a completely expressionless face.

"Yes. Due in about four months."

"That's great, man."

Sam nodded, waiting for Steve to go, because why had he come here in the first place? He hadn't forgotten, had he? No, there was no way he could have. He'd bullied Sam mercilessly several times a week at least for two *years*. No way had he forgotten that.

And Sam certainly hadn't.

Still Steve remained there, nodding and smiling and looking uneasy. Sam raised his eyebrows, waiting for more, because it seemed like he wanted something. Then, to his shock, Stephen said, half-mumbling, "Look, this might not be the time or the place, but…I just wanted to say sorry. For making your life miserable for a couple of years, back when we were little 'uns." He flushed, scratching his cheek. "I was a right little—" He stopped, glancing apologetically at Rose. "I wasn't nice."

Her lips twitched although there was a certain flintiness in her eyes. She gave a terse nod of acceptance, and Steve turned back to Sam.

"Anyway, I'm sorry. I treated you badly. Really badly. I know that. I shouldn't have, but I guess I was jealous of your life up at the castle. Seemed pretty golden to me, what with the way my dad was…" He shrugged. "But that's neither here nor there. I didn't come here to make excuses, just to say sorry." He gave a jerky nod and a kind of gulp, while Sam simply stared, trying to process what had just happened. What Steve wanted from him.

Was he supposed to say it was all okay now? *Was* it? Could it be that easy, after two years of torture and twenty years of rage and regret?

Could one heartfelt sorry compel him to let it all go?

He had no idea. He couldn't speak.

"I understand," Steve said hesitantly, "if you know, you're still het up about it all. I would be, most like. I was a right little bastard."

Sam gave a little shake of his head and forced himself to reply. "I'm not het up."

Steve's eyes widened at his sharp tone. "Well, like I said, I'd understand. I just…wanted to apologise."

"Thank you."

Sam nodded, and after a few uncertain seconds Steve nodded back and then returned to the bar. Sam let out a long, unsteady breath.

"Are you okay?" Rose asked quietly.

"Yeah." He managed the smallest of smiles. "That was unexpected."

"Was he the worst of them?" Rose guessed, and Sam nodded.

"I suppose it's good he apologised," he said after a moment. "I could have been more gracious."

"You were taken by surprise."

"Yeah, but…" A sudden realisation crystallised inside him. He'd let those two years of bullying dictate so much of his life—the reluctance to return to Casterglass, the constant search for another way to prove himself. Even his reserve in relationships could probably be traced back to those two years, along with his fear of trusting people, of letting them see who he really was, the insecurity that had felt so deep-seated, so much a part of him.

It could end here. At least it could *begin* to end. He had a lovely, beautiful woman at his side, two children on the way, a life to live. A life full of happiness and hope, love and freedom. Only he could step forward and claim it. Only he could choose to shake off the past.

"Let's go," Sam said, rising from the table and reaching for Rose's hand. As they walked out of the pub, Sam stopped by the bar where Steve was standing with Louise. He stuck out his hand.

"Thanks for saying sorry," he told Steve, his voice a little rough with emotion. "I really appreciate it. Those years weren't easy, but we've both moved on, and I'm happy to accept your apology."

The relief and gratitude on Steve's face as he grabbed Sam's hand and shook it humbled him. He'd stepped forward to free himself, but he realised he might have freed Steve, as well. It felt good. It felt right.

"Thanks, marra," Steve said, and Sam smiled. *Marra.* The true sign of affection, the Cumbria slang for mate or friend.

"You're welcome."

They shook hands again and then, hand in hand with Rose, Sam walked out of the pub, smiling.

Chapter Nineteen

"THAT WILL BE four twenty-five," Rose said, palm out, smiling as she took a five-pound note and then made change. "Have a nice day!" The Americanism had stuck after a stint in Florida, and the café customers didn't seem to mind. In fact, they seemed to appreciate her cheerfulness, and Rose couldn't help but feel happy, even if she still couldn't help but feel cautious about it. About everything.

As the customer took her tray of coffee and cake back to her table, Rose rested back against the counter, one hand on her bump, and surveyed the happy, bustling scene of her domain. It had been three weeks since the twenty-three-week scan, when she'd felt so frightened, the future suddenly looming in front of her, with all of its unknowns—Sam, the babies, the café, Casterglass. It had all felt like too much to process, to get her head around, to *risk*. Because she cared about it all—so much—and she wasn't used to caring about things. It had felt frightening, like her heart was walking around outside of her body, but wasn't that what they said having children was like? And hers hadn't even been born yet.

Fortunately, she'd had another scan last week and it had been okay. Mostly. Baby number two was still measuring small, but growing, which was the important thing. And Rose was clinging to the important things—like the fact that her babies were healthy, even if they hadn't been able to find out whether they were having boys or girls, and Sam was committed to both her and their children. In the three weeks since she'd opened the café, it had been a big hit, with customers clamouring for cakes and raving about the cappuccinos. They'd been taking out books from the little library, too, and Rose had been heartened to see people curled up on one of the sofas, absorbed in a book.

Her mind was buzzing with more ideas—a bigger menu, a noticeboard for community events, hosting clubs or workshops... There was so much she wanted to do. And there was, she knew, so much to be thankful for. And she *was* thankful...even if part of her still felt a little nervous, a tiny bit hesitant to embrace it all. Trust it. She, of all people, knew how quickly life could go completely pear-shaped. How the best-laid plans could fall apart, or really, explode in your face.

And yet, things had been pretty wonderful on all fronts. She was starting to get to know all the Penryns a bit better, and *liking* them, with all their quirks and foibles. Noisy dinners around the table, impromptu chats with Poppy or Olivia or even Seph, who seemed to be softening slightly, evenings with Sam watching TV or taking a walk, hand in hand, under the stars. It had all been so much more than Rose had ever experienced before, in all her carefree, lonely travels.

It was changing, though, already. Poppy and Ben were both heading off to uni next week, and Rose knew she would miss them. Toby, Lally, and Jake had already started back at school, and the leaves were now tinged with yellow and red. There was a new crispness in the air, although admittedly it had been rather cool all summer, which was typical Cumbria. But Rose didn't mind. She was starting to enjoy Casterglass in all of its Cumbrian glory, from the violet, rainmisted fells to the wild, raging seas to the pale pink roses that grew up the garden wall and the rain that spattered against the windowpanes like a handful of diamonds.

And beyond Casterglass or the Penryns, there was Sam. She was, Rose knew, starting to fall in love with him, just a little bit. Cautiously, because she didn't know how else to do it, easing into it, inch by inch, the way you would into a hot bath. And enjoying the process, even as it scared the daylights out of her, because he was kind and loyal and funny and tender. She felt safe with him in a way she hadn't with anyone else before, and yet she was still scared to trust it. Trust him.

All the while she had to fight the feeling of waiting for the blow to fall, the punch to land, because that's just how she was, how she'd learned to be, and sometimes she wondered if she'd ever be any other way. If she'd ever know how, never mind risk it.

"Rose?"

Rose tensed at the sound of Althea's voice, as prissily demanding as it had been the first day she'd met her. She hadn't heard that tone in two months, and it made her both quake inwardly and start to fume. *What now?*

"Yes?" she asked, pasting a smile on her face.

Althea stood in the doorway of the half-full café, her hands planted on her hips. "Could I see you in the castle, please? In the drawing room? Ellie will take over the café for a few minutes." Ellie was already standing behind Althea, looking sheepish, while the oldest Penryn's brows were drawn together, her mouth as pursed up as a prune. Rose's mind started to race. What was going on? After starting to slowly feel accepted by the Penryns, she found herself suddenly cast back to being an outsider, and a suspicious one at that.

She didn't have any more secrets, no other parental skeletons in the closet, so she had no idea what Althea could be annoyed about, but she was sure it was something. Was Althea unhappy with the way the café was being run? Dissatisfied with its takings, which could have been better but were, Rose thought, a very good start? Or maybe she thought Rose was being a bit too friendly with the customers, with her 'have a nice days'. Or was it something else? Something worse? Rose's stomach plunged unpleasantly.

She watched as Ellie took over the till with a quick, alarmingly sympathetic smile, and Althea stalked off to the castle, clearly expecting Rose to follow. What on earth was going on, Rose wondered, and how afraid should she be? She'd been waiting for something to go wrong, telling herself she was silly for being so alarmist, and yet maybe she'd been right to be cautious. Not to trust. Because something had clearly gone wrong, even if she didn't know what it was.

The whole castle was silent as Rose followed Althea through the empty kitchen, down the corridor. Why the drawing room, one of the most impressive and intimidating rooms of the house? Was there going to be some sort of interview? A showdown? An expulsion?

Rose had managed to work herself into high dudgeon by the time she'd made it to the drawing room doors, pausing to catch her breath. Althea had strode ahead, practically bristling. Rose didn't know whether to pretend to be meek or come out swinging. She was trying out first lines—*What is this about, Althea?* versus the humbler: *Have I done something wrong?*—when Althea demanded querulously from inside the room, "Well? Aren't you coming?"

Rose took a deep breath and stepped into the drawing room.

"*Surprise!*"

She blinked, one hand pressed to her chest, as confetti was thrown in a shower of colour and balloons floated and bopped in the air above a pink and blue banner that read

Happy Baby Shower. A dozen people sat or stood around the room, grinning at her. For a second Rose could only stare. She was so shocked, so utterly surprised, that her mind felt blank and alarmingly, her eyes filled with tears.

It was a baby shower. For her.

"Are you all right, Rose?" Olivia asked kindly, and Sam slipped his arm around her.

"I think she's just very, very surprised," he said in a voice rich with tender affection. She had an urge to bury her head in his shoulder but she resisted it, blinked back the tears. Swallowed hard. And then swung round to face Althea. "I thought you were annoyed with me!" she exclaimed. "Like, really annoyed. I was..." She couldn't make herself say the word *scared*.

"I know," Althea answered with a laughing grimace. "Sorry for the panic, but I figured that was the best way to get you in here sharpish."

Roes shook her head slowly. She still felt flummoxed. "I could have gone into labour, you know," she said, only half-joking, because she was twenty-six weeks now and it wasn't impossible. She'd been having Braxton Hicks contractions and she was as big as a house. And she had actually been more than a little scared. She let out a trembling laugh, and then pressed her hands to her flushed cheeks.

"I can't believe it..."

Belatedly she saw the pile of presents—big boxes with shiny ribbons, expensive-looking gift bags, and several boxes that were almost as high as she was, wrapped clumsily in paper. All for her? She hadn't had a birthday present since she was about six. Her dad had never seen the point, if he'd even remembered her birthday, which he often hadn't.

"This is too much," she whispered.

"It's not nearly enough," Althea exclaimed. "Do you *know* all the things babies need? The list is endless."

"When I was born," Violet remarked dreamily, "I slept in a drawer for the first six months of my life."

Althea rolled her eyes good-naturedly. "Fortunately, these days we have Moses baskets and cots, Mum," she said, and Violet gave a little sigh.

"A drawer did just as well, or so my father said. But, to be fair, he didn't really know the first thing about babies. I was raised by a nanny—quite an indefatigable woman, as I recall. Quite intimidating."

"So, get started, then, girl," Olivia said, pulling her towards the massive pile with a laugh. "You've got a lot of loot to get through."

Rose looked around at everyone—Olivia and Will, Althea and John, Walter and Violet, Seph and Ben, Poppy and Toby and John's daughter Alice, Will's two children Lally and Jake, and Ellie from the pottery shop, who had closed the café to join the celebrations. Rose had come to know them all, some more than others, but right now every single person in the room felt incredibly dear to her. *Like family.*

Drawing a shaky breath, she sat down on the sofa in

front of the pile of presents, giving everyone a trembling, grateful smile. "Where should I start?"

"Start with mine!" Lally exclaimed, and she scrambled up to give Rose one of the presents—a messily wrapped box and an accompanying card sprinkled liberally with glitter.

"Lally is our house gift-wrapper," Will told her with a wry smile.

"I love it," Rose told the little girl, and she carefully opened the card, doing her best not to let glitter sprinkle the carpet. *Deer Rose, Good luck with yor babees!* She choked a laugh back and then read the rest: *Please if their gurls can yoo call them Lally.*

"I love the name Lally," she told the little girl sincerely. "It's definitely in the running if we have girls." Hopefully, if the babies cooperated this time, they'd find out at the next scan, scheduled for the following week. She'd be twenty-seven weeks by then, the third trimester. Or, as Sam had called it, 'action stations'.

She opened the present from Lally—a beautiful lemon-yellow sleepsuit in the softest velveteen, and another one in mint green, impossibly tiny, yet apparently sized three to six months, so there were even *tinier* sizes. She loved them both.

"Thank you, Lally," she said, smiling at the little girl. "Thank you so much."

"Mine next," Poppy said, handing her a gift bag from the boutique they'd visited in Ulverston. Smiling at her, Rose opened it—two sets of tiny leather baby booties, in navy blue with white piping.

"I know blue is, like, a boy colour, but I'm all about smashing those gender stereotypes," Poppy proclaimed, and Rose laughed.

"Me too, Poppy," she assured her. "Me too."

She continued opening the presents, amazed at the generosity behind each one, and even more, the thought, the *love*. There were countless outfits—sleepsuits, Babygros, booties and bibs—as well as two matching highchairs from Althea and John, two Moses baskets from Olivia and Will, and a double pram—brand new and probably costing a fortune—from Violet and Walter.

"But," Walter said, with one of his twinkly smiles, "we thought you might like to use this one, too." He went out into the hall and wheeled in the Silver Cross pram from the attics—cleaned and refurbished, with new rubber wheels, looking both ancient and beautiful, perfect for two tiny babies to snuggle in together.

Rose struggled not to cry. She had never, she realised, ever felt so accepted. *So loved.*

"Thank you," she managed, her voice thick, and Sam kissed her cheek.

"I think we're ready for these babies to arrive," he said, and Rose gave him a look of not entirely mock alarm.

"Not yet! I'm only twenty-six weeks."

LATER, WHEN THE wrapping paper and confetti had been cleaned up and the presents put away, they retired to the dining room for cake and champagne, or sparkling apple juice, in Rose's and the children's case. The talk, as ever, moved to the castle and its business—Sam was going to close the glamping sites at the end of September, which would give them time together before the babies came, and Althea mentioned some bright spark from Oxford who was interested in doing an internship at Casterglass.

"How did he hear about us?" Olivia asked, bemused, and Althea smiled a bit smugly.

"There was that article in *Cumbria Life* last month, about how a family transformed their fortunes by turning their estate into a tourist attraction?"

"Which has only been done about a thousand times before," Seph replied with a roll of her eyes. "Who is this kid, anyway?"

"Kid?" Althea looked amused. "He's twenty-five, just finished an MPhil at Oxford and is interested in transforming his uncle's estate, or something. He wanted to come here for three months, unpaid, to see how it all works."

"When?" Sam looked dubious. "Not much will be going on over winter."

"Now that's where you're wrong!" Althea whipped out the notebook she seemed to carry with her everywhere. "We've got spooky stuff planned around Halloween, nothing too terrible though, so don't worry, plus lots over Christmas and New Year's. In January and February Olivia will be doing a 'winter garden' theme, with tea outside in the heated summerhouse, where you can see the snowdrops." She put down her notebook. "I was thinking, Sam, what about a winter wonderland glamping experience?"

"Winter wonderland? You mean, in a freezing gale?" Sam shook his head. "The yurts are likely to blow away in mid-January, you know how the wind gets. I'm going to have to take them down at the end of September."

"Oh, well." Althea looked disappointed. "It was just a thought."

"A good one, if we were living in Dorset or Devon, maybe."

Althea sighed. "Drat the Cumbrian weather."

Rose sat back, one hand on her bump, happy to let the conversation flow over her as the family chatted and laughed, exchanging ideas about the castle, the future. And she would be part of it, she thought dreamily. Would her children grow up running through these meadows and playing in the river, the way Sam did? Would they have barbecues on the beach and croquet on the front lawn and happy, noisy suppers around the kitchen table?

It was the kind of future she'd never, ever dared to imagine for herself. For a long time she'd convinced herself she didn't want it, traipsing around the world and pretending to be as carefree as a lark. It had worked for a while, but the reality was this: She'd always wanted a home. She'd always longed for a family.

And now she had the dazzling possibility of both…if only she could trust it. Trust the people, trust Sam. And trust herself too, not to mess it up, not to get scared and overreact and ruin everything.

Sam glanced over at her, slipping her hand in his in a way that had become easy and felt right.

"Happy?" he asked, and Rose nodded, her throat suddenly tight, her heart filled with gratitude.

"Yes." She nodded and squeezed his hand. "Very happy."

Chapter Twenty

SAM GAZED DOWN at the twinkling sapphire, sitting between two small diamonds. The sapphire had belonged to his mother's grandmother, and his mother had given it to him years ago, in something of an offhand manner.

"Sadly, the Penryns don't have many jewels," she'd told him, "so I'm afraid there's no beautiful ring to pass down the generations. They sold most of their jewels over the years to pay for repairs to the castle—although I do believe there was a dastardly uncle somewhere in the line who absconded with a fair few of them. Pity." She'd smiled in her vacant way and patted his hand, and Sam had wondered what on earth he was meant to do with a sapphire.

Now he knew.

He'd bought the two diamonds himself and visited a jeweller all the way in Lancaster to design the perfect ring, spending hours obsessing over the details—the white gold band, the cut of the diamonds, how many prongs for the setting. Amazing, really, how concerned he'd become about all the little details, but he so wanted to get this right.

He was going to ask Rose to marry him.

She had been at Casterglass for nearly three months now; it was mid-October and she'd just passed thirty-two weeks. She was enormous, a slender frame with a huge belly, and he loved her shape. He loved the two babies kicking inside her—they'd decided, in the end, not to find out whether they were having boys or girls. At the last scan, the smaller twin had been measuring nine days behind, which was a little worrying but not too much.

"They're still growing," the OB had assured them. "That's the main thing. Their environment has not degraded; there's still plenty of amniotic fluid." She'd turned to Rose. "Let's get you to thirty-six weeks if we can. But it might mean you stay off your feet a bit more."

An instruction Rose had not welcomed but had still obeyed. After spending two months getting the café up and running, she was content to manage her little domain from one of the sofas. They'd hired a young woman from the village, Lizzy, to run the café most days, with Olivia, Althea, or Seph filling in as needed. Sometimes even Violet took a turn at the till, although by her own admission she was fairly hopeless about giving correct change.

All in all, though, things were going well. Really well. He and Rose had developed a routine they both liked—they had breakfast with the family, and then went their separate ways for work, with Rose to the café and Sam to his study, either to pick up some freelance work or to work on future plans for his part of the Casterglass Empire, as Althea liked to call it, only semi-jokingly. They checked in for lunch, and then spent an hour or two together in the afternoon, strolling through the gardens if the weather was fine or playing a game by the fire if it wasn't. Sometimes they just sat on the sofa and read their books, and Rose had once joked, "We're like an old married couple already." Then she'd bitten her lip, looking semi-horrified. "I mean…not really."

Sam had just smiled, not wanting to give the game away, but heartened that Rose had mentioned the M-word. Sometimes he didn't know how much of her fiery free spirit remained; he liked her feistiness, but did it mean she wouldn't want to settle down? He still wasn't sure if she could envision Casterglass as her home, not just for now but forever. Her home with him.

Did she love him? He knew he loved her, the real her, not just the laughing girl she'd shown him in Tairua, although he'd fallen for that version of her, too. But he loved the Rose who was both strong and fragile, damaged yet healing, funny but tender, frightened but brave. He loved her in all her weakness and strength, her beauty and frailty. He just hoped that one day she might love him in the same way.

They hadn't talked about love or marriage yet, although they'd skirted the topics, when they'd mused about their future, when the babies came. But it was all hazy and hopeful without actually involving any specific detail, and after two months together—not to mention the three months they'd had in New Zealand—Sam was ready to make it official.

He just had to ask.

He slid the ring back into the black velvet box and put in his pocket, just as someone tapped on the door of his study.

"Sam?"

It was his father. Sam tensed instinctively. In the five months since he'd been home, he and his father had maintained their polite yet distant relationship; everything had been so busy, establishing Casterglass, dealing with the reality of Rose's pregnancy and its ensuing risks, that it hadn't *felt* as if they'd been avoiding each other, even if they actually had.

"Yes?" he called, already feeling on the defensive although he knew he shouldn't.

"Sam?" his father said again, popping his head around the door with that kindly and slightly befuddled smile that always made Sam want to grit his teeth. His father always looked at him like he was a problem he'd never been able to solve. "Is now a good time?" he asked, closing the door behind him.

Sam shrugged as he closed his laptop. "As good a time as any, I suppose."

"Well." Walter looked around the small, rather cluttered space Sam had used as his study for the last five months. "You've done wonders with the camping and things, haven't you?"

You don't need to sound so surprised, Sam thought, but he merely smiled. "Thanks."

"You've settled in at Casterglass?" Walter asked. "You're…happy here?"

Sam thought of Rose, the ring in his pocket. "Yes, I am."

"I'm glad. I never thought to see the day when you were happy to take the reins."

"I think it's Althea who has taken the reins, actually." Sam spoke lightly, but he was remembering, with some discomfort, just how firmly he'd told his father he had no intention of ever living at Casterglass, about two years ago. Walter had floated the idea of him taking over the estate, and Sam had been more or less horrified by the idea. Back then Casterglass had felt like a living hell, something that made him realise how much things had changed. Although, he knew, Casterglass hadn't changed, not really. *He* had.

"Do you mind having us here?" he asked his father, the notion occurring to him for the first time. "It's been just you and Mum and Seph for a long time. I suppose you've got used to the peace and quiet."

"I'm delighted," Walter assured him with the broadest smile Sam had ever seen him give. "I never could have imagined such a happy occurrence in all my days—to have all my children living back at Casterglass, and happily occupied doing so."

"I don't think I could have imagined it, either," Sam

admitted. All of them under one no-longer-leaky roof—although Althea would be moving to John's farmhouse after their wedding in December. Perhaps Olivia would move in with Will too, if they got married, which seemed likely at this point, which would leave just him and Rose at the castle, along with his parents and Seph.

"Sam…" His father cleared his throat, his tone turning serious in a way Sam recognised. It was a tone that was laced with disappointment, with the deep sorrow his father never articulated. "I feel I have to ask…what are your intentions towards Rose?"

Sam stared at him. "What are my intentions?"

"Yes. Because she is the mother of your children…and I know you've said you will do your duty by them, but what about by her? She's in a uniquely vulnerable position here, one I wonder if you can truly appreciate, and I cannot help but feel sorry for her—"

"Rose is not your worry, Dad." Sam heard the anger bubbling beneath the words, and he knew his father heard it, as well. But his father's question had felt like a rebuke, an accusation even, as if Sam was some sort of rake taking advantage of Rose, when nothing could be further from the truth.

"But I am worried," Walter told him quietly. "I cannot help but be. It has been three months, and you seem content to leave things as they are. And as long as Rose lives under my roof—"

"Oh, your roof," Sam retorted bitterly, while his father merely raised his eyebrows.

"Yes, my roof," he said calmly. "I am the master and baron of Casterglass, Sam. One day you will be, but—"

"I'm not now—I get it." Sam spun away, feeling like a child. Why did his father reduce him to acting like a mere boy? Why did he let him?

Walter sighed, the sound of disappointment. A sound Sam was all too used to. He pressed his fists to his eyes, wondering why he was letting his father get to him this way. Why he didn't do anything to keep them from colliding—or really, missing each other, time and time again. He thought of shaking Steve Barwise's hand, something he'd never thought he'd do, not in a million years.

His father was far less of an enemy than Steve had ever been. He was his father, his *dad*. Maybe they'd never seen eye to eye, never wrestled in the den or thrown a ball in the back garden, never even had a proper heart-to-heart, but still. He knew his dad loved him, didn't he? And he loved his father. Those two truths had never changed, and yet…

Sam dropped his hands from his eyes. Slowly he turned around. "Dad," he said, his voice steady although inside he was quaking, "you know why I've never wanted to come back to Casterglass?"

Walter blinked, looking surprised, discomfited, maybe even a bit alarmed. But then he rallied, straightening his shoulders, meeting his gaze head-on. "Why, Sam?" he asked quietly.

"Two reasons, really. The first one—because I was bullied by a couple of boys at the village primary. Really bullied. They made my life completely miserable for two years—once they nearly drowned me in the river. I was…affected by it, more than I ever let myself realise, for years."

He didn't feel the expected flushing of shame when he admitted this to his father, only release. The secret was out. The burden was finally laid down.

Walter looked shaken, his face pale. "Why did you never tell me? At the time, I mean—"

"Because I was ashamed. And I know that's on me, not you," Sam said quickly. "It was my problem—"

"No, Sam," Walter replied with quiet force. "It was mine, too. I just didn't know it." He shook his head slowly. "You would have only been ten years old."

"Yes."

"I'm sorry," his father said with the same quiet force. "You should not have felt you had to bear that alone."

"I should have told you. I know that now. I knew that a long time ago. It just…" Sam took a breath, let it out slowly. This was the harder part to say. "I didn't want you to be disappointed in me." He paused. "Again."

"Disappointed in you?" Now his father didn't look merely shaken but stricken. "Sam…why would I be disappointed in you?"

"Why wouldn't you be?" Sam couldn't keep from replying, while his father just shook his head, looking so surprised, so sad, that for a second Sam wondered if he'd got everything wrong. But, no…all those sad, bemused looks…all those comments… *Sam's our least bookish child… He's not much of one for school, it seems… Sam prefers the outdoors to books…*

No. He hadn't got it wrong. Had he?

Slowly Walter walked over to the chair in front of Sam's desk and sat down. "Do you really think I would have been disappointed in you, to learn you'd been bullied?" he asked, and his voice was full of grief. "Even now?"

"Not now," Sam allowed, "but then. Yes. I wasn't…I know I wasn't like you. Bookish and academic and smart. I felt like I failed you."

"Sam." Walter swivelled around to face him, his eyes clouded with grief. "*I* wasn't like *you.*"

Sam shrugged. "It's the same difference, isn't it?"

"No. *No.* I…I always felt as if *I* were the disappointment. I wasn't the kind of father who would throw a ball or go camping in the garden. I've never been the outdoorsy, athletic type, not even when I was young. I always felt as if I failed you in that regard…and I suppose it was easier to let you go your own way and for me to go mine rather than for both of us to keep butting up against our differences." He paused, his expression turning reflective, sad. "That was my fault, not yours. As your father, the adult, I should have been bigger than my own insecurities and failings. I should have

259

made more of an effort. Much more of an effort."

Sam stared at him, his mind spinning. He'd never considered their relationship from his father's perspective...how *he* might have felt like the disappointment, and not Sam. It was as if his whole world had turned upside down, or as if he were viewing things from the wrong end of a telescope.

"But...what about when I cheated on my A levels?" he asked in a low voice. In twelve years, they'd never truly talked about it. "I know you were disappointed in me then. You had to have been."

"I was," Walter agreed after a moment, his voice heavy. "As I know you were disappointed in yourself." Sam bowed his head in silent acknowledgement. "But I was also disappointed that it had come to such a point...that you'd felt so pressured, that you hadn't been able to talk to me about what was going on. I'd been fooling myself, I think, that we had a perfectly adequate relationship before that...but I felt the lack, then. In myself, as a father. I felt as if I'd failed, as much, if not more, than you had." He paused. "And it only worsened when you took off to travel, and then seemed set on never coming back."

He held up a hand to forestall Sam's protest, although he wasn't even sure what he might have said.

"I didn't blame you. In fact, I understood. But I regretted all the events—spoken and unspoken—that had brought us to that." Another pause, this one weightier. "To this."

Sam was silent for a long moment, his mind reeling, his

heart aching. He wished they'd had this conversation years, even decades earlier—and yet he also recognised that perhaps they couldn't have. Perhaps it wouldn't have been possible, with the way they'd been. The way he'd been. Rose had helped him, he knew, to let go of the past. Changed him, and so much for the better.

"I'm sorry," he said, because they felt like the only words he could say, or at least the most important ones.

"So am I," his father replied. "So much."

They stared at each other for a long moment, the weight of the years lying heavily between them, and yet Sam had the sense they would get lighter with time. With effort. After a few moments, feeling it was the right thing to do, and more importantly wanting to do it, he put his hand into his pocket and drew out the black velvet box. Silently he handed it to his father, who took it with reverence.

"Is this what I think it is?"

"I think so."

Walter opened the box, gazed at the ring with its sapphire flanked by diamonds with obvious admiration. "Sam, it's beautiful."

"The sapphire is meant to represent Casterglass," Sam said, feeling a bit awkward and cheesy, but still wanting to say it. "And…and family. The diamonds are Rose and me."

Sam's throat thickened as he saw his father turn misty-eyed and blink a few times. He handed the box back. "It's beautiful," he said again, and then he took out an ancient, monogrammed handkerchief and blew his nose heartily. Sam grinned.

"I'm going to ask her as soon as we get a sunny day," he told his father.

Walter let out a laugh that was half honk as he put his handkerchief back in his pocket. "Then you might be waiting a long time," he warned, and Sam laughed, too.

IN ACTUALITY, HE had to wait a week. An endless week of scanning the skies, the box heavy in his pocket, his heart starting to skip a beat as soon as the clouds began to part. Then—a perfect day. Bright blue skies, a hint of warmth in the air even though it was October. Leaves the colour of rust and ochre, a hint of loss in the air that always came with autumn, but a thrill of hope, with the sunshine.

He found Rose, as usual, in the café. "How about a walk to the beach?" he asked brightly, his voice sounding a little strange, a little forced, because he was nervous.

She gave him an odd look. "A walk? More like a waddle."

"We'll take it slow. It's such a lovely day…"

The smile she gave him was slow and full of affection. "How can I resist such a proposition?" she asked, and Sam hoped she had the same reaction to the far more important *proposition* he was going to ask in just a little while. He still didn't feel entirely sure of her answer.

She lumbered up from the sofa, grimacing a little, one hand on the small of her back, her bump sticking way out. She really was huge, and he loved her for it. He *loved* her.

"Come on," he said, and hand in hand they walked out of the café, through the courtyard, across the front of the walled garden and through the meadow, towards the sea.

They didn't talk, which suited Sam because his heart had started beating rather hard and he was feeling more and more nervous. He'd been anticipating and dreaming this moment for weeks now, and yet it was still managing to take him by surprise. His throat was dry and all the things he'd been thinking of saying, all the flowery phrases and heartfelt sentiments—they'd evaporated, as if they'd been vaporised from his brain. His brain was completely, appalling empty, so all he could think of, all he could feel, was the beating of his heart, Rose's hand in his, the wind on his face. *Think...*

"Sam," Rose asked. "Are you okay?"

"Yes." His voice came out in a croak. His heart was thudding. "Why do you ask?"

"Just, you've gone a little funny. Pale." She eyed him in concern. "You're not coming down with something, are you?"

"No." Even croakier this time. "No, I'm definitely not."

It was late afternoon and unlike the endless days of summer, the sun was already starting to set, sending long, golden rays over the placid surface of the sea. The tide was out and the beach was a long, flat stretch of damp sand. The air held a bite.

"It's so beautiful here," Rose said softly, staring out at the sea, and Sam knew there was nothing for it. He got down on one knee.

"Rose…" His voice trembled. She turned around. Her eyes widened as she saw him there on the wet beach on one knee, the black velvet box between his shaking fingers. "Rose…" He struggled to find the words, and then he realised he already knew them. They were written on his heart. "Rose, I love you. I was enchanted by you back in Tairua, but I've fallen in love with you in Cumbria. With who you really are, and not just who you pretend to be. I love your kindness, your strength, your sense of humour, and even your frailty. And if you think you can one day love me in the same way—love me not just for my good parts but my bad and my weak ones…" He trailed off because Rose was starting to look panicked.

He should have known, he thought miserably, only to screech to a halt when she clutched her bump.

"Sam…I think my waters have broken!"

Chapter Twenty-One

ROSE WAS TRYING not to panic. Really, really trying, but it was hard, because her waters had broken and she was standing on a beach and already she felt a contraction banding her belly—a real one or a practice Braxton Hicks she didn't know, but it was *scary*. She was only thirty-three weeks. She had three more weeks to go, according to the various consultants they'd seen, before the babies could possibly be delivered safely. Right then, with her hands on her precious bump, three weeks seemed like a very long time.

"Sam…" Her voice wobbled.

"Okay." Sam snapped shut the lid of the black velvet box—*that box!*—and took her by the arm. "Let's get back to the castle, and then we'll go directly to hospital. See what's what. It's going to be fine, Rose, absolutely fine, I promise you."

His voice was steady, his arm strong, and Rose was thankful—*so* thankful—that she was going to marry a man who was great in a crisis.

Except she hadn't actually said yes yet, but surely that

was just a technicality. A mere detail. They could have the rest of that conversation later, when their babies were safe. She could tell him how much she loved him, all of him, and how happy and thankful she was to be his bride. But right now they had more pressing matters to deal with.

With Sam talking steadily to her, holding her arm the whole way, they made it across the meadow. Every time Rose had a contraction, she drew her breath in sharply. *It wasn't supposed to happen like this!* She felt like wailing the words aloud, but of course there was no point. It *was* happening.

Back at the castle, Sam helped her into his Rover and then jogged into the house for his wallet and keys. Rose eased back into the passenger seat, her hands laced over her bump, willing her babies to stay strong. To stay alive—legs kicking, hearts beating, bodies growing.

A few seconds later, Sam was sliding into the driver's seat, clearly in crisis mode. "I told Seph what happened, and she'll tell everyone else," he said calmly as he started the car and started to reverse. "You don't need to worry about that side of things at all."

"Okay," Rose said, and then let out a gasp.

Sam glanced at her, his forehead crinkled. "Another contraction?"

"Yes."

"They're happening about every eight minutes, which isn't too bad."

She let out a choked laugh. "How do you know that?"

"I was keeping time when we walked from the beach."

She shook her head slowly, smiling despite her fears, her tears. "You're kind of amazing, you know that?"

The grin Sam gave her was both heartbreaking and wonderful. He looked so *chuffed*, and she loved him so much. "Why, thank you," he said.

The contractions kept coming all the way to the hospital, a band of muscles tightening and releasing across her bump. It was so strange, to have her body acting of its own accord, springing into action mode without her say-so. And scary, because it was too soon.

As if he could read her thoughts—and perhaps he could—Sam stated in the same calm voice, "Thirty-three weeks is still a decent gestation."

"But the smaller one…" She bit her lip, not wanting to say it aloud. It was bad enough to let that dark fear skirt the edges of her mind.

Keeping one hand on the wheel, Sam held hers with his other, squeezing gently. "We're going to be okay," he told her firmly. "All of us."

And even though Rose knew he couldn't promise any such thing, she appreciated him saying it. A lot.

In the hospital they went to A&E and then were referred to the maternity ward, a place Rose had been before several times, but which now felt scary and real. Was she about to be one of those lumbering, labouring mothers, breathing through contractions, her hospital gown gaping at the back, and far too soon?

"We'll do a scan," the consultant on duty told her, his manner both efficient and reassuring. "And see where we are. Then we'll need to make some decisions. Our priority is to keep these babies safely inside for as long as possible."

"And can that happen?" Rose asked, hearing how high and thin her voice sounded, like a child's. "Even when my waters have broken and I'm having contractions?"

The doctor's expression was grave, which made Rose feel like shrieking. This was serious. Really serious. She knew it was; she felt it. *Her babies.* "It is possible," he told her, "but it will require some intervention. You'll need to stay at hospital, and we can give you antibiotics to prevent possible infection and also a steroid to help your babies' lungs develop more quickly. We'll get you on an IV to keep you hydrated, which can sometimes help stop the preterm contractions." He gave her a sympathetic smile. "I know this is frightening, but we'll do all we can to keep these babies safe."

All they can. But what if it wasn't enough?

The next hour seemed to pass in a blur of both terror and unreality. She had a scan, which showed, thankfully that the babies were not in distress. Yet. Then she was taken to a room on the ward and hooked up to an IV, given steroids and antibiotics, and told to stay in bed, that she'd be checked every hour.

Sam sat next to her, holding her hand, while Rose fought

tears. This wasn't the way she'd envisioned this at *all*.

"I'm scared," she whispered, trying not to cry.

"I know." His voice was calm, but she saw how pale he was, how dark and clouded his normally bright blue eyes. He was scared, too. Of course he was.

What if they lost their babies? It was a prospect Rose hadn't let herself consider—not when her waters had broken, not when the contractions had started, not when she'd had the scan. Her mind simply wouldn't go there, but now it did. If their babies died, what would happen to them as a couple?

The only reason they were together was because of their two children nestled in her womb. Yes, Sam had told her he loved her, but had it simply been a case of when given lemons, make lemonade? The best of a bad situation? If he was truly free from obligations and responsibility, why *wouldn't* he take off for Kathmandu or Kilimanjaro or wherever the next charitable adventure took him?

Rose was used to people not sticking around. Leaving her in the lurch when it mattered most. Why should Sam, who hadn't asked for any of this anyway, be different?

"Rose?" He held her cold hand between his own, rubbing it softly. "Talk to me. What are you thinking?"

She shook her head, not meeting his gaze. "I don't even know."

"It's going to be okay."

"You don't *know* that." She sounded irritable, but the

reassurance she'd craved earlier annoyed her now. There were no guarantees. She knew that, and so did Sam. "You can't know that it's going to be okay," she told him.

Sam looked down at their hands, seeming chastened. "That's true."

Rose slipped her hand from his and wrapped her arms around herself. "I'm cold."

"Let me get you a blanket."

She watched him leave the room to fetch an extra blanket, missing him already and yet also strangely glad he was gone. Maybe, she thought darkly, she'd need to get used to it. Maybe it was better not to depend on his company, make herself even more vulnerable.

And yet what was more vulnerable than this?

When he came back in the room, he had two blankets and a cup of tea, milky and sweet, the way she liked it. Tears filled Rose's eyes. Again. She almost couldn't bear him being nice to her, and she wasn't sure why. Maybe because every other time she'd been in a crisis, there had been no one to help. To care. To fetch her tea and hold her hand. And she didn't know how to handle it now.

"I'm sorry," she whispered.

Sam looked taken aback. "Sorry. What for?"

"For everything."

"Rose…"

"I dragged you into this—" she persisted stubbornly, feeling like she had to say it.

"Rose." Sam looked both hurt and exasperated. "You didn't drag me into anything."

"You didn't ask to be a dad—"

"I'm glad to be a dad. Rose, please. Don't talk like this, not now. I'm here. I'm staying here. You can trust me. Okay?"

She bit her lip, longing to believe him yet still afraid to, even now. "Rose?" he prompted softly, taking her hand once more, and she let him. She was being stupid, she told herself. Stupid and scared and unfair, to assume Sam wouldn't be there for her, just because other people hadn't. He'd shown himself trustworthy and true time and time again, and just as he'd had to shake off the burdens of the past, so did she. She wouldn't let old hurts and regrets taint the present or tarnish her future. She could *choose* to believe, to trust. Right now.

"I know I can," she said, and she squeezed his hand. "Thank you."

Sam smiled and then he leaned forward and very gently kissed her lips. Rose closed her eyes, savouring the caress. The closeness.

A quick tap on the door had them easing apart and a midwife came in with a briskly cheerful smile. "Time to check your babies' heartbeats," she announced, and Rose nodded while Sam sat back, his hands braced on his thighs.

A few seconds later they heard it, a steady whooshing sound that reassured Rose until she saw the midwife frown.

"Is something wrong?"

"The heartbeat is a little slower than we'd like," she said as she rose from her chair. "I'll just ask the consultant to have a listen."

Rose shot Sam a terrified glance, and she saw how stricken he looked for a second before he smoothed his features into a bracing look.

"We're getting the best care we can," he told her.

Which didn't mean all that much, she thought, the panic mounting inside her as the consultant came in the room and listened to the heartbeats. Then he was frowning too, and Rose felt as if everything was moving very fast, and yet also in slow motion. She was wheeled out for another scan, which passed in a blur, then the doctor was telling her that the babies were in distress, and she would need to have an emergency C-section immediately.

"Wait…now?" She gaped, scrambled to keep hold of her thoughts, and then turned to look pleadingly at Sam. *"Sam—"*

"I'll be with you, Rose." Sam's face was pale as he reached for her hand.

"I'm afraid your partner cannot be present in this situation," the consultant informed them both swiftly. "We have to act quickly. But he'll be waiting for you when you emerge from theatre."

"But—"

"We need your consent for this procedure before we begin. We wouldn't be recommending it unless we thought it was the best option for your well-being and your babies' survival."

Survival. She stared at the consultant wildly for a moment before she nodded. "Yes. *Yes—*"

Then she was scribbling her name on a form, and Sam was kissing her forehead with tears in his eyes, before she was wheeled into theatre, her mind racing so hard and fast she felt dizzy, while nurses and doctors moved around, setting up lamps, pushing in a trolley of instruments, erecting a blue tent over her chest so she couldn't even see her bump anymore and she felt as if she were drifting alone in an endless sea, even as people surrounded her, seeming so urgent and important.

"Count to ten backwards for me," the anaesthetist instructed.

Rose stared at him in confusion for a second before she began in wobbly voice, "Ten, nine…"

Then the world went black.

HE WASN'T GOING to panic. He was definitely *not* going to panic, Sam told himself as he took deep, even breaths and his mind raced and spun. Everything had happened so *fast.* Just a few hours ago he'd been down on one knee, the happiest man on earth, or about to be, with Rose looking down at him in teary-eyed wonder.

And now…now it felt as if everything was fragile, tenuous. *Breaking.* His phone buzzed in his pocket and a nurse walking swiftly down the corridor gave him a quelling look.

"No phone calls in the hospital, please," she told him briskly.

Sam glanced down at the screen. It was Althea, no doubt wanting to know what was going on. He wanted to tell her, but he couldn't leave Rose. What if something happened? He had to be there. One hundred per cent, he had to be. He knew that absolutely, knew it in his gut, his heart. He would not leave Rose now, not even for a moment. Quickly he thumbed a text reply: *At hospital. Can't take calls. Will text when there's news.*

Then he slid his phone back in his pocket and paced in front of the doors. How long did a C-section take? When would he know if Rose was okay? If their babies were?

Every second felt like an age, an absolute eternity, crawling past so slowly Sam felt like screaming. Instead he tried to focus on practicalities, what he could do, what Rose might need after the surgery. Would the babies need a specialist? Rose would need a room downstairs at Casterglass; he had a notion that stairs were to be avoided after a C-section, but maybe that was old-fashioned. She could use the morning room, perhaps. She'd like the sunshine that room got, since it faced the sea...

And what about the babies? All the clothes they'd bought would be far too big. He hadn't even set up the Moses baskets yet, or the cots, or the pram...but realistically, he knew, they wouldn't need any of that for some time. Their babies might be in the hospital for weeks…

Dear God, please keep them safe. Please keep Rose safe.

It was a prayer he felt in every atom of his being, from the deepest recesses of his heart to the tips of his fingers.

The doors to the theatre opened, and a consultant stood there, dressed in scrubs and smiling wearily, but it was a cautious smile, a smile of sympathy rather than congratulations…or was it?

Sam found he couldn't speak.

"The babies have been delivered," the consultant said. "Two girls."

Girls. He had daughters. "They're…" Sam's voice sounded scratchy and his lips felt funny, like he'd forgotten how to form words. "They're okay?"

The consultant's smile slipped, just a little. Sam felt as if he'd staggered, even though he hadn't moved.

"They're in good health, but they're very small," the consultant told him. "The smaller one weighs only a kilogram and a half."

A kilogram and a half! Just over three pounds. *Tiny.* How could a human being that small live? And yet they had to live. They *had* to.

"They're being taken to the NICU," the consultant told him. "While your wife recovers."

"Is she awake? Rose?" Sam asked, gulping.

The consultant shook his head. "Not yet. It will be another half hour or so before she comes round."

"And the babies—" *His daughters.* "Can I see them?"

"Yes, in a little while. They're receiving the best care possible right now, but it would be better for you to wait until they've been checked over and stabilised. The smaller one might need a breathing tube to help get her lungs going." He paused. "Look, I'll give you the bottom line, because I know that's what parents always ask for. Your daughters are in good shape for their gestation—the larger one weighed over two kilograms and could breathe well on her own. The smaller one is going to have more trouble, but my hope is she will get there."

"But how likely—"

"I'm sorry, but I don't deal in percentages. The next few hours and weeks will be crucial. A human being that small is understandably very fragile, very vulnerable. But babies are often stronger than we think, and premature girls tend to be better fighters than boys. So there's every chance you'll be able to take your twins home one day soon."

Sam gulped again and then nodded. The consultant wasn't promising him anything, and he was very aware of that. It all sounded so...tenuous. Even more tenuous than it had been when Rose had been in theatre.

"Thank you," he managed, and the consultant nodded and walked away.

With half an hour before Rose would wake up and no opportunity to see his daughters, Sam decided to call Althea back. His whole family would be desperate for news, he knew, and he needed to talk to someone. He had to share this burden.

Outside the hospital he leaned against the wall, swiping to call Althea with trembling fingers before he leaned his head back against the wall and closed his eyes.

"Sam?" She'd answered after only one ring. "What's going on? What's happened? Is Rose—"

"She had a C-section. The babies are…they're girls. They're alive."

Althea's breath hissed between her teeth. "Alive…"

"The bigger one seems okay. The smaller one…" They didn't even have names, he thought. He and Rose had never discussed names. Maybe they hadn't wanted to jinx themselves, but he wished they'd thought of names now. He wanted his children to have names. "The smaller one," he resumed, his voice wobbling just a little, "is having more of a struggle. I'm not sure how much. She'll probably have a breathing tube. They said the next few hours and days are crucial…"

That was when he lost it. He, who had always tried to be strong, who had been proving himself over and over again to anyone who cared, who couldn't bear to show his weakness or fear, broke down and wept. He pressed the bridge of his nose with his forefinger as he tried to stem the sobs and found he couldn't. He didn't even want to. This was too big for him.

"Oh, Sam," Althea said softly. "Sam, *Sam*. Let us help you. Do you want someone to come—"

"No." He drew a clogged breath. "No, I need to get back to Rose. She'll be waking up soon, and I have to be there when she does." He wiped his eyes with the back of his hand as he drew another breath. "I'll call you when I have more news."

"We're thinking of you, Sam. Praying—"

"I know."

He ended the call, slipping his phone into his pocket and wiping his eyes again. Then, squaring his shoulders and lifting his chin, he headed back into the hospital, to find his family.

Chapter Twenty-Two

Rose woke slowly, as if she were swimming up through murky waters to a distant light. Her body felt heavy, detached, no more than a collection of lifeless limbs. She blinked slowly as the room around her came into focus—a hospital room, shadowy and dark, the last of the sun's rays slanting through the blinds. A machine marking time with its relentless beeps. Her body felt so *strange*…

Rose lifted her arm from the bed; it flopped as if she wasn't in control of it, but she managed to touch her stomach, wincing as she did so, and then gasped. Her bump was *gone*. Her babies…*her babies were gone!*

She let out a sound that was half sob, half moan. Why was she alone? Where were the nurses, doctors, her children?

Where was Sam?

Realisation thudded through her. She'd been here before, hadn't she? And yet this was so much worse. That dark moment of complete despair, when she realised she had absolutely no one. She'd felt it back at boarding school, when she'd walked through the front doors and realised she had nowhere to go, no one who was willing to help her. She'd thought she'd felt alone then, but it had been nothing on this. Nothing.

Where was her family?

He's gone, she thought numbly. Sam must have left. Had the babies not made it? Had he decided to cut his losses? *No, of course he didn't,* her inner voice of reason asserted. *He would never do that. Never. He loves you. He asked you to marry him...*

But only because you were pregnant.

She let out another choked sob, too weak and lonely and scared to battle those inner voices, those inner demons whispering their vicious lies. This was her worst nightmare...the nightmare she'd lived once before, had never wanted to live again—being as vulnerable as it was possible to be, and utterly alone. Forgotten. Forsaken. Yet part of her, she realised, wasn't even surprised. Part of her, a large part even, had been waiting for a moment exactly like this. She'd thought she could shake off her old fears, but maybe she couldn't. Maybe she *shouldn't.*

Sam...

"Rose!"

She turned her head against the pillow and saw Sam rush into the room. Tears slipped silently down her cheeks, and she found she was too overcome to speak, and she wasn't even sure what emotion she was feeling.

"Rose, Rose." He crouched by the side of her bed, cupping her cheek, kissing her face. And still Rose could not keep the tears from coming.

"I…I thought you'd gone," she whispered.

"Gone?" He looked thunderstruck, but also hurt. She saw it, felt it. One more person who'd been disappointed in him. "Gone?" he repeated. "You think I'd leave you like this? Leave our children, as soon as they've been born?"

Now that he'd said it aloud, she knew how absurd it was. How utterly impossible. And yet for those few awful seconds, she'd let herself believe it, out of fear.

"No…no…I'm sorry. I don't think that. I couldn't. It's just…I felt so alone." She reached out one trembling hand to touch his face, felt the rasp of his stubble against her fingers. "I know you wouldn't do that, Sam."

"Never, Rose." He pressed his lips to her fingers. "Never."

"The twins?" She almost didn't want to ask, was afraid to know. Because there was hope in ignorance, there was still possibility.

"They're doing okay. They're girls, Rose. Two beautiful little girls."

She let out a sound that was half sob, half laugh, full of both wonder and fear. "Have you seen them?"

"No, they wouldn't let me, not yet. We can see them together, when they've been seen to and are stable. The smaller one…she's a fighter. And she needs to fight."

Rose felt as if a giant hand had squeezed her heart. "Is she in danger…?"

"The consultant said the next few days are important."

Important…for survival. She closed her eyes, and felt Sam cup her cheek again. "We'll fight for them, Rose. Together. We're a family, the four of us. Nothing will ever, ever separate us."

And Rose thought she'd never heard more wonderful words.

AN HOUR LATER they wheeled her to the window of the NICU, Sam at her side, to see their daughters, tiny and swaddled, with caps on their heads, mittens on their hands, and all sorts of tubes snaking out of them.

"They're so *small*," Rose said, her voice choking as she reached for Sam's hand.

"Yes," Sam replied, "and they're ours."

"You can hold them, if you want," a nurse said kindly, and Rose goggled at her in incredulous hope.

"I can…?" She felt as if she'd been given the world. She *had* been.

"Yes, skin-to-skin contact is very good with premature babies, as long as they're well enough. It's called kangaroo care."

Moments later Rose was in the NICU, with the bigger twin curled up on her chest like a little frog. Rose stroked her tiny head and pressed her lips to her forehead, the skin impossibly soft, heartbreakingly fragile. Sam reached down and touched their daughter's hand, letting out a wondering laugh as the tiny, tiny fingers slowly curled around his.

"Would you like to hold daughter number two?" the nurse asked, and now it was Sam's turn to stare.

"I can? She's not too small?"

"She's a fighter, this one," the nurse told him. "She's doing fine."

Sam sat in a chair next to Rose as they brought the baby and laid her tiny form on his chest. Her eyes were scrunched closed, her mouth nuzzling against him as he let out a sound like Rose had, half laugh, half sob.

"Can you believe this?" he asked her, and Rose gazed at him, her face full of love, her eyes full of tears. They really were a family now.

IT WAS THREE weeks before they were able to bring their daughters—now named Michaela, meaning gift of God, and Beatrice, meaning she who brings happiness—home. It was a banner day, to buckle those two tiny girls into their car seats, laughing as Sam grew exasperated with the fiddly straps before Rose leaned in and explained the five-point harness system to him.

"How do you know how to do that?" he demanded.

"YouTube," Rose told him smugly, and he rolled his eyes.

They'd been going back and forward from Casterglass to Kendal every day for nearly a month, spending as much time as they could with both Michaela and Bea, trying to get as much 'kangaroo care' in as possible, and also for Rose to keep trying to breastfeed. It hadn't been easy, and had involved pain, tears, and quite a few lactation aids, but finally her two girls were nursing like champs. Bea, the smaller one, was clearly trying to make up for lost time.

"She'll be pushing Michaela out of the way soon enough," Sam predicted, and Rose envisioned a future where two tow-headed toddlers were elbowing each other in their race to get to their dad. A future where she held Bea's hand and Sam hoisted Michaela onto his shoulders. A future where they were a family, just as they were now, strong together.

Three weeks on, it still felt almost too good to be true, too wonderful to be real. And yet it was. The last three weeks had been hard in so many ways—Bea had developed a chest infection, and Michaela had refused to feed for a little while, but they'd navigated those bumps successfully. Rose had been exhausted by her own recovery as well as the emotional toll of worrying about her two daughters, but she'd found the reserves, along with the conviction, to write both her mother and father and let them know where she was and that they had two grandchildren. She didn't know if either of them would be in touch—they hadn't yet—but the door was open. Family was family, after all, and she was grateful for her new one. Grateful for the man who had stood by her side the whole time and fought for their family.

Everyone was lining the drive as they drove up to the castle, waiting for a glimpse and a cuddle of the newest Penryns. They'd all been to the hospital themselves for a visit, but Rose knew how eager everyone was to welcome these two to Casterglass, their true home.

"It's like something out of *Downton Abbey*," Sam muttered as he saw his family lining up outside the castle, and Rose grinned.

"They're excited."

And she was excited to have her daughters home at last. Sam lifted the car seats out of the back of the Rover, one after the other, while Althea cooed at Bea and Olivia held out her arms.

"I am dying for a cuddle," she told Rose. "Absolutely dying. How are you holding up?"

"Good. Tired." And a bit achy still, but nothing she felt like complaining about. "Grateful, mostly."

Olivia squeezed her hand, and then laughed as she caught her finger on the ring Sam had slipped on Rose's finger two weeks ago, when they'd finally caught their breaths and she had said an absolute, heartfelt yes to his proposal.

"Now *that's* a sparkler," Olivia said, and then she leaned closer to whisper in Rose's ear. "And actually…I think I might have one of those soon."

"Ooh, Olivia!" Rose looked at her keenly and Olivia blushed.

"Not to jinx it or anything, but subtlety isn't Will's strong point, thank goodness. He's dropped a few hints."

Rose squeezed her hand back. "I'm so happy for you, Olivia. Happy for you both." Her gaze was caught by a stranger in the line-up outside the castle, a young man about her age, tall and lanky, with dark hair and green eyes, like a grown-up Harry Potter. "Who is that?" she whispered to Olivia.

"That's the intern! He arrived a few days ago—did you not notice?"

Rose shook her head. She'd been too taken up with going to and fro from the hospital and getting things ready for the girls. She and Sam were taking up their own wing of the castle, with two bedrooms and their own sitting room, for a little privacy.

"Nothing like that babymoon," Althea had told her with a roll of her eyes. "And those sleepless nights."

Now Rose gave the newcomer a curious glance—so this was Oliver Belhaven, nephew to an earl somewhere or other, wanting to save his own family pile by coming to Caster-glass? Or so Althea had claimed, when she'd first received his email.

"Interesting," she murmured to Olivia.

"Yes, especially because Seph can't stand him. Thinks he's soft or something. But she blushes whenever he's nearby."

"Ooh, *very* interesting," Rose said, and they both laughed.

"What are you two gossiping about?" Sam asked good-naturedly. Olivia leapt for the handle of one of the car seats.

"Just about how darling your babies are. This is Bea, right? Can I hold her?"

"Of course."

"And I want to hold Michaela," Althea exclaimed, liberating the second car seat from Sam's arm.

"Good thing there are two," he told them, "because then you don't have to fight over them."

"There are quite a few more arms wanting to hold these babies," Violet informed him rather severely, and Rose gave a little laugh. Yes, she had no doubt there would be a long queue of family members eager to cuddle their little ones. She had never, ever dared to dream that she'd have so much family, so many people to love and be loved by.

As they strolled across the courtyard, Sam put his arm around Rose and she leaned into him, revelling in the easy caress, in the peace and joy of this moment, as perfect as a pearl, as pure as a diamond.

"Welcome home," he murmured in her ear, and she smiled as he kissed her cheek. Hand in hand, they walked together into the castle.

The End

Discover the final book in the Keeping Up with the Penryns series, with Seph and Oliver's story in *The Last Casterglass*!

Join Tule Publishing's newsletter for more great reads and weekly deals!

If you enjoyed *The Casterglass Heir,*
you'll love the next book in the...

Keeping Up with the Penryns series

Book 1: *A Casterglass Christmas*

Book 2: *A Casterglass Garden*

Book 3: *The Casterglass Heir*

Book 4: *The Last Casterglass*
Coming in August 2022!

Available now at your favorite online retailer!

More books by Kate Hewitt

The Return to Willoughby Close series

Book 1: *Cupcakes for Christmas*

Book 2: *Welcome Me to Willoughby Close*

Book 3: *Christmas at Willoughby Close*

Book 4: *Remember Me at Willoughby Close*

The Willoughby Close series

Book 1: *A Cotswold Christmas*

Book 2: *Meet Me at Willoughby Close*

Book 3: *Find Me at Willoughby Close*

Book 4: *Kiss Me at Willoughby Close*

Book 5: *Marry Me at Willoughby Close*

The Holley Sisters of Thornthwaite series

Book 1: *A Vicarage Christmas*

Book 2: *A Vicarage Reunion*

Book 3: *A Vicarage Wedding*

Book 4: *A Vicarage Homecoming*

Available now at your favorite online retailer!

About the Author

After spending three years as a diehard New Yorker, **Kate Hewitt** now lives in the Lake District in England with her husband, their five children, and a Golden Retriever. She enjoys such novel things as long country walks and chatting with people in the street, and her children love the freedom of village life—although she often has to ring four or five people to figure out where they've gone off to.

She writes women's fiction as well as contemporary romance under the name Kate Hewitt, and whatever the genre she enjoys delivering a compelling and intensely emotional story.

Thank you for reading

The Casterglass Heir

If you enjoyed this book, you can find more from all our great authors at TulePublishing.com, or from your favorite online retailer.

TULE
PUBLISHING

Printed in Great Britain
by Amazon